EXCEPT *the* DYING

THE MURDOCH MYSTERIES

Except the Dying
Under the Dragon's Tail
Poor Tom Is Cold
Let Loose the Dogs
Night's Child
Vices of My Blood
A Journeyman to Grief

THE DETECTIVE INSPECTOR TOM TYLER MYSTERIES

Season of Darkness
Beware this Boy

MAUREEN JENNINGS

Except
the Dying

A Murdoch Mystery

MCCLELLAND & STEWART

First published by St. Martin's Press 1997
First McClelland and Stewart mass market paperback edition 2004
This trade paperback edition 2012

LIBRARY AND ARCHIVES CANADA CATALOGUING IN PUBLICATION

Jennings, Maureen
Except the dying / Maureen Jennings.

(A Murdoch mystery)
Originally published: New York : St. Martin's Press, 1997.
ISBN 978-0-7710-4302-4

I. Title. II. Series: Jennings, Maureen. Murdoch mystery.

PS8569.E562E93 2012   C813'.54   C2012-902334-5

We acknowledge the financial support of the Government of Canada through the
Canada Book Fund and that of the Government of Ontario through the Ontario
Media Development Corporation's Ontario Book Initiative. We further acknowledge
the support of the Canada Council for the Arts and the Ontario Arts Council for our
publishing program.

Published simultaneously in the United States of America by
McClelland & Stewart, a division of Random House of Canada Limited,
a Penguin Random House Company

Library of Congress Control Number: 2012937163

Printed and bound in the United States of America

McClelland & Stewart,
a division of Random House of Canada Limited,
a Penguin Random House Company
www.penguinrandomhouse.ca

6   16

*For Iden, without whose love and support I would
never have got to this point*

The last night that she lived
It was a common night,
Except the dying; this to us
Made nature different

–Emily Dickinson

Prologue

They started with the boots, which looked new. They tried to hurry but their fingers were already stiff and clumsy with cold and the buttons were troublesome. The second boot was particularly difficult. She was curled up on her side against the fence and the leather had fastened to the earth in an icy bond. It took both of them to get it off, one holding on to the frozen leg, by now stiff as stone, the other tugging until the boot came away. Next was the waist, a decent black sateen, but in their haste they pulled on her arm too sharply and they heard the bone snap as the elbow dislocated. "Be more respectful," said the younger one.

THE SMELL OF THE extinguished candle lingers sharp and sour in the cold air. At the high, small window the night is a paler square but in the room Therese can see only the massy shapes of the wardrobe and the dresser by the door. Since Mrs. Foy left she has been lying like this under the bedcovers, praying for guidance.

It is not the housekeeper Therese fears, it is the other, who, full of solicitude and wine, has already come to her twice this week. The memory makes her tremble and she sits up suddenly, thinking the stairs have creaked. Not so, just the stable door opening in the yard below. Faintly from the dining room, she can hear the booming voice of the guest, the faint interspersing of her mistress's replies.

She pushes back the quilt and gets off the bed. Except for her outer garments she is fully dressed, but she shivers. Moving fast so there is no room to regret, she packs her meagre belongings into the valise: her second chemise, a pair of drawers, her other grey silk waist for church that she made herself and her plaid wool skirt. Everything else she possesses she is wearing. On the bedside table is the Bible that Claudette gave her when she left the farm. It is a gift that gives her great comfort even though she cannot read a word. Next to it is her rosary, which she picks up, touching the crucifix to her lips. Then she falls to her knees by the bed and begins to tell her beads.

Hail Mary, full of grace,
blessed art thou among women,
Hail Mary, full of grace,
blessed is the fruit of thy womb, Jesus.

They removed the felt hat next. The pink velvet flowers around the brim were crushed by the weight of the head and dusted with snow light as sugar. The skirt came off easily, as did the woollen stockings. There were no gloves and, disappointingly, there was no jewellery to speak of – small silver earrings, which they left, and a pretty bead necklace of green glass that had broken and was wrapped around the rigid fingers. One of them started to pull out the wooden combs that pinned up the girl's hair. "No, don't," said the other. "She won't need them now," her companion replied. In the darkness their breath came from their mouths like smoke.

She takes a serge jacket from the hook on the door. She can see her own breath in the cold room, and she wraps her muffler tight around her face. All evening the ice-laden wind has been building, sweeping across the city from the dark lake, worrying at the house. There is a portable oil heater in the corner but she hasn't used it tonight, not wanting to be held accountable for the additional expense. She does not want to leave with any blot on her name.

Father Alphonse said to her, "If you have difficulties, go to talk to the priest, Father Corbiere. He is my friend, he will assist you." But she found that this priest has departed and the new one is an English. He appears hurried and has impatience with her language.

She cannot tell him her troubles even in the confessional box. But last Sunday she found a French-Canadian church and she wept with the joy of the familiar tongue. Perhaps there she can find succour.

At the last moment she returns to the narrow bed, plumps up the pillow and slips it beneath the blue counterpane. From the door in the dark, it looks like a sleeping figure.

The corpse was clad now only in white flannel drawers and chemise, the blue-grey skin of legs and arms blending with the snow where she lay. They considered leaving her, considered stopping at the final indignity, but the cloth of the undergarments was good and they had gone this far. Awkwardly they manoeuvred the body, unyielding as a large doll. The one was shamed by the triangle of hair in the fork of the legs and she tried to bend the knee up to give the girl modesty, but it was impossible. They bundled up the pile of clothes and slipped away into the darkness.

She crosses the bare floor to the door, opens it and peers out, clutching the Bible against her chest as if it could be a shield. She makes her way to the narrow back stairs the servants use and runs down, her feet made light and fast by fear.

Chapter One

THE WIND CUT TO THE BONE and Alice Black pulled her shawl tight about her head and throat. The hot gin was a fire in her stomach but no defence against the cold of the winter night. She grumbled to herself, trying to expose as little of her face as she could. She'd expected to do some business at the John O'Neil but none of the piss-makers wanted to pay for a bit of dock tonight. She wiped the back of her hand across her dripping nose. She hoped Ettie had fared better, else it was potato-peel soup for the next few days.

It was getting late. Although the hotel officially closed at the legal Saturday time of seven o'clock, there was a backroom where the regulars could go to top off, and for a cut of the dash, the proprietor, James McCay, usually allowed her and Ettie to stay on.

Alice edged closer to the houses. She was afeard to

5

go past the churchyard where the bodies of the Irish immigrants were laid out in their eternity boxes. Even though the epidemic had happened almost fifty years earlier, for sure ghosts lingered in the area. Not so the cholera. She always held her nose as she scurried by. On this stretch of Queen Street the shops were interspersed with vacant buildings and the boarded-up windows were blinded eyes. The gas lights were few and far between and what with that and huddling into her shawl, she didn't see the young woman walking in front of her until they almost collided.

"Mind where you're goin'," snapped Alice. She heard a muttered "Pardon" as the other one moved out of the way. She had a thick muffler wrapped around her face, but Alice had an impression of youth, and she wondered where the girl was going by herself at this time of night. A country piece, by the look of that hat and valise.

Alice glanced over her shoulder. The girl was hovering on the sidewalk. She looked lost, and for a moment Alice considered stopping to offer help. But sod it, it was too cold. A gust of wind blew her skirts up about her knees and she struggled to hold them down. At that moment she heard the jingle of harness as a carriage came around the corner heading east onto Queen Street, going a good clip considering the state of the road. The iron-hard ruts had a light covering of snow and they were slippery and dangerous to the horses.

6

"Get out of the way, you bloody bint," yelled the driver. Alice jumped back onto the sidewalk just in time. She lost her balance on the snowbank and fell backwards, landing on her tailbone. For a moment she remained sprawled on the hard ground, groaning, then angrily snatched up a handful of snow and threw it in the direction of the carriage. The wind tossed it back in her face. Sodding toady. She shook her fist and suddenly the driver pulled his horse up sharp, wheeled around and headed back in her direction. She shrank back, prepared for recriminations, but the carriage went right past her and halted beside the girl. The door opened and a gloved hand reached out. After a moment's hesitation, the young woman accepted the help and climbed in. In the flickering yellow light of the gas lamp, Alice saw that the carriage was a smart burgundy colour with brass fittings, the high-stepping horse light-coloured, but the blinds at the windows were pulled down tight and she couldn't see the occupant.

The driver cracked his whip, wheeled the horse around, and they set off again at a brisk canter back along Queen Street.

Alice got to her feet, rubbing at her rump. She brushed the snow off her skirt, rewrapped her shawl and started to walk. Her stomach was cramping badly and she needed to get home soon. She should've known better than to trust those snaggy sausages of McCay's. If there was a morsel of real pork in there at all she'd

7

be surprised. More like rotten horsemeat, by what it was doing to her stomach.

She was going by the Dominion Brewery now, the pleasurable part of her route. In spite of the increasing urgency of her indigestion, she paused in front of the entrance. The smell of hops hung heavy and sweet on the night air. She sniffed hungrily but the cold made her cough. Sod it. She headed up Sumach Street. Her toes had gone numb. Even though she'd stuffed newspaper into her boots, they were so split they were useless.

"Lucky for that little tit, whoever she is. Gettin' a ride to some warm place. Why'd it never happen to Alice?"

Constable Second-Class Oliver Wicken was looking forward to the end of his shift, when he could warm his feet at the station woodstove. His thick serge uniform and cape kept his body warm enough but his feet were frozen and a chilblain itched painfully on his right heel. He stopped for a moment and stamped to restore his circulation. Since the early hours of the morning a steady snow, soft and pure, had been covering the grey detritus of the week. Now with dawn approaching the wind had got up again, burning his face, and tiny icicles had formed along the edge of his fine blond moustache.

At this hour the streets were empty. He hadn't encountered another living soul during his entire beat

8

except for a bread man in his dray rumbling down River Street. Privately, young Wicken always hoped for a little excitement he could relate to his sweetheart. She was a romantic girl and was always after him to tell her his adventures. Like he'd told her, the graveyard shift in the winter wasn't going to be lively. The citizens were sealed up tight in their snug houses. Summer was different. Larceny, pickpockets on the increase, violations of Sunday bylaws. And, of course, the flood of drunk and disorderly. Over three thousand cases of D-and-D charged in 1894. Made you want to take the Pledge. Almost.

This month his main task was to check the vacant houses to make sure no vagrants had broken in to get shelter for the night. Toronto was just climbing out of bad times and there were over a thousand properties standing empty throughout the city. The police were placed in charge of protecting them.

He turned north on Sumach Street. He badly needed to relieve himself and he wasn't sure he could hold it until he got to the station. Just up a ways was a dark laneway, and he walked in for a few feet, intending to use one of the outside privies that served the row of houses along St. Luke Street. However, the pressure in his bladder became too urgent and he stopped by the tumbledown fence.

In a hurry to unbutton his trousers, he didn't notice the body immediately, as the whiteness of it was blended

9

into the snow. But two large rats were sniffing at the girl's head, and at Wicken's approach they scurried away like shadows and attracted his attention. He had placed his lantern beside him on the ground and it was only when he raised it aloft that he fully comprehended what he was seeing.

He went close enough to confirm the girl was dead and then spun around and ran as fast as he could to the telephone signal box that stood on the corner of Wilton and Sumach. Panting, he tugged free his key, opened the box and grabbed the receiver off the hook. He turned the crank and waited for what seemed endless moments until the police operator at central headquarters answered. Wicken could hardly hear him above the usual static and hiss of the telephone. He yelled, "Connect me with number-four station. It's an emergency."

Chapter Two

ACTING DETECTIVE WILLIAM MURDOCH crouched beside the dead girl and lifted the dark hair away from her face. Despite the pallor of death, there was still a sweetness in the curve of her cheek, the skin unmarked by life's experience. He felt a pang of pity at the sight. Behind him Constable Crabtree shifted nervously and the ambulance driver leaned over from his seat to gape. Fortunately, the gathering crowd at the entrance to the laneway were being kept in check by young Wicken, but even at this early hour on the Lord's Day a ragtag mob had formed, roused by the clanging alarm. One man had even brought out a stool to stand on so he could see better.

"Fetch a blanket, will you, Crabtree?" Murdoch called over his shoulder to his constable.

He sat back on his heels, shielding the body as best he could. The girl was lying on her back close to a rickety wooden fence. On the left side of her body were the purple marks of lividity. Rigor mortis was advanced, the head unmovable, the arms and legs frozen. Her eyes were closed, and he lifted one eyelid. The pupil was a mere pinprick in the light blue iris. The right eye was the same. He bent and sniffed at her mouth but there was no detectable smell of liquor. At first sight the cause of death was not apparent, no blood or obvious wounds. He leaned closer. There were three small bruises at the left wrist. He placed his own fingers on the spots. They fit. There was also a largish contusion on the inside of the forearm and another at the elbow. Gingerly, he examined her hands. The nails were cut short and there was nothing caught there that he could see. He ran his finger over the cold flesh of her palm, feeling the slight roughening. He brushed aside the snow and checked her feet. The toenails were likewise clean and there were no scratches or marks on the soles.

"Here you go, sir." Crabtree handed him a grey hospital blanket. "She looks to be about the same age as my sister. Fourteen, if that," he said.

"I'd put her older, myself."

The face was youthful, especially with the thick dark hair loose about her shoulders, but her body was voluptuous, the breasts full and the hips and buttocks rounded. Murdoch covered her over and straightened up, frowning.

"Bloody peculiar, Crabtree, her eyes . . ."

He stopped as the police horse whinnied. There was an answering neigh from the street. Wicken was pushing the onlookers back as a two-wheeler turned into the laneway. The constable went over to hold the horse, and the elderly driver got down stiffly. He was wearing an old-fashioned houndstooth cloak and stovepipe hat and his lower face was wrapped in a white silk scarf. When he reached Murdoch he muttered, "Abscess tooth," and indicated the scarf. He looked down at the body.

". . . happened here?"

"I don't know, sir," answered Murdoch. "One of our constables found her about forty minutes ago."

He pulled away the blanket so the coroner could see.

"Whoze she?"

"We haven't determined that yet."

"A doxy?"

"I don't think so, sir. She's quite clean and the constable on this beat says he hasn't seen her before."

The coroner indicated the purple stains on the side of the body. ". . . you move her?"

"No, sir, somebody else did."

"Clothes?"

"Nowhere around. Probably stripped."

"Heathens." He tried to bend closer but the movement caused pain in his jaw and he straightened quickly. "She's dead . . . right enough, but I . . ." He frowned at Murdoch. "Where've . . . seen you before?"

13

"Last December, sir. The Merishaw case."

"Course, remember now. Shocking . . . heathen!"

The Merishaws' servant girl had given birth to a stillborn child and tried to bury the body in the neighbour's front yard, where some children had found it. Arthur Johnson had been the attending coroner in that instance and without the excuse of an abscessed tooth he had been just as perfunctory.

"Bring the body . . . morgue postmortem examination . . . too cold here . . . Get a report . . ."

Murdoch didn't make out what he said. "Beg pardon, sir."

Johnson pulled the muffler away from his mouth, then winced as the cold air hit his tooth. There was a waft of oil of cloves in the air. "I'll get an examination done at once and send you the report."

He quickly wrapped himself up again and started back towards his carriage, muttering something else undecipherable. Crabtree gave him a lift up into the seat, and he slapped the reins at the docile bay mare, which trotted off briskly.

Murdoch replaced the blanket. He'd never encountered a situation like this before, and although he'd felt pity for the dead girl he was also keenly aware that it might prove to be a noteworthy case. The notion was agitating. Promotion was difficult to come by in the city's police force. The last few years had been hard economically for the city and the council had refused

14

Chief Grasett's request for a bigger budget. The police force could not expand. Murdoch had been acting detective for three years and unless somebody above him in rank died or retired he was stuck there. Lately he had fretted beneath that yoke, hating the need to kow-tow to men he despised. There was a chance the dead girl could bring him some glory if he handled himself well.

The constable in charge of the ambulance called out. "D'you think you'll be much longer, Mr. Murdoch? It's perishing cold for the horses."

"Put their blankets on, then."

Richmond was a chronic complainer and lazy to boot. Murdoch had no time for him.

Grumbling, the constable got down from his seat, took two blankets from the back of the wagon and threw them over the horses. Their breath smoked in the cold air. The snow continued to drift down and bits of ice were crusting on Murdoch's moustache from the moisture of his breath. He was grateful for the warmth of his long sealskin coat and forage hat, which he'd acquired in exchange for three plugs of Jolly Tar from a dying prisoner. The nap was gone under the arms of the coat, but it wasn't obvious and his landlady had managed to remove most of the stains.

He motioned Constable Crabtree to come closer.

"We'd better find out who she was. Take down some notes, will you?"

15

Crabtree took out a black notebook and inserted a piece of carbonized paper between two pages. He was a giant of a man, made taller by his high round helmet and wider by the serge cape. His broad, ruddy face was guileless as a farmer's, but he was shrewd and Murdoch liked and respected him.

"Righto, sir."

"The body is that of a young female between fourteen and sixteen years of age. She has light blue eyes, dark brown wavy hair. She is approximately five foot three inches, and would weigh about nine stone. There is a small wen to the right side of the nose. No scars or pockmarks. She is wearing silver ear hoops. Got that? Before the postmortem examination we'll get some photographs just to be on the safe side. Cavendish is the best for that, and Foster can do the drawing in case we need it for the papers. When the rigor has passed we'll take proper Bertillon measurements."

Crabtree was surprised. "Is it worth it, sir? You said you don't think she's a slag."

"We might as well. You know how the chief feels."

Chief Constable Grasett was very keen on Bertillonage, and he'd sent all the detectives and acting detectives on a special course the year before. In fact, Murdoch thought the laborious system had its faults, but it was better than nothing, and there were reports, probably exaggerated, of some resounding successes. Murdoch had heard that the American police were experimenting with a method of identification using fingerprints, but so far the Toronto police had no knowledge of it.

He called to Richmond. "Bring over the stretcher."

The constable pulled it out of the wagon and placed it on the ground beside the body. Crabtree went to help him. As they began to lift, the blanket slipped and the forearm and hand appeared, pointing toward heaven as if in supplication. The other man tried to get it covered over again. Murdoch snapped at him.

"Take care with that arm, you'll break it."

Richmond swore under his breath but finally managed to slide the girl over. Crabtree seized the lower handles of the stretcher and the two of them carried it into the ambulance. The driver jumped up on the front seat, clucked to the horses and set off down the lane. There was a burst of excited chatter from the watchers. At the same time a carillon of bells sounded from St. Paul's Church, signalling the Mass. Murdoch sighed to himself. He was a Roman Catholic, but last Sunday he'd stayed in bed reading, and it looked like he'd miss this week too. Father Fair wouldn't be happy; nor would Mrs. Kitchen, his devout landlady.

As Crabtree joined him, Murdoch pointed to the depression where the body had lain.

"Before she was moved, she was lying on her left side facing the fence. Her head was west towards Sackville, feet easterly towards Sumach Street. Her legs were

17

drawn up close to her body and her arms were folded against her chest."

He stepped aside and dropped to the ground, curling himself into the position the girl had been in when she died.

"What does it look like, Crabtree?"

"Like she might have tried to get a bit of protection from the wind here where the shed juts out."

"That's what I thought."

Murdoch clambered to his feet and brushed the snow from his coat.

"Was she hickey?" asked the constable.

"Don't think so. There was no smell of liquor. We'll have to wait for the postmortem examination to be sure. But something was wrong. I don't like the look of it at all. As far as I know, you don't die naturally and have pinpoint pupils. And she was bruised. Could be from somebody gripping her arm hard. If this is a crime we have to be careful. I don't want his nibs using my stampers for boot cleaners, if we've missed something. At the very least we're dealing with desecration of a dead body. Back east they used to say, when you're not sure which way the wind is going to blow, keep your deck clean, your sail up and your Man Thomas down."

Crabtree grinned.

Murdoch took out a retractable tape measure from his inner pocket.

The snow of the last few hours had been steadily filling up any dints, and the coming and going of the constables overlaid whatever prints had been there previously. However, at the edge of the depression where the girl had lain, he saw one clear toe print. It was narrow and pointed, as from a fashionable boot. He measured it carefully.

"Let's have a gander down the lane."

"Are we looking for anything in particular, sir?"

"Fresh droppings of any kind. Nothing'd last more than two days in this place, so we don't have to worry whether it's new or not."

The dirt lane ran parallel to Shuter Street from River Street as far as Yonge. Over at that westerly end within sight of the cathedrals, Shuter was respectable and well tended, most of the residents professional men. You could find more doctors per square inch on Shuter and adjoining Mutual Street than bugs on a pauper's pillow. Here, though, the houses shrivelled in size and demeanour, taken over by working-class families who were too tired or too indifferent to maintain them. Not even the covering of snow could prettify the narrow-faced, drab houses and untended backyards where the outhouses sat.

Slowly the two officers walked down the lane on each side, but there was nothing out of the ordinary that they could see. At the Sumach Street end they halted, and the people jostling against the rope barricade stared at them. One woman had her child with her, clinging sleepily to her chest underneath her shawl. There was the usual sour odour from clothes that were never washed or removed.

"What's going on, Officer?" the man on the stool called out.

Murdoch recognized him. "Hello there, Tinney. You're out early."

"I didn't want to miss anything, Sergeant. What's happening? We heard some tart got a nubbing."

"You heard wrong."

"She's dead, though, ain't she?" interjected a scrawny red-nosed youth.

"Unfortunately she is that. So listen, all you folks. The police will need your cooperation. I'm going to give you a description of the girl and if you know her, know of her, or saw her anytime last night, speak right up. Is that clear?"

All eyes were on him, and a few of the crowd nodded eagerly.

"Is there a reward?" asked a short, round man who was protected against the weather by a long moth-eaten raccoon coat and fur cap with earflaps.

"Shame on you, Wiggins," hissed one of his neighbours.

"Lay off, Driscoll. You'd shat your own mother if there was a dollar to be got."

Mr. Driscoll scowled, but the crowd who heard the repartee laughed.

"Stop this at once," roared Wicken. "You're not at a music hall."

Murdoch continued. "If there's any reward it's the one of knowing you might be saving some poor mother hours of heartache from wondering where her child is. Now listen. The girl is about fifteen or sixteen years old, dark hair, blue eyes. A bit over five feet. Same height as Wiggins. She has a small mole to the side of her nose. Anyone know her?"

There was a murmur and buzz but nobody answered him.

"Well? Poor girl died in your laneway, you must know her."

Then Tinney offered, "There was a widow woman lived at the corner of Sackville and St. Luke's a few months back. Could be her."

At least four voices shouted him down.

"You're leaky, John Tinney," jeered his friend Driscoll. "That woman was on the downhill side of forty, for one thing, and she was as long as the copper, for another. Six foot if she was an inch. The sergeant says the poor girl was short."

Tinney shrugged. "You never know." 21

"When would she have passed on?" a woman asked Murdoch.

"Last night, probably between eleven and twelve o'clock." He pointed to Crabtree. "This officer is going to write down all of your names and addresses and any information you can give him. Honest information, mind. No queer or you'll find yourself with a charge. If you prefer a bit of privacy you can come to the station. You all know where that is, don't you?"

There was a mixed response to that question. Some of them knew only too well.

He turned to Crabtree. "When you've done with this lot, stir up Cavendish, then trot over to the station just in case anybody's come asking. Join me as soon as you can. I'm going to start knocking on doors."

He went back down the laneway to where the body had been. Directly across from him was a row of six narrow, two-storey houses with sharp gables, each one leaning slightly towards its neighbour as if for comfort. All of the houses showed candles or lamps except for the end one, which was in darkness. Murdoch wondered if the inhabitants were sound sleepers. He decided to find out.

There was a ramshackle fence with more boards missing than standing. The gate had long gone and Murdoch stepped through the gap into the yard, taking careful notice of the tracks in the snow. From the back door, the snow was trampled down into a narrow path, unfortunately with so much overlay he couldn't make out anything distinctly. Maybe that was the top of a needle-toed boot, maybe not. He straightened up and turned his back to the house. The place where the girl had died was easily visible.

Suddenly an angry voice shouted.

"Oi. What you doing? Get out of here."

A woman was at the back door watching him. She was carrying a covered chamber pot that she was presumably about to empty into the outhouse.

"Detective Murdoch. I'd like to ask you some questions."

The courteous address wasn't really necessary, given the sort of woman she was. Her stained yellow wrapper was carelessly fastened and her unkempt hair straggled around a face that looked none too clean. She was young but her thin face was haggard.

"What sort of questions?" she said, not moving from the doorway.

"Tell you what, it's cold as Mercury out here. Why don't I come inside where we both would be more comfortable. And miss, if you can scrounge me up a mug of tea, I'd be right grateful."

"I haven't even lit the Gurney yet," she said, yawning widely and showing discoloured and chipped teeth. "I just got up, matter of fact."

"Lucky you. I've been up so long I'm ready for bed."

"That's not an invite, is it, Sergeant?"

Murdoch grinned, still willing to appease the woman, but he remained out of reach in case she decided to

23

fling the contents of the pot in his direction. It wouldn't be the first time.

"What do you want to know?" she asked as she emptied the chamber beside the door, turning the snow yellow.

"Like I said, we'd both be more comfortable inside."

"Suit yourself."

She stepped back and Murdoch followed her into the gloomy hallway. Two closed doors were to the right and at the far end was a curtained archway through which came the dim glow of a candle. The air was cold and stale.

The woman deposited the chamber pot in her room.

"We're in here," she said and led the way through the portieres into the kitchen. Here a second woman was bending over a large black range, fanning at a meagre fire that she had started in its belly. She was trying to get it to blaze but succeeding only in wafting clouds of smoke into the room. She turned around, coughing, when they came in.

"Bleeding hell, Ettie, will you see to this shicey stove. It won't go." She saw Murdoch. "Who's he?"

"Copper. Wants to ask us some questions."

"What about?"

"Don't know, do I? Says he wants some tea." She went over to the stove and peered at the fire. "Sod it, Alice, I told you to wait 'til it draws to put the coal on. You've smothered it."

24

Murdoch stepped forward. "Let me. I'm good with fires."

"That's a surprise. I thought frogs were good for nothing." Alice scowled. She too was in a day wrapper, this one a dingy green flannel. It gaped open at the neck, revealing her breasts, but she made no move towards modesty. She looked older than the young woman she had called Ettie by a good ten years.

There was a pair of tongs in a bucket beside the stove and Murdoch took them and removed the big lump of coal. Then he propped up the few bits of kindling and began to blow on the smouldering paper. A couple of good puffs and a bright flame appeared. When the wood began to crackle, he fished out some smaller pieces of coal from the bucket, put them on the fire and closed the stove door.

"Give it a few minutes," he said, dusting off his hands.

The two women had been watching him silently.

"I suppose he deserves his chatter broth after that," said Alice. She went to the sink and pumped water into a blackened pot. "It'll take a while. Stove isn't hot yet."

"You'd better sit down before you knock out the roof," said Ettie. The ceiling was low and Murdoch was six feet tall.

"Here." She pulled forward a wooden chair. The back slats were almost all gone and Murdoch didn't fancy the thing collapsing underneath him.

25

"I'll stand," he said, but he unbuttoned his coat and put his hat on the chair. Then he took his notebook and fountain pen from his inner pocket. The silver-nibbed pen had been Elizabeth's Christmas present to him before she died, and it was his pride and joy. Both women took stock.

"First off, I need to know your names."

"Why?" asked Ettie.

"Because, miss, the body of a female person has been found in the laneway. Practically in your back garden, as you might say."

He paused for their reaction, but there was none. No expression of any kind, except stillness. They reminded him of two cats who'd come into the yard of his lodging house last winter. Lean and tattered, with pale, wary eyes. When he'd tried to befriend the starving creatures, they had growled and spat at him and would have bitten his hand if they could.

Alice shrugged. "This weather'll kill you, that's for certain. Poor old dolly."

"Who do you mean, miss?"

"The stiff mort."

"I doubt she was a tramp, and she wasn't old. Possibly no more than fifteen or sixteen."

26 "Shame that."

They stared at him but he didn't say anything.

"What's it to do with us?" Ettie said finally.

"That's for you to tell." He paused. "We don't know

who the girl is as yet. I'm making enquiries."

He wanted to see if either of them would offer information that they shouldn't have or try to mislead him in any way. Ettie spoke again.

"What kind of girl was she, then? A working girl, for instance, or a young lady?"

Alice guffawed. "Bleeding hell, Ettie. Young lady? What would a lady be doing in the lane?"

Ettie shrugged. "Takes all sorts," she said.

Murdoch knew this exchange was entirely for his benefit. He decided to play out the line a bit longer.

"We can't tell yet. She was mother naked."

Alice grimaced. "Couldn't have had much in her idea pot if she was stark in this weather."

She was overtaken by another fit of coughing, and she grabbed a cup from the table and spat into it. Dispassionately, she studied the sputum she had deposited.

"Just phlegm."

"What's your last name, Alice?" Murdoch asked.

"I'm Alice Black." She pointed at her partner. "She's Ettie Weston."

"Bernadette Weston," the other woman corrected her. "They just call me Ettie."

"Just come over did you?" he asked Alice.

She shrugged but the other woman laughed. "She's been here since she was a nipper but you'd never know it."

"And you?"

27

"I'm homegrown."

"Do you both live here?"

"Yes. We've got a snug down there." She pointed down the hall.

"You get use of the kitchen?"

Alice snorted. "Use! That's a joke, that is. We supply the rest of this shicey household, if you ask me. We have to fetch the coal scuttle into our room at night, else it'd be empty as a cripple's stomach by morning. Don't notice Mr. bloody Quinn bringing in a bit of coal, do you? But he's quick enough to come in here and warm his chilblains when we've got it up, isn't he?"

"Come on, Alice, he helps us out in other ways."

"You maybe, not me."

"Who is this Mr. Quinn?" Murdoch interceded.

"One of the other dudders that lives here. He's got the room next to us."

"Who else?"

Ettie answered. "There's two brothers upstairs. Say they're lumberjacks. Don't know what they're doing here if that's the case. Aren't going to cut down many trees in this neighbourhood, are they? And they're both lumpers. Bang around like horses up there."

She looked as if she was going to continue with a diatribe against the absent brothers but Murdoch stopped her.

"What's your occupation?"

Ettie grinned at him. In spite of her bad teeth she

28

had an attractive face when she smiled. Youth still lingered there.

"I'm a glover. Alice the same."

"Where do you work?"

"Here. We work from home, don't we, Alice? We mend and clean."

"That's right. We specialize in men's articles. Of the best pigskin." She met his eyes impudently. "We fit them."

Murdoch knew that sexual protectors were made from fine pigskin, but he didn't take the bait. They were toying with him and the slightest sign of annoyance or embarrassment on his part would be seen as a victory they would chortle over for weeks to come.

"Who employs you?"

"Mr. Webster, the tailor. He's over on Queen Street."

"We're always in demand," added Alice. "The shops are using machines these days but we find most gentlemen still like the work done by hand, don't we, Ettie?" She laughed. "It's hard work, Sergeant. At the end of the day we're spent many times over."

"Alice, don't be vulgar. What'll the sergeant think?"

"I'm thinking I've had enough of you two. This is a serious matter I'm investigating."

In spite of his resolve, he'd got irritated.

Alice was still laughing. It became a coughing fit that shook her scrawny body so painfully Murdoch winced.

29

"Bad cough you've got there, Alice. Have you seen a doctor?"

She thumped herself on the chest. Her face had turned almost blue with the effort to get breath. "It's just a cold. Winter does it to you."

Murdoch went back to his notebook.

"Do either of you know anything about this young girl, then?" He went through the description again. "Fullish figure but short. Bit shorter than you, Ettie."

"Don't know her, do we, Alice?"

"No."

"Did you hear anything last night? Any cries? Shouts?"

They both shook their heads emphatically.

"You were home all night?"

"Yes," said Alice. "Tucked up in bed, good as gold."

"No, Alice!" the younger girl spoke sharply. "He means earlier. You were at the hotel 'til almost ten." She stared her companion down.

"I will be checking," said Murdoch.

"See. Don't confuse him."

"Oh yeah. Sure I didn't know what you meant, Constable. I did spend the early part of the evening at the John O'Neil with friends. But I was here with Ettie the rest of the night. Didn't move."

"What about you, Ettie?"

"In bed at eight, I was. Not a peep 'til just half an hour ago."

"And nothing disturbed you?"

Ettie went to the stove and poked at the fire even though it was blazing merrily. She didn't turn around. "No, not a thing."

Alice giggled. "Come on now, Ettie. Don't give him the queer."

Ettie swivelled around, staring.

Alice continued. "Truth is, we was disturbed in the night. 'Bout two o'clock." She eyed Murdoch expectantly.

He sighed. "Get on with it, Alice. What woke you?"

"Terrible cries."

"Well? What was it?"

"Probably the Virgin Mary."

She laughed again so heartily at her own feeble joke, she went into another coughing spell. This produced another gob of sputum, which she tried to deposit in the cup and succeeded only in catching the edge.

He looked at her sharply. There was no possibility she could know his religious affiliation, but she was teasing about something.

"Would you please explain what –"

At that moment a loud yowling cry resounded down the dark hall. Pitiful moans and howls. Not quite human, though, as if some animal were in pain. Alice and Bernadette grinned at each other.

31

"Jesus save us," said Alice. "There it is again. Exact same cries as last night."

"Sounds like a dog," said Murdoch. "Must be hurt."

He went into the hall. The racket seemed to be coming from the far room.

"Who lives down there?" he called to the women.

They came to the archway, arms around each other.

"Samuel Quinn," said Alice.

"Does he own a dog?"

"He does. He's a regular dog fancier." She smiled but Murdoch didn't miss the quick warning poke from Ettie.

"I'll be right back," he said.

The noise stopped abruptly; then a soft plaintive howl filled the air, eerie, full of sorrow. He banged hard on the door.

"Open up. Police. Open up."

The piteous howling suddenly changed to the every-day identifiable barking of a dog. A lighter treble joined in, the yapping complementing the loud, deep warnings of the first dog. Murdoch kicked the door.

"I'm going to break down this door if you don't open it."

That did the trick. As fast as it might have taken the occupant to get out of bed, the door opened a crack. A young man stood there in his nightshirt. He was holding on to the collar of a small black and tan dog. It was hard to believe so loud a sound could come from an animal that size.

"Is something wrong with the dog?" Murdoch bellowed.

Before the man could answer, the animal gave a quick twist of its head and moved backwards, leaving the man holding an empty collar. In a flash, it slipped between his legs and darted off towards the kitchen.

"Princess, stop!" the man yelled. At that moment another dog, tiny and long-haired, appeared from behind him and scampered off in pursuit, yapping excitedly.

"Ettie, catch him!" the man shouted again.

At the kitchen threshold, the bitch halted and began to jump up and down, barking at top volume. The little one was right behind and reared himself up on his hind legs in an attempt to mount her. His erection was bright scarlet. The hound turned her head and snapped at him over her shoulder as indifferently as if he were a fly. Not daunted, he gripped her more tightly, a difficult task as she was easily twice as tall as he was. Ettie, with Alice peering over her shoulder, burst out laughing. The young man in the nightshirt pushed past Murdoch and ran down the hall. Quickly, he snatched the tiny dog up in his arms, where he wriggled wildly, trying to get back to his pleasure.

"Grab Princess."

Ettie tried to oblige but it was easier said than done; the dog was dancing round her feet, barking non-stop. She shouted to make herself heard above the din. "Does she want a bit of meat, then?"

33

The dog stopped barking as if a switch had been thrown and sat down abruptly, her tongue out, tail wagging. Ettie smiled lovingly, her voice as tender as if she were addressing a beloved child. "Come on, my chick, I'll see what I can find."

She went over to the pine cupboard next to the sink.

The dog in Quinn's arms was still yipping shrilly but Quinn smacked him smartly on the nose and he shut up, snuffling in surprise.

"Thank God for that," said Alice. "What a din."

Quinn became aware of Murdoch standing behind him and smiled disarmingly. "Sorry about all the noise."

"Sounded like she was being tortured."

"I know. It's 'cause she has hound blood in her. Really she just wanted to get out and see if Ettie had any treats."

Alice scowled at that. "Dog has a better life than I do," she said. "What a fuss."

Quinn was standing barefoot in the cold hall, dressed as he was, in his nightshirt, and he started to hop from one foot to the other.

"Didn't I hear you shout 'Police'?" he asked Murdoch.

"He's a detective. Mr. Mud something. He wants to ask you some questions," said Alice. "Hope your pot's clean." Her glance at Quinn was full of malice.

"Oh? What about?" Quinn looked decidedly uneasy.

"Let's go to your room, and I can speak to you there,"

said Murdoch. He was keen to regain some control of the situation.

Ettie came back from the kitchen, Princess behind her.

"Is that all you want from us?"

"For now. But Quinn here will catch his death if he doesn't get some clothes on."

The little dog was struggling wildly to get free, and suddenly Quinn thrust him into Murdoch's arms.

"Carry him, will you? Hold him tight."

Murdoch had no choice but to obey. It was a small dog but it must have weighed a good ten pounds, most of the flesh in its portly belly. The dog's long, silky coat was caramel-coloured and smelled like violets, as if he'd recently been bathed with perfumed soap. He had a squashed-in face, long ears and bulging eyes that were nonetheless bright with intelligence. Or lust. His major aim at the moment seemed to be to get back to the bitch. Quinn caught Princess by the scruff of the neck and half dragged, half pushed her down the hall to his room. He stepped back to usher in Murdoch.

"My humble abode, as they say."

The room was stiflingly hot, and the warm air poured out into the chill of the hall. A fire was blazing in the hearth and a candle was lit. There was one tall, narrow window currently hung with a piece of torn cloth that might have once graced a table. No fresh air had entered via the window since the house was constructed but

35

Murdoch didn't expect anything else. Fresh air was a prerogative of the wealthy, who in the winter could afford coal to heat cold rooms and in the summer employed servants to deal with the dust that sifted through every aperture.

Quinn pulled forward a wooden box that had formerly contained lye and placed a red plush cushion on top of it.

"Sit yourself down," he said and plucked the dog out of Murdoch's arms. Ignoring the beast's protests, he thrust him into an old hat box that was beside the bed. Airholes were punched into the sides and Murdoch could see a keen brown eye as the dog stared out at them. The bitch collapsed with a sigh and a smacking of lips and promptly closed her eyes.

"What's his name?" asked Murdoch, indicating the yapper.

Quinn looked bewildered. "Name? I, er, oh sure, Prince – his name is Prince." He grinned. "Looks a bit like him, doesn't he? Pop eyes, fat stomach."

"He certainly has the same appreciation for females," said Murdoch. "Looks like a quality dog. Where'd you get him?"

"Actually, he's not my dog. Belongs to a pal of mine. I'm taking care of him for a few days."

36

"That's kind of you."

"Eh?"

"It must be a lot of trouble."

"Not really. Good little dog, aren't you, Bertie?"

"Thought you said his name was Prince?"

"What? Yeah. It is. Prince Albert. Got bloodlines, this animal."

He had perched on the edge of his bed but he jumped up nervously and went over to the fire, where an iron kettle was hissing away on a spit. "I was going to make myself a pot of char. Can I offer you a mug?"

"Thanks, that would be appreciated."

Quinn reached under the bed and pulled out another box. This one was cardboard and advertised gloves. He took out a tin of tea, a brown, chipped china pot and two mugs, placing them on a japanned table next to Murdoch where there was a silvered milk jug and sugar basin.

"What can I help you with, Officer?"

"I'll wait for the tea, then we can get down to it."

"Be ready in a jiffy."

Quinn spooned the black tea leaves from the tin into the pot, filled it with boiling water from the kettle and covered it with a blue, knitted cozy. His movements were the deft, practiced habits of a bachelor. He was a short, stocky man, rather bandy-legged. His complexion was swarthy and badly pockmarked but there was something open and humorous in his expression. Murdoch couldn't help but take a liking to him.

"Could you go for a bun with your tea? I'm a baker. They let me have the leftovers."

37

"Don't mind if I do."

Murdoch could feel a trickle of sweat down the back of his neck. With the two of them in the tiny room and the fire roaring like that, it was becoming unbearably hot.

"Here, give me your coat," said Quinn. He took the seal coat and laid it across the bed. An old army blanket, heavy and greasy looking, seemed to make do as a cover. Murdoch hoped the coat wasn't going to collect any livestock.

Quinn pulled forward the single chair in the room, removed the pair of trousers that was draped across the back and sat down. He had produced a biscuit tin from the window shelf and he opened it, revealing two currant buns and one half-eaten slice of bread. Princess opened her eyes and raised her head, recognising the possibility of food. Murdoch took one of the buns and bit into it. His teeth made no impression. Quinn grinned.

"Better dip it into your char to soften it up a bit. Here."

He poured some tea, thick and black, into one of the mugs, added two spoonsful of sugar and a splash of milk and offered it to Murdoch. Princess sat up on her hind legs and begged. She let out one demanding yelp. Quinn broke off a piece of his bun and gave it to her. Murdoch followed suit.

"Alice called her the Virgin Mary," he said.

Quinn grinned nervously. "Did she now?"

38

Murdoch sipped at the hot tea, almost burning his tongue. Quinn drank some of his, not looking at him. Murdoch gave the end of his bun to Princess.

"All right, to business, then."

He told Quinn about the dead girl.

The man put down his cup. "Why, that's terrible, that is. Just terrible. Young, you say?"

"No more than sixteen."

The candle and the fire cast so many shadows it was hard to read his expression completely, but as far as Murdoch could tell, Quinn was genuinely shocked.

"How did she die?"

"We don't know 'til we get the postmortem examination."

Quinn shook his head in disbelief.

"I'm trying to find out if anybody heard or saw anything last night. Between ten and midnight particularly."

"I wasn't here, myself. Like I said, I'm a baker. I have to work from ten-thirty to seven. I've not long got home, as a matter of fact." He indicated his nightshirt. "I sleep during the day."

"Do you usually leave by the back door?"

"Eh? Oh, er, no. By the front. To Wilton Street. She was in the laneway, you say? I wouldn't have seen her at all."

"Don't you have to relieve the dogs before you go to work?"

39

"Yes, that's right. I did that. Yes, I did take them out but it was earlier. Weren't no dead body there then, I promise you."

Murdoch made a note. "Can you be precise as to the time?"

"Yes, I can. I was thinking I'd better start getting ready for work. Looked at the clock. Ten minutes before ten. 'Come on, Princess,' I says, 'let's go for a bit of a stroll.' So we did. Didn't see nothing, like I said." Suddenly he slapped his thigh. "No, what am I thinking? I saw Alice coming home." He winked and tapped the side of his nose. "As she would put it, she was hickey as a lambskin."

Murdoch wrote that down. It confirmed the time Alice had given.

"Where do you work, Mr. Quinn?"

"The Union Hotel on King Street. I do all their dinner rolls for them. And the pies and tarts. Very tasty, if I say so myself. You can't tell from that one, it's a bit stale. Drop by for breakfast one of these days. I'll serve you a Bath bun like you've never had. Melt in your mouth."

"Thanks, I might do that." Murdoch wiped at his sweaty face. "I'd better get going. I've got to talk to a lot of people."

"Wonder what the poor girl was doing in the laneway at that time of night. Not to mention it was colder than Beelzebub's bottom. Was she a, er, lady of the night?"

"I don't think so. Course it's hard to tell with no clothes. She was naked."

"Sweet Jesus, you don't say. How did that happen?"

"They were stolen, most likely. Which is a serious offence in the eye of the law." He put away his notebook and stood up. "By the way, didn't you take Prince Albert out last night?"

"What?"

"You know, to relieve himself. He must have needed to go as well. You just mentioned taking out Princess."

"Oh, no . . . Fact is I just got him this morning. From me pal."

"He must be quite a swell to own such a nobby dog. Bloodlines and all that."

Quinn tugged at his sidewhiskers. "Oh, no. This dog ain't worth a dime. Who'd pay money for a funny-looking tiddler like him?" He drummed his fingers on the arm of his chair. "Fact is, the fellow, this pal of mine, is going on his honeymoon. Didn't want to leave the little fellow with his mother 'cause she doesn't see so good. What the heck! I felt sorry for the man. And I do like dogs, as you can probably tell. Said I'd take care of him 'til he got back."

The words had come tumbling out and now he stopped, eyeing Murdoch. His full cheeks glistened in the firelight.

Murdoch went to the door.

41

"If anything else comes to you, drop in at the station and give us a report. Do you know where we are?"

"Sure. The corner of Parliament and Wilton."

"That's it."

"I will. For certain I will. Terrible pity." Quinn ran his fingers through his already dishevelled dark hair. "Best of luck."

Murdoch stepped out into the hall, which seemed wondrously refreshing after the furnace of Quinn's room. He headed back toward the kitchen. The man might be a likeable fellow, but his guilty conscience was as thick in the air as the smell of the dogs.

Chapter Three

DONALDA RHODES WOKE ABRUPTLY, forcing herself into consciousness away from the terror of her dream. It is the same nightmare over and over. She is walking by the river that flowed at the bottom of the field where she grew up. She is accompanied by another woman. Usually this woman is her dear friend Marianne, but this time it is Harriet Shepcote. Owen, a child still in skirts, is skipping ahead of them. Suddenly he falls and disappears. She runs over and sees that he has tumbled down an old well. She can see him at the bottom, hear him crying. She struggles to reach him but cannot. "Help me, Harriet," she cries, but the young woman only stands frozen in fear. As Donalda looks into the dark mouth of the well she sees that it is no longer her son crouched there but a little girl with long dark hair. She is sobbing and her anguish enters Donalda's own body.

43

She pulled herself into a sitting position. What time was it? Her bedroom was dark, the curtains drawn and the fire gone to a few dull embers in the grate. She fumbled on the bedside table for the box of matches, struck one and lit the lamp. She felt almost ashamed. She was behaving like a frightened child in the nursery.

She got out of bed and put on her velvet wrapper and slippers. The mantel clock said a quarter past nine. She went over to the window and pulled back the curtains. Outside, the street was empty, the bare maples charcoal etchings against the grey sky. Fine snow danced by the window. She leaned her forehead against the cold pane and her breath made a patch of mist in front of her.

There was a discreet tapping at the door and Edith Foy entered, manoeuvring the breakfast tea trolley.

"Good morning, Mrs. Rhodes."

"Good morning."

Edith wheeled the trolley to the fireplace, where there was a bowlegged Chinese table and a plush-covered armchair.

"I hope you slept well, madam."

"Yes, thank you."

"Shall I build up the fire?"

"If you please."

Donalda poured herself a cup of tea from the silver pot and added a slice of lemon and a piece of sugar. There was a bread roll and a dish of stewed compote on the tray for her breakfast.

"Is Master Owen awake?"

"Not as yet, madam. Shall I have Foy call him?"

"No, I'll do it. But you can start drawing his bath."

She sipped at her tea, enjoying the warmth of the cup in her hands. "Where is Theresa? Is she still unwell?"

The housekeeper was poking at the fire, her back to Donalda.

"To tell the truth, madam, I don't rightly know."

She turned around and there was a strange expression on her face, a hint of pleasure curling at the side of her mouth. "She's gone."

Donalda stared at her. "I don't understand. To church, you mean?"

"No, madam." Edith took a piece of paper out of her apron pocket. "I went to her room first thing, seeing as she had not yet shown her face in the kitchen and I was concerned she might still be feeling poorly." She handed Donalda the note. "This was on her bed."

Donalda unfolded it. The message was written in pencil in childish big letters.

I HAVE GONE BACK HOME. I MISS EVERYBODY TO MUCH. YOUR OBEDIENT SERVANT, Therese Laporte.

"Good gracious. What does it mean?"

"Just what it says, I think, madam. She's gone off back to Chatham, most like."

"But why?"

"Like she says there. She was homesick."

45

"I know she was at first, but not lately. She seemed to have settled down nicely."

"Not really, madam. She put on a good face with you because she knew that it bothered you to see her carrying on so, but I heard her weeping away nights."

"You should have told me."

"I didn't want to trouble you with such silly matters, madam. I kept expecting she'd get over it."

"When did she leave?"

"I can't rightly say. I was concerned about her last night and looked in, as was only right. The room was dark and I thought she was sleeping and didn't disturb her. However, this morning I found that she'd put a bolster under the quilt to make it look like she was in bed. She didn't want her getaway to be discovered too soon. Cunning child that she is. Not giving a care to those who would worry about her."

"I find it so hard to believe that she wouldn't say anything."

"Ungrateful, if you ask me. She should have given notice at least. And you taking her under your wing the way you did, madam."

Donalda wanted to snap at her housekeeper, speak out in the girl's defence, but she knew that would be foolish. There was bad feeling enough. Donalda had taken to Therese from the start. She was sweet-tempered and eager to please, whereas Mrs. Foy, efficient though she was, often had an aggrieved put-upon sort of air that was unpleasant.

The housekeeper came over to the tea trolley and, unasked, poured more tea into Donalda's cup.

"I haven't wanted to say anything, madam, because I know you showed a fondness to the girl, but she was a sly one . . ."

"Why do you say that?"

"She looked like butter wouldn't melt in her mouth, but –"

"Yes, do go on." Donalda couldn't hide her irritation.

Edith tightened her lips. "Little Miss Laporte was a thief."

"I don't believe that!"

"It is quite true, madam. Last Thursday my silver brooch went missing from my room, and also my husband's watch fob. A real gold piece it is, that he's most fond of. I found them in the girl's room. Tucked into the back of the wardrobe."

"How do you know they were stolen?"

"Begging your pardon, madam, I don't see as how they could have walked there."

"Why would anyone steal jewellery only to leave it behind?"

"I can't pretend to understand the mind of a thief, madam. I only tell you what I found . . . There was another thing, madam."

47

Edith sounded as if she had something delicious in her mouth. Donalda was positive she actually smacked her lips.

"I found a box of handkerchiefs in her drawer. Untouched. I distinctly remember they were the ones Dr. Rhodes himself gave you yourself as a Christmas present. Lovely Irish linen they are. If that isn't proof I don't know what is."

"Nonsense. I gave them to Theresa myself."

"Oh, I see. I beg your pardon, madam, I didn't realize –"

"I didn't much care for them."

"Of course, madam. You can do whatever you wish with your own belongings."

"Thank you, Edith, I shall keep that in mind."

"Yes, madam. Will there be anything else?"

"I assume you plan to inform the police about the thefts."

Edith lowered her eyes quickly. "I don't wish to be uncharitable. I have them back and as long as there's nothing else missing I am willing to let the matter drop."

"In that case we had better question the doctor and Mr. Owen. Neither has reported any loss so far, but perhaps they should check their cufflinks and pins."

"Yes, madam. Will you be wanting me to advertise again?"

"I suppose so."

"Perhaps this time we could request an orphan girl? They appreciate a good position more than most young women do these days. The Wrights got someone from the Barnardo Home in Peterborough and she has worked out most satisfactorily."

"Very well."

"I'll see to it tomorrow." Edith picked up the note from the tea trolley. "We don't need this, do we?" Before Donalda could protest, she threw it into the fire. The flames devoured it in a moment.

"What dress would you wish me to lay out this morning, madam?"

Donalda was staring at the black fragments of paper as they floated up the chimney. "What did you say?"

"Your dress, madam? Which one today?"

"My wool plaid, I think. The church is never warm enough."

"Perhaps your cashmere undervest, then, madam?"

Edith went into the adjacent dressing room. Donalda was glad to be out of her sight. She could feel tears stinging at the back of her eyes. Inappropriate tears, she knew, but the anguish of her dream was still close and she was hurt by Theresa's callous behaviour. In spite of the inequality between them she thought there had been real affection. She was obviously wrong.

49

When Edith returned to the kitchen with the breakfast tray, her husband was sitting at the table with Joe, the stable lad. The boy was gulping down hot porridge and John Foy was sipping noisily from a mug of steaming tea.

"'Bout time you stuck your head out of the den," she said.

Foy spooned more sugar into the mug, took another drink, smacked his lips and wiped his mouth with the back of his hand.

"I said it was about time you got down here," she repeated.

"I heard you," grunted Foy.

"It's almost a quarter to ten. Master Owen needs his bath drawn and you should get the doctor's breakfast going."

Foy sipped his tea slowly. His wife glared. "What's wrong with you? You look like something the cat brought in."

"Don't go at me, woman. I was up late last night."

"Oh?"

"Oh, yourself. What do you know? You were whistling at the angels."

"Why were you up late, then, Mr. Clever?"

"Because the doctor couldn't get in."

"What do you mean he couldn't get in?"

50   Her husband was spinning out his tale, knowing it would irritate her to no end if he was privy to something she wasn't.

"The door was bolted. Fortunately for him, I was awake."

"What time was that?"

"Must have been at least two o'clock."

"Where was he 'til that godforsaken hour in the morning?"

"At his consulting rooms. He enjoys it there. It's quiet and peaceful."

"How do you know?"

"How do you think? Because the doctor speaks English and I understand English. He told me."

"Who bolted the door?"

"Must have been Mr. Owen. He took Miss Shepcote home. Poor thing was very poorly, sneezing all over the china the entire evening. I suppose when he come back he shot the bolt, not knowing Doctor was out."

Edith took a pair of gloves out of her pocket and wriggled her fingers into them. They were a tight fit.

"Where'd you get those?" asked Foy.

"I found them."

"Where?"

"It don't matter where." She smoothed the black leather gloves. "What were you doing going round the house at two o'clock in the morning?"

"I couldn't sleep. Not with the racket you were making. So I got up. Thought I might as well make sure everything was tidy downstairs. Good thing I did too.

51

The doctor had been out there knocking the wood off the door. Could have got his death of cold."

She spoke sharply. "I hope you're watching yourself, John Foy. This is a good position for us."

Neither of them had acknowledged the presence of Joe Seaton, who had not raised his eyes from his bowl of porridge. He finished, picked up his dish and went over to the sink. Edith noticed him.

"See you give it a good rinse."

He didn't say anything. He never did, and they had got into the habit of treating him as if he were deaf and dumb, which he wasn't.

"You'd better go and get the carriage ready," continued Edith. "They'll be leaving soon. I don't know what's the matter with you stableboys. You couldn't find your way out of a maze if a string was tied to your whatnot."

Joe's predecessor had left the Rhodeses' employ the summer before without any warning. Although Joe had never clapped eyes on the boy, Edith always spoke as if they were in a wilful collusion.

She tapped her husband on the shoulder. "As for you, if you don't hurry up with that bath, they'll all miss church. And we wouldn't like that to happen, would we?"

"I haven't finished my tea yet. Where's Tess? She can do it."

Edith stroked the sleek kid of her gloves, finger by finger.

Foy watched her over the edge of his mug of tea. "Is she still poorly?"

"She's gone. She's left."

"Gone? What the Jesus do you mean?"

"What I say, and I'll thank you not to take the Lord's name in vain . . . She was homesick. Couldn't stand it here a minute longer. She's gone home."

"Home?"

"There's an echo in here."

"To Chatham, you mean."

"That's where she's from, so I assume that is where she is heading."

"Will you please explain what the Christ you are going on about? How d'you know she's gone home?"

Edith reached over and put her hand on top of her husband's. There was no affection in the touch. "I told the mistress that the girl ran away because she was homesick. I told her she left a letter. She left it on her bed. For me to find. Said she missed her home. You know how she was always going on about that sister of hers . . ."

Joe made a strange grunting noise, and the Foys stared at him.

"What's wrong, lost your sweetheart?" asked John maliciously.

"Leave him alone."

"It's true. I seen him making sheep's eyes at her."

"Never mind that. Listen to me. I also told the mistress that Therese stole some of our jewellery."

53

"She didn't do that."

"Oh yes, she did. You see I found your fob in her bedroom."

"Oh, get away . . ."

She gripped his hand hard. "That gold bit went missing weeks ago. You said you'd dropped it at the lodge. But there it was. How would it have ended up in the girl's room if she didn't steal it?"

He stared at her, then jerked his hand out from beneath her gloved one. "You've got all the answers, haven't you?"

She began to peel off the tight black gloves. "One of us has to, don't we . . . Now, why don't you get along and draw that bath. You, Joe, swill out your bowl and get going. You'd think the royal princess had vanished, to see the both of you."

Joe pumped out some water and washed his bowl and spoon. If the other two had paid him any attention at all they might have noticed how slumped over he was. They might have seen that his thin, pale face was taut with misery.

Joe already knew that Therese had gone.

Chapter Four

AT SIX O'CLOCK MURDOCH SENT CRABTREE to bring
Cavendish to the morgue so he could do a likeness of
the dead girl. He and two constables had called at all
the houses on the nearby streets with no success. There
were the usual number of unlikely identifications but
nothing he could believe. Nobody had come in to
number four with information, and telegrams to the
other stations had so far yielded nothing. When
Murdoch finally left for home the brief grey winter day
was long gone. The street lamps were lit and the
persistent snow swirled around the posts, shining in the
gas light. His lodgings were on Ontario Street, an easy
walking distance from the station. He was tired and
hungry and glad not to have far to go.

Three years ago Father Fair, the priest at St. Paul's,
had referred him to the Kitchens, who were also Roman

55

Catholic. His previous digs had been with a Presbyterian widow whose faith was as hard and uncompromising as the Rock on which she claimed her church was built. It was a relief to Murdoch to live with his fellow parishioners. There was no frown of disapproval when he left for Mass. No muttered prayer of fear when he hung his crucifix above his bed. And he didn't have to find ways to dispose of the roast beef his previous landlady had always served on Fridays.

The Kitchen house was one-half of a double with white bargeboards edging the brown gables. In the summertime both dwellings were covered with grape-ivy, but now the runners were like tracings on the orange brick. He let himself in.

The hallway was redolent with the smell of fried meat, and a burst of saliva filled his mouth. On Sunday all restaurants and shops were closed and the only food he'd eaten all day was half a cheese sandwich that the duty sergeant had shared with him. His stomach rumbled. He was looking forward to his tea.

The far door opened and Beatrice Kitchen came out to greet him. She was a tiny woman, as neat as a nuthatch, with fine grey hair worn flat and smooth to her head.

56 "Mr. Murdoch, you're so late. You must be famished. I'll wager you didn't have a thing to eat all day."

"You are absolutely right on all counts."

She took his hat and coat and hung them on the

coat tree. "You've been dealing with that poor murdered girl, I'm sure," she was tut-tutting as she dusted the snow from his hat and coat.

"You heard about it, then?"

"Yes, I did. May Brogan – you've heard me mention her, I'm sure; she was so poorly all winter – well, in any case she came to Mass late and she was all of a fluster, I could see that right away. After the service she told me about the police finding a dead girl in St. Luke's Lane. May lives at the corner of St. Luke's and Sumach, so she heard all the commotion. She wondered if I knew anything, seeing as how you live here, but I said I was in the dark myself. A constable had come to fetch you early this morning, but that was all I could say."

Murdoch hovered awkwardly in the narrow hall, pinned by his landlady's excitement.

"Not that I would tell May anything that I shouldn't, as you know. Oh, dear, look at you shivering here. All in good time . . . Come on down to the kitchen and get yourself warm. I made you a nice bit of liver."

Murdoch rubbed his hands together to restore the circulation. "Thank you, Mrs. K. Right now I could eat moss off a rock." He nodded in the direction of the parlour. "How's himself?"

"Not so good today. But he'll cheer up when he knows you're home. He was very interested in the story of the dead girl. He's got all sorts of ideas already. You know what he's like."

57

"I'll be glad to hear them. We've got nowhere so far."

Murdoch meant what he said. He'd come to value Arthur Kitchen's shrewdness, and talking over the incidents of his day had become a routine they both looked forward to.

Last winter Arthur Kitchen had developed a hacking cough, and it soon became apparent he had the consumption. Until then he'd had a good job as a railway clerk, but when his condition was known, he was fired with some paltry excuse. A tiny pension from an insurance company was all he had to live on. Over the last six months his health had deteriorated to the point where he no longer left the house, spending his time confined to the small front parlour. Murdoch was the only lodger now; others had moved out when they realized what the sickness was.

Murdoch followed his landlady to the kitchen and as they passed the parlour, he could hear the bubbling cough.

"I'll just say hello," he said. With a knock, he opened the parlour door.

The room was icy cold. Mrs. Kitchen had heard that fresh air was good for tubercular patients, and she kept the window open day and night. Murdoch wasn't convinced the sooty blasts that came in from the Toronto streets were equivalent to fresh Muskoka breezes, but Arthur found the cold air relieved the discomfort of his constant fever. When he saw who it was, his gaunt face lit up.

"Evening, Bill. Late tonight."

He was seated in a wicker Bath chair, wrapped in a quilt. Handy beside him was a spittoon. The room was thick with the rotten odour of consumptive lungs.

"Evening yourself, Arthur. You've heard about the case, I understand –"

Beatrice interrupted. "That'll keep 'til you've had your tea. Come on now."

Murdoch grinned. "All right. Be back shortly."

He followed her down to the kitchen, which was blessedly warm and filled with the delicious smell of fried onions. A place was set at the small pine table and he sat down obediently while Beatrice took his plate out of the warming oven. The Kitchens and he had become good friends but he was still the boarder and, as such, certain formalities were observed. He was served separately from the two of them and always got the best cuts of meat and the choicest vegetables. He'd given up protesting. Arthur seemed to subsist on broth and junkets but Murdoch worried that Beatrice didn't eat enough herself. Even birds couldn't subsist on air.

"The water's boiling when you want it and there's a lemon pudding for your sweet. Join us when you're done."

She left him to eat alone.

He eased his chilled feet out of his boots into the slippers she had warmed for him and tackled his meal. The liver had dried out to the consistency of gutta-percha but he was too hungry to be fussy. He sliced off a piece, loaded onions on top of it and shovelled it into his mouth. He demolished the meal in no time at all, then sawed off a thick hunk of bread from the loaf beside his plate and mopped up the grease from his dish. The kettle was whistling shrilly and he got up to make a pot of tea. The sweet was lumpy but he wolfed that down too, then sat back to drink his tea. Usually he read the newspapers while he ate but there were none today. Instead he propped up the book he'd taken out of the library the week before. It was a biography of the explorer Henry Stanley.

He turned the page but realized he hadn't really taken in the words. He was finding it hard to concentrate. Images of a young naked body kept intruding. Images of raw flesh where the skin had torn from the knees and elbows as they pulled her from the winter's deadly embrace.

The three of them were seated in the parlour. The window was closed and Beatrice had lit the fire but it hadn't yet touched the chill air. Arthur, the lines on his face as dark as scars, was wearing a woollen nightcap and mittens, and Murdoch was huddled under a blanket. The single oil lamp hardly made a dint on the gloom. For the past hour, they had been discussing the day. Murdoch had no worries about them being indiscreet. Arthur didn't go out and although Beatrice enjoyed hearing gossip, it was from an avid interest in humanity, not to revel in another's misfortune. He knew she had never repeated any information that she'd gleaned from their chats together. He also knew that her friends and neighbours often pressed her to be forthcoming but she wouldn't.

"What's your next step, then?" asked Beatrice.

"Wait and see, really. Cavendish did a good likeness and I sent the drawings over to all the newspapers. The *Herald* and the *News* should be able to print it in the morning editions. If we're lucky we'll get a response soon."

"What's himself have to say about it?"

"He hasn't had a chance to say anything yet. He wasn't in. Bad stomach again."

Thomas Brackenreid was the inspector of Murdoch's division, and there was no love lost between them. Many an evening Murdoch had poured out his anger and frustration to his sympathetic friends.

Mrs. Kitchen moved her worktable closer to the lamp and spread out a box of shells on the surface. She picked up a small wooden box and arranged the shells on the lid. She added to their tiny income by making craft items and selling them to the fancy goods stores on King Street.

61

"What do you think?" she asked the two men.

"Very artistic," said Murdoch.

"The scallop would look better in the centre," said Arthur.

"I think you're right." She dipped the brush into the glue pot.

"Best thing is if you find her clothes," said Arthur.

"Might be best but he doesn't know what to look for, does he?" his wife said.

"You're right there, Mother. I wasn't thinking."

He coughed violently, then spat into the spittoon. There was a fleck of blood on his lower lip and his wife reached over and wiped it away as calmly as if he were a child with a crumb on his face.

"Well, whoever or whatever she was, I'm sorry for her," Beatrice continued. "So young. Somebody somewhere will be worrying."

She added a brown auger shell to the rim of the box.

"Not necessarily at this moment, Mother," said Arthur. "She could have come from the country. Her family might not be expecting to hear from her for a month or more."

"You could be right, Father. God rest her soul," said Beatrice, and she blessed herself.

"Amen to that," said Murdoch, and he did likewise. There was silence in the room except for the soft hiss of the coals burning and the quiet tick of the mantel clock. Murdoch glanced over at Arthur, who was staring into the fire.

"I almost forgot. There was something I wanted to ask you. What kind of dog is about this big?" He indicated with his hands. "Long-haired. Caramel-coloured with pop eyes and a squashed-in nose. Long ears."

Before he got sick, Kitchen had been quite a dog fancier. He considered for a minute. "Sounds like a Pekingese. Wouldn't you say, Mother?"

Beatrice nodded. "That or a King Charles."

"Not that colour. Why'd you ask, Bill?"

"Just curious."

He related the story of Samuel Quinn and the Virgin Mary, although from delicacy he called her the proper name of Princess. Mrs. K. tutted and exclaimed several well-I-nevers, but they both were diverted by the tale.

"I miss having a dog," said Mrs. K. "And Arthur's always wanted a greyhound, haven't you, dear? As soon as he's better we'll get one."

Arthur nodded, the pretense hovering in the air like a miasma.

Murdoch yawned. Time for bed. "Do you want more coal on?" he asked.

"If you please. I must finish this box, and Arthur has promised to read to me."

Arthur grunted. "She says she wants to hear *Paradise Lost*. I told her it was written by a Protestant and she won't understand a word, but she insists."

"You can explain what is necessary. You like doing that."

63

Murdoch smiled and started to load lumps of the black shiny coal into the red maw of the fire. The supply was low in the bucket and he made a note to himself to have some delivered for them. Then he shook hands good night and left.

Beatrice had put a candle ready for him on the hall table, and he lit it from the sconce and went upstairs.

Last summer, Murdoch had insisted on renting the extra room upstairs for a sitting room. It was a squeeze for him to manage on his wages but it helped out the Kitchens and he liked having the luxury of a separate place where he could sit and read if he wanted to. He went into that room first.

It was simply furnished with a flowered velvet armchair and matching footstool, a sideboard and two lamp tables. The oilcloth-covered floor was softened with a woven rag rug courtesy of Mrs. Kitchen.

He placed his candlestick on the sideboard, then bent down and rolled the rug back to the wall. Even though it was getting late he had to do his practice before he went to bed.

Two years ago last June, his fiancée, Elizabeth Milner, had contracted typhoid. Within five days she was dead, gone as quickly as a shadow on the lawn. He mourned silently, deeply. Still did. But he was a healthy, vigorous man and of late his body had begun to clamour for normal satisfaction. Many a night he tossed restlessly, listening to the church bell mark out each hour until

64

the dawn seeped over the sleeping city, blotting up the darkness, and he sought a relief that not even the threat of confession could stop.

Shortly before Christmas he decided he had to make some attempt at renewing a social life and enrolled in a dance class given by a Professor Mansfield Otranto. The professor was evasive about his educational credentials but, as he taught dancing and did phrenology consultations, Murdoch didn't think it much mattered if his mastery of Greek and Latin was shaky and his accent slithered all over the place before coming to rest in the flat vowels of Liverpool. They'd had three waltz lessons so far. After five lessons Murdoch would be allowed to attend the soiree that the professor gave for his best pupils on the second Saturday in the month.

He took his patent-leather dance slippers out of the shoebox and slipped them on. Ready? Arms up to shoulder height, right hand resting lightly on the lady's back.

"Mr. Murdoch, pul-leez! Don't push. You're not trying to get a cow into a barn. Ladies are like thoroughbreds. Skittish and sensitive. You must *persuade*. And again! Pul-leez, sir, don't stomp. A person would think you were killing cockroaches. Glide, always glide. Like skating . . . And with the right . . . Forward, two, three. Left again, two, three . . ." The professor's wife, a plump, well-coiffed woman, thumped out the waltz with

65

military precision on the out-of-tune piano tucked into the corner of the third-floor studio. Otranto took the female part, surprisingly graceful for such a corpulent man. He was short, and the overpowering smell of his violet pomade wafted upwards beneath Murdoch's nose. The oil, however, could not disguise the sparsity of the hair plastered across his crown, nor could the sweet cachou he sucked on mask his cigar-tainted breath.

In spite of this, Murdoch was enjoying the lessons immensely and was looking forward to holding an honest-to-goodness woman in his arms.

Humming some bars from Strauss, he began to dance around his tiny room.

"Glide! One, two, three. Forward, two, three. Lightly, lightly, like it's air you're treading on. Think of clouds, light fluffy clouds . . ."

He did this for twenty minutes more, then executed a tricky half-turn and, pleased with his progress, decided to call it a night.

Chapter Five

He recognized the portrait immediately, although in it, Therese looked older and of course the artist could not capture the glow of rude health on the lightly freckled cheek that made her so attractive. Fear shot through his body. Had anybody seen him? Could he be linked to the dead girl? He lowered the newspaper, struggling to gain control. Guilt came like acid in his stomach, but it was really the fear that gripped him. If there was one jot of sorrow for the young interrupted life, it was so fleeting he could not have acknowledged it.

MONDAY, FEBRUARY 11

LIKE ALL THE OTHER POLICE OFFICERS, Murdoch spent long hours at the station. When he entered the station hall early the next morning and caught the usual whiff of sawdust, coal stove and winter clothes, it was as familiar as home.

"Good morning, Sergeant," Murdoch greeted the duty sergeant, who was perched on a tall stool behind the high counter. The other man's dour face changed and he grinned at Murdoch.

"Would you believe I rode on the Singer this morning?"

"No! You must have wheeled it all the way."

"I did not. I told you, it'll go through anything."

Variations of this conversation had been happening all winter. Because the detective branch of the police force was so new, the status of detectives, especially acting detectives like Murdoch, was unclear. Technically he ranked above all the other officers but below the two sergeants and the inspector. As the only detective he often felt isolated. Then last summer, by chance, he and Sergeant Seymour had started to chat about the merits of the Singer versus the Ideal bicycle. It turned out that Seymour was also a keen cyclist and on that basis the two men had struck up a friendship. The rivalry wasn't serious and they had gone on a couple of strenuous bicycling trips when their days off coincided.

"Anything for me?" Murdoch asked.

"Foster sent over a photograph. I put it on your desk."

He nodded in the direction of the three ragged men who were sitting on the bench. They were all watching the two officers.

"They're here about the girl." Suddenly, the sergeant raised his voice. "Hey you! Yes, you in the tartan cap. I told you no spitting on the floor. Do it again and you'll be charged."

The man addressed scuffed his boot into the sawdust on the floor like a scolded schoolboy. The other two shifted their stare into the space ahead of them.

"Let me get a cup of tea and look at the photograph and then I'll talk to them," said Murdoch. He pushed through the gate and walked back to the orderly room.

The station was not large. On the first floor was the public hall, lit by narrow grimy windows. Most months of the year, the wall sconces had to be lighted and the room was stifling winter and summer. A large black stove dominated the centre, and around the walls ran a wooden bench, rubbed smooth by the rear ends of countless nervous occupants. Across one end of the room ran a high wooden counter, a barrier between police and public. Behind it sat the duty sergeant with his big cloth-bound daily register, and behind him was a desk with a telephone and the telegraph machine, manned this morning by a young constable named Graham. At the rear were two small holding cells for those brought in as drunk and disorderly. Some nights these also had to make do as a place for waifs and strays, as part of the duty of the police force was to give temporary shelter to the homeless. Last year number-four

69

station had handled over a hundred and twenty souls, most of them single men who weren't vagrants – not yet, anyway – but had no home to go to.

The backroom where the policemen ate or on occasion questioned suspects was also dark, but there was a cheery fire going in the hearth and, as usual, a kettle of water boiling on the hob. Murdoch poured some hot water into a large teapot. The tea grouts were used over and over, fresh leaves being added to the pot as necessary. The tea thus produced varied from weak as pauper's gruel to so strong it could take the enamel off teeth. This morning it was a tolerable strength.

As Murdoch was pouring himself a mug, the ginger station cat rubbed against his legs, purring like a swarm of bees. He bent down and scratched her head.

"No, I'm not going to give you anything to eat, you slacker. See those mice droppings on the table? How come? There shouldn't be a one around here."

The cat smiled complacently and rubbed her gums harder against his leg.

"I mean it, Puss. Go find your own breakfast."

He picked up his mug and walked on back to his office.

Barely more than a cubicle, there was room for a desk, scarred and chipped, a chair with the upholstery poking out of the seat and a wooden filing cabinet with two broken drawers. Facing him were last year's posters from the annual police athletic tournament. Murdoch had won the one-mile bicycle race against stiff opposition, and he enjoyed the memory every time he glanced at his poster. Behind the desk were hung two obligatory portraits. One was of Her Majesty Queen Victoria in ceremonial attire, the other of Chief Constable Grasett, whose patrician face lent authority to the proceedings and also covered a crack in the plaster.

He sat down and, as he did every day, pulled open the top drawer and took out the silver-framed photograph of Elizabeth. He'd taken it himself with his new Premo camera just after they were engaged. Unfortunately, she'd moved and her face was out of focus, but it was the only picture he had. He gazed at it, said his prayer, planted a kiss on the glass and returned the picture to the drawer.

Then with a sigh, he picked up the envelope and pulled out the photograph of the dead girl. Foster had propped open her eyes for better recognition and used tints to get a good approximation of her natural colouring. There was a light dusting of freckles across the straight nose and the cheeks were pink. Foster was guessing there but Murdoch thought, given the girl's strong body, it was likely she'd had a rosy complexion. Probably fresh from the country. He had to admit he was relieved he wasn't the one who had to notify the family.

71

By nine-thirty, he'd interviewed four people and more kept arriving. It was only Seymour's formidable presence that prevented the front of the station from sounding like a music hall.

Murdoch knew the body was not that of Simon Poyner's wife, who'd never returned from a visit to her aunt in Detroit and who'd now be about forty. When shown the photograph, however, Mr. Poyner had been caught in a timeless world and said it certainly could be Agnes with some meat on her. Likewise the girl was not Martha Stone, daughter of Ezekiel, who'd walked away from the household ten years ago. She would be fifty-five if she was living. One old woman, all agog with excitement, swore the portrait was that of a school-teacher from Kingston who'd boarded with her last year. "Lovely young woman, lovely. So tragic." Unfortunately, the old lady's testimony kept changing according to what she thought he wanted to hear. One moment the schoolteacher had brown eyes, the next blue, yes, blue, of course. The age didn't fit here either but he decided to send a wire to the Kingston police anyway. You never knew. There was an outside chance the dead girl might be related to the "lovely schoolteacher."

He was considering going to make some more tea when there was a knock on the wall in the hallway. The office was too small to permit a regular door and Murdoch had to make do with a reed curtain. It was Constable Crabtree who pushed through. The curtain clacked and snapped behind him.

"There's a gentleman out front, sir. Come about the

72

notice in the newspaper. He claims the girl was his housemaid. Says she disappeared on Saturday night. The description does fit."

"Who is he?"

"Quite a swell. Dr. Cyril Rhodes. Lives up on Lowther Avenue."

"Bring him in. I've not had much luck so far. How many more now?"

"A good dozen, I'd say. Constable Graham and me are sorting out the wheat from the chaff for you."

The constable left, the reed strips swaying in his wake. Murdoch turned to a fresh leaf in his notebook and placed his pen at the ready.

In a minute there was another tap and Crabtree pulled aside the curtain.

"Dr. Rhodes, sir."

Behind him hovered a short, middle-aged man. Murdoch stood up and reached across the desk.

"Detective William Murdoch here."

They shook hands. The doctor's grip was light. Murdoch indicated the chair and Rhodes sat in it quickly. He pulled off his gloves, removed his silk top hat and fumbled with his silver-headed walking stick as he tried to find somewhere to lean it. He obviously wasn't accustomed to being interviewed by policemen in dingy cubicles where the sour smell of vomit wafted over from the holding cell, courtesy of last night's resident. The stables adjoined and they added their own contribution.

73

"Can I get you a cup of tea, sir?" asked Murdoch.

The doctor shook his head and reached inside his coat, which was of fine sheared lamb.

"My card."

Murdoch studied the piece of cardboard. Substantial, glossy white, plain black script.

DR. CYRIL RHODES
(Specializing in nervous diseases)
387 Church Street

He took his time, allowing the doctor to settle down.

"I understand you can identify the dead girl we're seeking information about?"

Rhodes nodded. "I do believe she is, er, was, our maid Therese."

Murdoch held out the photograph. "Was this her?"

Rhodes swallowed nervously. "Yes. Regrettably it is."

"Her full name?"

"Therese Laporte."

"French-Canadian?"

"Yes. She was from somewhere near Chatham, I believe." Rhodes tugged on his trim beard. "W-what happened?"

74   "We don't know yet. One of our constables found her body in the early hours of Sunday morning. Over near Sumach Street. You live up in Yorkville Village, sir?"

"That's right. Birchlea House on Lowther Avenue."

Murdoch wrote that down. "She seems to have been a long way from home. What would she be doing over this way?"

"I can't-t say. I heard on Sunday morning that she had left. Sort of run away, really. She's been with us for the past six months but apparently she was home . . . er, home . . . homesick. Our housekeeper, Mrs. Foy, found a note she'd left. My wife will be very distressed when she finds out. She was fond of the . . . the girl. Spent a lot of time with her. Training and whatnot."

His words trailed off and he gazed at Murdoch anxiously. Then he patted his coat. "Sorry, I can't linger. I was at my office when I saw the notice. I had to postpone my appointments. Th-thought this was im-important. You'll want me to make a formal identification, I presume?"

"Yes, I will."

Rhodes was about to stand up but Murdoch frowned at him.

"I have to ask you a few more questions, sir."

"I don't know much more than I've already said."

"What were the exact contents of the note?"

"What?"

"The note that your cook found – what did it say?"

"Didn't look at it myself, but apparently it was about wanting to return home. She was from the country, you see. Got quite homesick. Often do these, these . . . they often do, these girls."

"Indeed. Toronto must be a big change for them. When did you yourself last see Miss Laporte?"

"Hmm. I suppose it was shortly before the evening meal. Fiveish on Sat-Saturday. She was setting the table."

"Did she seem herself?"

"How do you mean?"

"Did she seem ill in any way?"

"Not that I noticed, although she didn't serve that night. Mrs. Foy said she was indisposed. Seems now as if that wasn't true. She was probably planning her getaway. Dratted inconvenient. My wife spent considerable time training her. She seemed most suitable. Now we've got to start all over again."

"So you do."

Murdoch thought he'd kept his voice neutral, but the doctor glanced at him sharply and blushed suddenly like a boy. He was not quite so self-centred and impervious as he seemed.

"You d-do . . . you don't understand," he said.

"Understand what, sir?"

Rhodes waved his hand. "No m-matter. It is not relevant."

He patted his coat again, which seemed to be a habitual nervous gesture. "I do have appointments to meet . . ."

"Of course. I will need to come to the house and talk to your servants afterwards." Murdoch thought this was a good time to give out some more information, and he explained about the body being naked. Rhodes seemed suitably shocked.

"We'll need a description of her clothing," added Murdoch. "I don't suppose you could help us in that regard, could you, Doctor?"

"I'm afraid not. She was the, er, maid . . . after all."

"She wore a uniform, didn't she, sir?"

"Yes, of . . . of course. A dark skirt, or dress rather, white apron, white cap. The usual sort of thing."

There was another knock from the hallway and Crabtree came in and handed Murdoch a cardboard box.

"The postmortem report, sir. Just delivered."

Murdoch hesitated for a moment. "Do you mind if I take a quick look at this, Doctor?"

Rhodes pulled out his watch again and studied it. "If you must . . ."

Murdoch was already reading the report.

Toronto. February 11, 1895

This is to certify that I, Robert Moffat, a legally qualified physician in the city of Toronto, did this day make a postmortem examination upon the body of a woman, not yet identified. The body is that of a well-nourished young woman about fifteen or sixteen years of age. There were no clothes on the body when it was brought into the morgue. The abdominal organs, kidneys, and liver are normal in size. Bladder is contracted and empty.

77

The immediate cause of death was asphyxiation. This was brought about by the extreme cold weather, which caused the lungs to go into contraction and therefore no oxygen reached the brain and heart. There were injuries to the left elbow, which was dislocated, and the left ankle, which was severely bruised. These injuries may have occurred after death and are consistent with limbs being displaced while in the grip of rigor mortis.

Murdoch finished reading while Rhodes fidgeted.

"Bad news, is it?" he asked finally. "She wasn't, er, wasn't attacked, I hope?"

Murdoch put down the paper. "No, she froze to death. However, as I'm sure you know, Doctor, a person doesn't just lie down and take a nap in freezing weather."

"Great heavens, she wasn't inebriated, was she?"

"Apparently not. Did she have a history of drinking?"

"Not that I know of. Young g-girl, after all."

"It's not unusual. Anyway, that's beside the point. . . ." He looked Rhodes squarely in the eyes. "She was with child. About six weeks along."

Rhodes recoiled. "Dear Lord!"

"I gather this is a surprise to you, sir?"

"Of c-c-course it is. I mean, she d-didn't seem that sort of girl, not at all. Good gracious, my wife will be very upset."

"Perhaps that was the real reason Miss Laporte left your house so abruptly."

"I . . . well, I suppose it could be."

"Did she have a sweetheart that you know of, sir?"

Rhodes blinked. "Mr. Murdoch, I am dreadfully sorry for the girl but she was only my maid. I do not concern myself with the private lives of my servants."

"Did your wife ever mention it?"

"No, she did not."

Murdoch picked up his pen. "Would you give me the names of the other members of the household?"

"Are you only interested in the males?" There was an unexpected note of sarcasm in Rhodes's voice, but Murdoch liked him better for it.

"Everybody, if you please," he said politely.

"There is my wife, Donalda, my son, Owen. The butler, John Foy, and his wife, Edith. A stableboy, Seaton, er . . . I don't recall his Christian name. Those are all the servants we keep. We live quite simply."

"How old is your son?"

Rhodes raised his eyebrows and looked as if the question were too forward, but he answered. "Twenty-t-two."

"And the stableboy?"

"I have no idea. About thirteen, I would imagine."

Rhodes patted his watch pocket. He was going to wear a hole in it at this rate.

"Doctor, you said you saw Miss Laporte at the dinner

79

hour. Were you at home for the rest of the evening?"

"I'm sorry, Mr. Murdoch, I fail to see . . . Why do you ask?"

"Answer the question if you please, sir."

The doctor flushed at his tone. "Well, let me see . . . In fac-fact I was not at home that evening. Miss Shepcote was not well and the evening ended fairly early. I had some important work to do at my consulting rooms so I went there afterwards."

"Miss Shepcote?"

"She and her father, Alderman Shepcote, were our dinner guests. She and my son are, er, well, we, er, hope they will be betrothed fairly soon."

"What time did you leave your house?"

"I don't know exactly. Somewhere after nine. Owen took Miss Shepcote home in our carriage and I left a little later with Mr. Shepcote, who let me off at my office."

"And when did you return home?"

"Detective Murdoch, I must say these questions are s-starting to sound impertinent. What does it have to do with the girl's death?"

"Allow me to read this section of the doctor's report:

> I was suspicious about the state of the deceased's pupils,
> that is to say they were contracted to the point of
> pinpricks. There was a distinctive odour to the organs

which I recognised as that of opium. When I examined the bruise on the right forearm under a glass my suspicions were confirmed. There was a tiny puncture in the vein consistent with the mark of a syringe. I then tested blood samples and found significant residue of the drug opium or a derivative such as morphine . . ."

Rhodes gasped, but Murdoch kept on reading.

"My estimate is that there was not sufficient amount of the drug to bring about death but certainly enough to have induced unconsciousness. It is difficult to say when this would have occurred but might have happened anywhere from ten minutes to half an hour after injection. If she lost consciousness on the street, as seems to be the case, she would have been unable to withstand the freezing temperature. The stomach was empty. She had not eaten recently, which would also contribute to the power of the drug. There were what looked like bruises from a hand-grip on her arm as well. My surmise is that she was held forcibly while the injection was administered. Some person or persons is criminally culpable for her death.
I am your servant, R.D. Moffat, M.D."

Murdoch paused and regarded Rhodes. "Perhaps now you can see the need for me to ask questions no matter how impertinent they seem?"

Before the doctor could respond there was another tap and Crabtree thrust his head through the reed curtain.

"'Scuse me, sir, but there's a gentleman out in the hall. A Mr. Shepcote. He won't wait."

Murdoch looked at Rhodes. "Could this be your dinner guest?"

At that moment the man himself appeared. He wasn't as tall as the constable but he was as wide, and a heavy raccoon coat made him wider. "Rhodes?"

He had a booming voice, and Murdoch didn't miss the almost involuntary flinching that occurred in Dr. Rhodes. Or the look of utter distaste that crossed his face. However, he got to his feet.

"Shepcote, I'm in here."

Crabtree backed away, squeezing past the newcomer, and Shepcote pushed through the curtain into the little cubicle. He ignored Murdoch and addressed Rhodes.

"Must be true, then? It *is* your maid that's been found. Harriet said it was her. What in Hades happened to the girl?"

Murdoch intervened. "Mr. Shepcote, I'm Detective Murdoch, the investigator on the case."

The alderman had a red wind-whipped face, thick blond sidewhiskers and prominent blue eyes. He considered Murdoch for a moment, then thrust out his hand.

"'Pologies for bursting in like this. But it was a shock,

82

seeing as how it was Saturday when I saw the girl alive. I thought I'd better do my duty and get over here. What in Hades happened?" he asked again.

Murdoch turned to Rhodes. "Would you mind waiting for me outside, Doctor? I'd like to talk to Mr. Shepcote in private for a moment."

"Outside? In the h-h-hall?"

Rhodes was reacting as if Murdoch had suggested he go sit in the privy.

"Did you come by carriage? There, if you prefer."

Rhodes left and Shepcote took the chair, undoing his heavy coat. Murdoch knew who he was. He owned the *Signal*, a popular morning newspaper, and he'd used it as a vehicle to get himself elected to the city council, splashing the front page for a month with his portrait and highly flattering endorsements from local business-men. As far as Murdoch was concerned the man was welcome to the job.

Shepcote was watching him with his head turned to a slight angle, as if one eye was sharper than the other.

"What's the story? What happened to that poor girl?"

Murdoch avoided a direct answer. "I understand you dined with Dr. Rhodes on Saturday. Is that where you saw Therese Laporte?"

"That's it. She's their maid, or was, I should say."

"How did she seem?"

83

"I can't say I paid much notice. She took my hat and coat and I went into the drawing room."

"Did she appear distressed? Ill? Disturbed in any way?"

Shepcote gave a snort. "Strange question, isn't it? Like I said, I didn't pay her any attention. I was there to visit Rhodes and his wife, not to hobnob with the servants."

Murdoch kept his head down as he made notes. "I can take that as a no, then, can I, sir?"

"You can."

"I understand you gave Dr. Rhodes a ride in your carriage at the end of the evening. You left him off at his office."

"That's it."

"What time was that, sir?"

"I've no idea. Must have been before ten."

"Where did you go then?"

Shepcote's face went even redder. "Look here! I came here as a good citizen because I thought I knew some poor dead girl. Why the hell are you questioning me like I was a candidate for St. Vincent's?"

Murdoch would have dearly liked to tell him to sod off but that was too dangerous a thing to do with an alderman.

"Because I'm investigating a serious incident. At the least we're dealing with manslaughter, at the worst, murder."

That shut his nab. Murdoch pulled over the postmortem report and read it aloud again.

Shepcote tugged a large bird's-eye handkerchief out of his inner pocket and wiped at his face. "Good God! Shows you can never tell with wenches. One in the basket! She didn't seem like a willing tit."

"We can't make assumptions, can we, sir? Connections could have been forced on her."

"Wouldn't she have said something? Told her mistress?"

"Not necessarily. She'd be afraid to lose her position."

The alderman stared at him for a moment in his lopsided way, then shook his head violently. "Terrible thing, terrible. But see here, Sergeant, you can count on my help. I'll make it front-page news."

And it'll sell you more papers, thought Murdoch.

"Thank you, Mr. Shepcote. If Dr. Rhodes confirms the identification at the morgue, I can go right over and get a description of the clothes she was wearing. It'll help us to trace her movements. Perhaps I could bring that information to the paper later today?"

"Of course."

Murdoch flipped the sheet of paper in his notebook. "And where did you go after you let off Dr. Rhodes?"

"What? Oh, yes. I went over to my club."

"Which one is that, sir?"

"The Yeoman Club on River Street. I stayed there 'til midnight or so, then went home. I suppose you'd like my address? One hundred and twenty Berkeley Street."

"Did you drive the carriage yourself?"

"I did not. Them days have long gone. I've got a man, George Canning. You can ask him, if you doubt my word."

"It's not a matter of doubt, sir."

There was the sound of footsteps out in the hall and again Constable Crabtree loomed outside the curtain. "Dr. Rhodes wants to know if you'll be much longer. The horse is getting cold."

"I'll be right there."

Shepcote stood up to leave.

"Just one more question, sir," said Murdoch. "Do you have any opinion as to who might have had connections with the girl?"

"Hardly."

"You're a shrewd man, Mr. Shepcote. Did you notice anything at all? Anyone eyeing the girl? Any little glances, a brush of the hand, that sort of thing?"

"You're sounding like a novel, sir. Our encounter must have lasted a minute. Didn't see her after that. But if you're looking for a culprit, you should go talk to the Rhodeses' stableboy. He's a home boy and we all know they have the morals of dogs." His voice grew louder and with a certain ring as if he were addressing eager members of the Mechanics Institute. "As a matter of fact, I'm bringing a bill to the council as soon as I can. We've got to limit our intake of immigrants. These

86

children they send us are the offspring of degenerates and criminals. It's in their blood. You only have to take one gander at that boy and you can tell. Shifty-eyed as they come!"

"I understand the boy's only thirteen."

"So what? I've known boys like him and younger who've sired naturals like rutting dogs."

"I'll speak to him, sir. Thank you for coming."

"Yes, of course. Terrible business it is for certain. But I'll wager a month's salary that boy's the culprit."

And I'll wager we'll see that in your paper tomorrow morning, thought Murdoch. *And a lot of people will be only too ready to believe you.*

He was also struck by the fact that neither Rhodes nor Shepcote had commented on the presence of opium in the girl's body.

Chapter Six

OWEN RHODES FINISHED FASTENING the skate blade to Harriet's boot.

"There you go. Ready?"

He pulled her arm through his and they glided off onto the ice. The rink was a cleared patch of the frozen river Don. Later it would get crowded, young men and women meeting after working hours to skate in the torchlight, but now in the morning the other skaters were mostly boys playing truant from school. A ragged bunch nearby had one pair of skate blades among them, and a fierce quarrel erupted as they tried to determine whose turn it was next. Some other boys were sliding on pieces of cardboard and shouting with delight.

Owen and Harriet skated past them.

"Your cold seems better," said Owen.

"It is. Sometimes I think it's better to ignore colds, don't you?"

"Absolutely."

In fact, when he had come to call on her late this morning, Harriet had been feeling wretched, but she wouldn't dream of forgoing the chance to be with him and had quickly agreed to spend a couple of hours skating on the river.

"You're an excellent skater, Harriet."

"Oh, I'm not. You lead so well." The exercise had whipped colour into her cheeks and her eyes glowed with pleasure. Owen felt a rush of affection for her. He squeezed her arm.

"Shall we waltz?"

"I'm a bit shaky still on the turns."

"Don't worry, I'm a master."

It was true. His hold on her was firm and confident and his strokes effortless. She gazed up at him. Even though the closeness of his body made her almost breathless, she liked it. He made an easy half-turn and smiled at her.

"There, well done . . . Harriet, dear, I have a small favour to ask you. You must say at once if you can't do it because it might mean telling a little fib."

"Yes?"

She was thrilled that he wanted something from her. That she had something to offer.

"I've mentioned my friends Sprague and McDonough

89

to you before. They are fine chappies. The best. And, well, you see, we've all developed quite the passion for billiards. A fellow needs some pleasure once in a while, don't you think? Whoops!"

She almost stumbled but he pulled her around easily into a glide.

"I think billiards is a fine sport."

"So do I. Anyway, what I wanted to ask you is this. After I left you on Saturday night I dropped in at Hugh's house and we got into a few rounds. He gave me no quarter, nor I him. Before I knew it the clock was strik-ing twelve. And like Cinderella I knew I had better be getting home . . . If anyone were to ask, could you bring yourself to say that you and I were together, chatting?"

Harriet looked bewildered. "Who would ask?"

"To tell you the truth, Mother entirely disapproves. She's afraid I'll be distracted from my studies, that sort of thing . . . Shall we have a breather?" He manoeuvred her towards a bench. "Would you do that for me, Harriet? Say I didn't leave your house until midnight?"

"That would be very late, wouldn't it?"

"We were in the parlour the entire time."

She sat down on the bench, and a boy appeared at once at her elbow. His clothes were dirty and too big for him and he was shaking with cold. He had a bundle of newspapers under his arm.

"Latest news, miss. One cent."

"No, no, she doesn't want one. Shoo."

90

"Exciting stories today . . . The *Gascoyne*'s come in to New York all safe –"

"No."

"A lady's been found dead as a doornail. Nobody knows who she is. There's a big reward for news . . ."

"The young lady doesn't want to hear any of that sordid nonsense. Go away."

The newsboy kept his eyes fixed on Harriet.

"If I don't sell nothin' I won't eat nothin', kind missus."

"What a story. You look well-fed to me," jeered Owen.

That wasn't true. The boy's face was thin and pasty. Not even the wind could bring colour to his cheeks.

"Please, mister . . ." His voice dropped to a whisper. "I heard as the girl was naked as a jaybird –"

"Get out of here. We don't want to hear about it." Owen handed the boy a five-cent piece. "No, keep the newspaper. Sell it to somebody else."

The boy grinned in delight. "Thanks, mister." He trotted off to where the boys were skating, dropped his bag of papers and started to beg for a skate.

Harriet looked at Owen. "I wonder what that was about, the dead girl, I mean?"

"Some sensationalism, as usual. Those boys are clever little beggars when they want to pump up a story."

He sat down close beside her on the bench and took her hand in his. "I'm sorry, I shouldn't have

91

asked what I did just now. It's too –"

"No, it's not at all. I quite understand. Father can be quite severe when he wants to. What you're asking is such a small fib. It doesn't matter at all." She lowered her head and he could see the blush flood her neck and cheeks. "Besides, we were together in my thoughts."

He leaned over and gave her a quick kiss on her cold cheek.

"And mine. Bless you. The subject mightn't come up but if it does, don't forget, Mother can winkle the truth out of an oyster if she sets her mind to it."

She smiled. "I can actually be quite good at dissembling . . . I simply become very vague."

She wrinkled her forehead and pursed her lips to show him and he burst out laughing. "That answer deserves a bag of chestnuts. Don't move."

On the other bank a man had set up his brazier and was calling his wares. "'Taties, chestnuts, get them hot."

Harriet watched Owen as he skated off. He was wearing dark brown knickerbockers, a brown ribbed sailor's jersey and a matching cap, and she thought he was easily the best-dressed and handsomest man on the rink. And by far the most accomplished skater. Of course she could tell a small lie for him. There was no question.

At four o'clock, Murdoch and Constable Crabtree were seated in Brackenreid's office. The inspector claimed to have dragged himself in from his sickbed to attend to the matter at hand. True, his hands shook and there was a yellowish cast to his eyes, but Murdoch doubted his motives were so noble. He sensed the inspector was torn between ambition and nervousness about a case that touched so closely on a well-to-do family like the Rhodeses. Not unlike Murdoch himself.

Thomas Brackenreid's father had emigrated from County Cork during the potato famine of '51 and by luck and ruthlessness carved himself a living as a dry goods merchant. Young Thomas had known hardship from an early age and was determined to hoist himself up the social ladder, not much caring what heads he used as struts. He joined the police force as a young man and rose steadily up the ranks. Late in life he married the indulged daughter of a local lawyer, and gleeful gossip around the station claimed she led him a merry dance. Before his demons overtook him, he had been a shrewd, hard-working man with a certain meticulousness about detail that served him well. Now, those qualities were more and more obscured.

As inspector, Brackenreid wore a fine wool jacket with brocade epaulettes and frogs down the front. Murdoch could see stains on the brocade and even across the table he could smell the beery stink of the man's breath.

There was a blazing fire in the hearth and the small room was uncomfortably hot. Brackenreid, however, hadn't given the other men permission to undo their jackets. Sweat was running down Crabtree's forehead and he had to keep wiping at his face, and Murdoch was feeling unpleasantly sticky. His stiff celluloid collar had started to chafe his neck. The inspector was also buttoned up but he seemed impervious. He took a noisy sip from the mug he was holding. His face relaxed a bit and Murdoch wondered what else was in there besides tea.

"Now, according to your report nobody laid eyes on the girl after five o'clock, and Mrs. Rhodes was the last to see her, when she was making sure the gal had set the table properly."

He had rigorously tried to expunge his native brogue but it slipped out now and again, through the *r*'s particularly.

He turned a page. "You say you're checking the dockets of the cabbies to see if she hired a cab."

"Yes, sir. She'd travelled a goodly distance from Birchlea."

"Don't mean much. She looks like a bonnie gal to me. She could have walked easily."

"True." Murdoch eased into the sensitive area. "Or she could have been driven in a private carriage."

Brackenreid frowned. "According to this, all the carriages at Birchlea are accounted for, and anyway they're all saying they never saw the kinchin."

"If they're telling the truth, sir."

"For God's sake, Murdoch, let's not tread into that

sort of muck. It won't do us any good. I know for a fact Colonel Grasett and Shepcote are close as dilberries on a beggar's arse. The colonel attends the alderman's salons all the time." He gulped on his tea. "Of course the fact that she had her apron up might not have anything to do with the opium thing."

"I realize that, Inspector."

"None of them have an idea who rogered her?"

"Apparently not. Mrs. Rhodes was shocked. She couldn't believe the girl hadn't confided in her."

Brackenreid shook his head. "That's a fanciful notion. Her mistress would be the last person a maid would get snug with. She'd be more likely to deny it 'til she popped out the little bastard."

"Mrs. Rhodes said the girl had never had any callers. She was a Roman Catholic and was allowed to go to Mass on Sunday morning. They dropped her off at St. Michael's while they went to St. James's. They met her on the corner afterwards and brought her home. She didn't have any other day off and according to Mrs. Rhodes she never reported meeting anyone or talked of any new acquaintances."

Brackenreid chuckled. "Perhaps it was the Holy Ghost that did for the girl. Don't the Catholics call it Immaculate Conception?"

"Yes, we do," said Murdoch.

"Oh, beg pardon, Murdoch. No offence. I forgot for a moment."

"No offence taken, sir."

Brackenreid was perfectly aware of his detective's faith but always tried to get in a jibe or two at Murdoch's expense if he could. His own family had brought the politics of their country with them and he was a staunch Orangeman.

Crabtree shot a glance at Murdoch and wiped surreptitiously at his neck. He thought the detective skated close to the thin ice sometimes, and Brackenreid and he often eyed each other like two fighting dogs. Murdoch wiped a droplet of sweat from his nose.

"Can we unbutton our jackets, Inspector? It is very warm in here," asked Murdoch.

"What? Oh yes. Take them off if you like. It is hot, now that you mention it."

He unfastened the top button of his jacket.

Crabtree opened up his uniform, revealing a glimpse of red flannel underneath and an impression of redoubtable muscle development. He was the station's prize athlete in the heavyweight division of shot put and tug-of-war, and even though the next police games weren't until August, his chances were the subject of much speculation and interest among the other policemen. Murdoch could see the keen glance that Brackenreid sent that way, but he didn't want to spend the next half hour discussing the possible condition of Sergeant Anstell, who was number-one station's pride and joy. He unsnapped his collar studs and got back to the subject.

96

"I went to talk to the priest at St. Michael's this afternoon, but he didn't know the girl. It's a big parish. However, he gave me his tithe list and tomorrow we can start calling on the parishioners."

"Maybe she didn't actually go there. She could have been lying. Taking that time to get up to mischief."

"That's possible, sir. But given that she was a Roman Catholic I think it's more likely that she was reluctant to say much about her church at all in a family that was not of the same faith. People can be prejudiced."

Brackenreid waved his fingers irritably at the detective. "And they don't know anything about opium, I suppose?"

"Dr. Rhodes admits to using it in his medicines, which he makes up himself at the surgery."

The inspector stared at Murdoch. "That don't mean anything."

"I didn't make any implications. I'm stating the facts. The son, Owen, is a medical student and it's quite likely he could acquire the drug if he wanted to."

"It sounds to me like you're trying to stick a pin on a donkey's rear end, Murdoch. Just find out who seen the girl and we'll have the answers. Why don't you get out there and start asking some proper questions?"

"That's what we've been doing for the past day and a half, Inspector."

Crabtree wiped a damp spot from under his chin and shifted uncomfortably in his chair. He knew only too well the extent of Brackenreid's temper. His colour was rising, and it wasn't only the heat and his "tea."

"Have you gone to the Sheenies about the missing clothes?"

"Yes, sir. Two constables went to all the Jewish merchants on Queen and King but nobody has received anything resembling the goods. She left her uniform behind, but according to Mrs. Foy she would have been wearing a grey serge skirt, matching jacket with blue velvet trim –"

"I have no need to know all that. Can we get along? I'm still feeling poorly, I should remind you. Constable, what about you?"

"You've got my report there, too, sir," Crabtree answered quickly. "I questioned the servants and it's the same story. Nobody knows anything."

"What about the stableboy? He's a Barnardo Home boy, isn't he? I'd say he's a likely possibility."

"He's a timid little creature. Frightened of his own shadow. He never takes his eyes off you. Makes you think of a dog that's been ill-treated." Crabtree looked a bit embarrassed at his sortie into simile. "He's only thirteen and small to boot."

"That's old enough. Boy in my father's village had spawned two brats by the time he was eleven. Boys like that have no more Christianity in them than dogs."

Murdoch was reminded of Alderman Shepcote's words. Perhaps he and Brackenreid had had a good chin about it at one of the salon evenings for Miss Flo Wortley.

"By boys like that, do you mean orphan boys, sir, frightened boys, or boys from Ireland? As I understand, this one is English."

Brackenreid stared at his detective for a moment, trying to determine whether or not to take offence. "Gutter boys, that's who I mean." He contemplated his mug, which was now empty. "Is that everything, Constable?"

"I'd say so, sir. The Foys claim they didn't leave the house that evening and neither did the boy."

The inspector fished a cigar out of a silver box on the desk and lit it. "Has anything come up with the Bertillon?"

"Not yet. The regular clerk is off sick and we don't have anyone else who understands the system. By Friday, we should know if she has a file."

Brackenreid blew a cloud of smoke towards the two officers. "I presume we are trying to get in touch with the family?"

"I sent a wire to the Windsor police and they'll try to contact the local priest in Chatham. We don't know exactly where the girl lived. It was a farm near there, but they've had a bad storm and the police don't think they can get through until Thursday or Friday."

99

Murdoch's envelope was sitting on the table and Brackenreid took out the photograph and studied it for a moment.

"Perhaps she was a light-heeled gal, but she doesn't look it. She's got a sweet face." He drew thoughtfully on his cigar. "Needless to say, I'd like to show that this station can work as well as any other, if not better. I want answers soon but I don't want any feathers ruffled. Is that clear?"

Murdoch managed to bite his tongue. "Quite clear, sir."

The inspector flicked some ash into a dish on the table. "Dismissed," he said.

Murdoch and Crabtree went back to the orderly room downstairs, where Murdoch poured them both some tea. It had been steeping for a while and was as dark as molasses. Puss was cleaning herself diligently underneath the table. Crabtree added two spoonfuls of sugar and some milk to his mug and took a gulp of the tea.

"When I was there in the kitchen a-telling of the girl's condition the air was so thick you could've cut it with a butter knife. The boy looked like he was about to flash his hash any minute and the housekeeper almost choked on the soup she was tasting."

"I had a similar feeling with the Rhodes family. The son stammered and stopped like he was imitating his own father. Then he finally confessed that he had stayed visiting with Harriet Shepcote until midnight. They weren't chaperoned, and maybe that's why he was acting so guilty. His mother was furious. Not going to show it in front of me but she got very tight-laced, I can tell you."

"Do you think the young master got into the maid's drawers, sir?"

"Could be. He's a handsome fellow. Wouldn't be hard for him to steal the heart of a young country lass. Then again, she could've met some cove at church. It might take nine months to grow a babe but it only takes minutes to plant the seed. As you know," he added.

The constable had four children and another on the way.

"You're right there, sir," he said and he looked so glum Murdoch was sorry for teasing him. He motioned to him to continue.

"There's a back window. Faces onto the stable yard and opens into the passageway behind the kitchen. You could climb in there and be up those stairs like a bolt of lightning."

Both men sipped on their tea in silence for a minute. Then Murdoch said solemnly, "We can't totally overlook the other possibility."

"What's that, sir?"

"The Holy Ghost, of course."

Crabtree smiled.

Chapter Seven

MONDAY, FEBRUARY 11

OWEN WAS SPRAWLED at one end of the sofa, his foot tapping restlessly, watching his mother while she fastened bands of black crepe along the mantel of the sitting room fireplace. The pictures were similarly festooned, the mirrors covered and the curtains drawn all afternoon.

"Shall I light another lamp?" he asked.

"No, thank you, Owen. This is sufficient."

Suddenly she stopped what she was doing and picked up one of the framed photographs from the mantel.

"Owen, look. How could I not have noticed before?"

She brought the photograph over to the sofa. "Can you see the resemblance?"

Puzzled, he studied the picture and shook his head. "Don't know what you're getting at, Mother."

"Theresa and Marianne. You must see it."

He shrugged. "Sorry, dear, I don't."

"It's not so much a resemblance of features as expression. See, the openness about the eyes. The mouth. Marianne always looked as if she were about to burst into laughter. Theresa had that look sometimes."

"If you say so. 'Fraid I can't quite see it myself."

Donalda replaced the picture on the mantel. "Marianne was not much older than Theresa. Far too young to die, both of them."

She hadn't really looked at the picture for a long time, and she saw it now with fresh eyes. The photograph was a small *carte de visite*, more popular years ago than now. They had gone down to London, to the best studio in Belgravia. Her father was able to indulge in such things in those days. Both girls had worn their most fashionable dresses, shot silk taffeta with a high collar and ruched bodice, the new tight-fitting sleeves. They had only put their hair up that month, she remembered. Marianne had led the way as she always did, bossing her, determining what she would wear, even rubbing the merest hint of rouge on her cheeks.

Donalda touched the glass of the picture frame. A lock of dark hair was curled around the bottom of the photograph. Who would have known that before the summer was over, Marianne would be dead, the victim of a stupid accident? All their endless, earnest talks about dying an honourable old age, "full of pride at our noble deeds," as Marianne had put it, had come to naught.

103

"What are you thinking, Mother?"

"That the dreams of youth so rarely materialize."

"Dear me, that is gloomy."

"I feel that way today."

"That's understandable. Ever since I can remember you've told me stories about yourself and your friend." He hesitated. "Perhaps that's why you're so distressed now. About Therese. It's sort of like losing her twice."

Donalda glanced up at him. "I hadn't thought of it quite like that."

She sat down in the armchair opposite and stared into the fire, watching while the flames danced and jumped around the coal. And told her son the story again because she needed to.

The particular day was one of the glorious August afternoons that happen only in England. The blue sky was dotted with puffs of white cloud and the air was golden with sunlight. Marianne had wanted to go to the ramshackle hut that perched on the riverbank. They had played there since they were children and she had taken to calling it their summer house. "How utterly pretentious," said Donalda scornfully. She didn't like the spiders or the musty gloom inside. She wanted to sit in the shady gazebo and read together. However, as usual, Marianne had overridden her objections. "It will be cool in there. It's an adventure, Addie. Don't be a slug." Finally, Donalda agreed on condition they play "Jane Eyre," from their favourite book. They'd played this game

104

before and Marianne always wanted to be the mad Mrs. Rochester. The first time, she cried and wailed so convincingly that Wilson, the gardener, had rushed down to the hut to see what was the matter. Donalda preferred the part of Jane but they always squabbled about her interpretation. "She is afraid, timid," said Marianne. "You must wring your hands like so. Perhaps even faint. Then Mr. Rochester sweeps you up in his arms and carries you away." Donalda demurred, "She is made of tougher mettle than that," and insisted on addressing the crazed Bertha in a loud, commanding voice. "Stop that at once." Marianne scolded her in exasperation. "No, Addie, not like that. You sound exactly like Miss Thompson. You are not speaking to a naughty pupil, you are facing a woman in the grip of violent insanity."

But Donalda would only modify her tone slightly, and they played out the scene over and over, adding more and more embellishments until they fell to the ground sated with drama and imagination.

On this afternoon Marianne ran ahead and took up her position at the glassless window of the hut. Donalda followed more sedately along the towpath through the willow trees that bent to touch the gently moving water. Even on hot days the air inside the green tunnel was cool and damp, smelling of the river. She smiled when she saw her friend, dark hair dishevelled and tumbling down from its pins, face alight with fun, beckoning to her with a theatrical gesture. "Let me in," she cried, "let

105

me in." Suddenly, she yelped and withdrew her hand. A rusty nail had torn the skin at the cuticle of her thumb. Donalda hurried over to examine the wound. There was a tiny blob of blood. "It's nothing," she said. "Not nearly as bad as my knee when I fell last week." She donated her new linen handkerchief to bind the scratch. "I hope the bloodstain comes out."

Marianne wrapped her thumb and they entered into the game, Marianne waving around her bandage with great gusto.

When they returned to the house in the early evening, however, she complained of pain. Her thumb was throbbing and had become red and swollen. Donalda was not overly sympathetic, as her friend exaggerated everything.

The next morning she came to visit and Marianne showed her the angry red streaks running down her forearm. "Betsy says if they travel above the elbow, I'm done for," she said.

"That's a stupid old wives' tale," Donalda scoffed.

But Betsy was right, and neither contempt nor reason could protect her beloved friend. The infection raced through the young girl's body, the doctor could do nothing to stop it, and within the week she was dead.

Donalda stood up, reached behind the picture and picked up the tiny glass bottle, beautifully coloured, that was behind it.

"What's that?" asked Owen.

"For my tears. We used to catch our tears and keep them as mementos."

"Let me see." He held the bottle to the light of the fire. "I do believe there is still a tiny drop of liquid in the bottom. How wonderful."

He gave the vial back to his mother and she touched it to her lips. Then she pressed her fingers into the back of her neck.

"Do you need your medicine? I can soon fetch it."

"No, thank you."

"Perhaps you should lie down for a little while. All those questions this afternoon, what happened . . . it's been terribly upsetting."

"Owen, please stop addressing me as if I were an elderly invalid."

"That's not fair, Mother –"

She cut him short with a frown. "I hope you are intending to wear something other than that suit."

"What? Oh, yes, yes, I will, of course. I haven't had an opportunity to change."

She herself was wearing a plain, charcoal-coloured gown that emphasized her pallor. The shadowy room also intensified the lines of fatigue on her face. He regarded her anxiously.

107

"Such a shock. You could have knocked me down with a goose feather when the detective – what's his name?"

"Murdoch."

"Yes, Murdoch, when he said she was, er, she was in the, er, family way. I had no idea."

"I sincerely hope not, Owen," his mother said dryly.

"Beg pardon? Oh, I see . . . right. Who do you suppose is the guilty party?"

"I don't care to know. It is irrelevant now."

The silence fell heavily, and Owen shifted his position on the sofa. He wanted desperately to check his watch but he didn't dare. Donalda was contemplating the fire.

"There is so much I don't understand. Why was she going home? She told me there was nobody there for her except an elderly father, and she was quite forthcoming about how strained their relationship was. He was terribly strict."

"It must have been because of her condition. An unmarried young girl and all that shame. Where else would she have gone?"

"She could have stayed here."

"Mother, that wouldn't have been right."

"I don't see why not." Again she rubbed at her neck. "And the opium! It is unbearable to think what happened to her."

108

"I, er, I hate to say, but is it possible she wasn't quite as innocent as you have thought –"

"No! I know what kind of girl Theresa was. Something dreadful happened to her that she could do nothing about."

"If you say so, Mother."

Donalda looked over at him. "You seemed quite nervous while Mr. Murdoch was questioning us."

"Did I? Well, I'm not exactly used to having police officers perched on our best chairs demanding to know one's every movement. It's unnerving."

Donalda sighed and sat back in her chair. "I'd have thought Harriet was too ill to stay up so long chatting."

"She felt better when she was home."

Donalda stared into his eyes, grey-blue, so like her own.

"Is that the truth, Owen?"

"Of course it is. Stop worrying. You can ask her yourself." He patted the seat beside him. "Come sit down, there's a dear."

She joined him on the sofa and he leaned his head in the hollow of her shoulder.

She stroked his hair, then pushed him away, shaking her fingers. "Ugh, Owen. You really do use far too much pomade."

He smiled up at her, glad that the danger had passed. "I'm sorry. I promise I will abstain completely if you don't like it, and my locks will stand up on end like the wild man from Borneo."

109

She studied him for a moment. His skin felt rough at the jaw where he hadn't shaved yet and there were delicate tracings of lines at the corner of his eyes. She felt a sudden pang of longing for the boy who was no more.

He pretended to pout at her. "Do I deserve a kiss at least?"

She laughed at that and, drawing him closer, kissed him. "I'm sorry, dearest."

At that moment, the door opened and Cyril came in. He stiffened immediately when he saw them.

"Shouldn't you be at your l-lecture?" he asked his son.

"Not at this hour, Father. Just talking with Mother a bit."

"Y-yes. Of course. Yes. That's why I came down myself. How are you, Donalda?"

The expression of love she had shown her son disappeared at once. She had caught the look of jealousy on Cyril's face, and it ignited an old anger.

"How do you expect?" she snapped.

"Beg pardon?"

"How do you expect me to be, Cyril? I am extremely distressed."

He indicated the signs of mourning in the room. "But she was merely our ser-servant, Donalda. Don't you think this is a bit excessive?"

110   Owen groaned to himself. He knew what sort of response his mother would give to that. She placed her hands in her lap and laced the fingers tightly together. "Theresa was an exceptional young girl, and I had

become very fond of her. I cannot brush off her death as if she were a failed kitten. 'Oh dear, what a pity. Well, let's get another.'"

"Please, D-Donalda, such hyperbole is unwarranted. I am a-attempting to show you some sympathy. One would think I were responsible for the girl's death the way you are carrying on."

There was a light of anger in her eyes but her voice was still controlled, the sharp edge of the knife only hinted at. "How could you be? You were safely ensconced at your office, weren't you? Where we can always be sure to find you."

Owen got to his feet abruptly. "I'm off. I promised Hugh I'd go over some cribs with him before tomorrow's class."

"Surely you're not go-going in that outfit?" asked Cyril.

Owen was dressed in a light check suit with slim-fitting trousers and a high stiff collar with a gold-striped silk four-in-hand. He smoothed the cravat nervously.

"All the fellows are wearing these, Father."

"You look b-bloody ridiculous."

"He's going to change," intervened Donalda. "Considering what has happened."

Owen bent over and gave her a quick peck on the cheek, which felt fiery beneath his touch.

"I won't be late, I promise. And I'll come and say good night. Good evening, Father."

He nodded at Cyril and left. Donalda waited until the door closed behind him, then turned angrily towards her husband.

"Must you always address him as if he were a misbehaving child?"

"It is not I who maintain our son in perpetual puerility."

"Stop it, Cyril, please."

He was not to be gainsaid. "You know what I-I say is true, Donalda. He is most immature for his age."

"He is not. You have sung that tune ever since he was born. 'You are nursing him far too long, Donalda. Why isn't he walking yet, Donalda? What? Can't he read yet?' If you had your way, he would have been at his desk doing sums when he was six months old."

"Don't be ridiculous."

"It is not ridiculous to love your own child, Cyril. To want to give them some protection from the harshness of the world."

"What you have given is not protection, it is mollycoddling."

"He seems to be doing quite well in spite of it."

Rhodes tugged angrily at his moustache. Lips tight, he said, "I am not as sanguine as you are, my dear. I ran into D-Davidson at the club. He said he was concerned about Owen. It seems that he has been missing many of his lectures. Not doing the work."

"Davidson said that? Why . . . it can't be true. You

heard him. Two or three times a week he stays late and works at the college."

"According to his teacher, that is not the case."

Donalda stared at her husband. She wanted to go on arguing, to deny what he said, but she knew it was pointless. There was a gleam of triumph in his eyes that meant he considered himself unassailable. Stiffly, she said, "There has to be an explanation. Perhaps he is with a friend. He is a young man. He cannot work every minute. Perhaps –"

"Perhaps the truth is we have raised a slacker. Afraid of hard work. Interested only in the intricacies of his toilet."

"Cyril! How can you be so cruel about your own son?"

"Unlike you, D-Donalda, I believe in facing the truth."

"What a pity you acquired such virtue so late in life."

He closed his eyes, tilted his head towards the ceiling as if in prayer. "I see. Am I now to get my annual castigation?"

"How dare you demean my feelings in that manner."

"Donalda, I have begged your f-forgiveness over and over. I might as well have spoken to a stone. There is no more I can say or do."

He walked towards the door, and she called to him.

"How very fortunate that with such a barren domestic life you can find satisfaction in your work. Where you are universally admired. Perhaps even *adored*."

Rhodes's face flushed and he bowed, coldly, as if she were a disagreeable acquaintance he wanted to cut. "Please inform Edith I will be dining at the club."

He left. Donalda remained seated, fighting to subdue the trembling of her body. She and Cyril hadn't had such a bitter quarrel for a long time. His words began to repeat themselves in her head. She knew that what he had said was true, and the thought was like bile in her stomach. Would someone else have forgiven him? Would another woman have restored love and respect between them? She breathed in sharply. The questions were useless. The fact was her marriage had been destroyed many years ago and whether it was primarily her fault or his was a moot point now. It was far too late to retrieve.

She got up to tend to the fire, and her eye was caught by the silver-framed wedding picture at the far end of the mantelpiece. She had married Cyril Rhodes, a young Canadian medical student, the year after Marianne's death. She was barely eighteen, and she knew now that she had rushed into his arms in the naive expectation that life in a new country would bring her the happiness she craved. Had that young bride ever been happy, she wondered? She seemed so in the photograph, smiling and lovely in her dove-coloured

114

silk gown with its delicate lace and beads. Cyril also was beaming with pride.

With a sigh she replaced the photograph. It was such a long time ago and those two young people full of promise and expectation were no more.

Owen was born eighteen months after the wedding, and by the time he was two she was carrying her second child. Had it lived, she would have named it Marianne.

She returned to the *carte de visite*. There was a resemblance, there really was, there in the full mouth, the round chin. Perhaps that was why she had become so fond of Theresa, had confided in her one night the way she had once talked to Marianne. She had whispered to her maid the old sad secret that she had told no one else.

She leaned her head against the mantelpiece. The crepe ribbon smelled faintly musty and the fire was hot against her legs, but she was impervious.

How could Cyril wonder why she never forgave him?

Chapter Eight

WITH A HEAVE WORTHY OF A CABER TOSS, Crabtree lifted the mattress and flung it to the floor.

"Hey, watch what you're doing," yelled Alice. "You could have broken my statue. That's worth a lot of dash, that is."

She snatched up a chipped plaster figurine, gaudily painted in gilt and blue.

"Sodding, shicey frogs," Alice muttered.

"Watch your language or you'll find yourself up on a charge," said Murdoch.

Alice glared at him. Both she and Bernadette had been asleep when the officers arrived, although it was well past eleven o'clock. Ettie had pulled on her frowzy satin wrapper, but Alice remained in an unclean flannel nightgown that had long ago lost its buttons.

Murdoch surveyed the rusty iron bedsprings. There

was nothing hidden there except a couple of squashed cockroaches and a crumpled five-dollar banknote. Bernadette Weston snatched up the money and stuffed it into her bodice.

"I told you there was nothing here."

"You'd better give those other coves as good a bleeding going-over as you've done us," added Alice, waving her hand in the direction of the wall to indicate their next-door neighbours.

"Why are you picking on us?" snapped Ettie. "There are half a dozen other houses as back onto the bleeding alley. Frigging coppers."

"I said to watch your language," said Murdoch. "One more remark like that and you'll be in for the night."

Alice put her hand on Ettie's arm. "Don't go on so, Ettie. They're only doing their duty. Can't help themselves. Gents never can."

Her voice was suddenly arch, and she leaned forward in her chair so that the placket of her gown opened, revealing a flaccid breast and pink nipple. Ettie laughed and began to pull at the forefinger of one of the wooden forms on the mantel, which they used to hold the gloves when they were cleaning them. The constable abruptly concentrated on the upended box that served as their dresser. Triumphantly he held up a piece of pasteboard.

"Been visiting F. and J.'s, have you?"

He handed the card to Murdoch. It was a pawn ticket

117

from Farrance and Jenkinson, a well-frequented shop on Queen Street.

Ettie scowled. "No crime, is it?"

"What did you pawn?" Murdoch asked.

Alice snorted. "My best drawers." She leered at them. "I can get on without them. See?"

Crabtree ran his finger around his tight collar. He was a young man and the needling of the two prostitutes was getting to him. Murdoch refused to give them that satisfaction. There was also a date on the back of the pasteboard from two weeks previous, which meant it couldn't be Therese's belongings that had been pawned.

The few spare clothes the women had were hung on hooks on the far wall. Under the bed, as well as the chamber pot, which was full, were two pairs of boots, one of newish black leather with needle toes. The ends were well scuffed and a button was missing, but the soles were not worn and the leather still stiff.

"I'll need to commandeer these."

"No you don't. They're mine," Alice said.

"Where'd you get them?"

"From Mr. Eaton's."

"How much did they cost?" asked Murdoch.

"Three dollars. I saved up."

"I didn't notice them before."

"That's you being nocky, isn't it. They were there."

"I'll have to check them out."

Alice wailed. "And what am I supposed to do without

118

my boots? Some of us have to work, you know. I don't have no others."

Murdoch frowned, then took out his tape and measured the boots, making a careful note of the length and the appearance.

"All right. I'll let you keep them. Think yourself lucky."

"Father Christmas now, is it," said Alice sullenly.

Murdoch looked around the room again but there wasn't anywhere else they hadn't checked. In spite of poverty there had been some attempt at prettifying. A piece of flowered cotton served as a curtain at the only window, and the candle stub sat in a tin lid in the middle of a handmade paper doily. Another piece of cheap bright cloth was draped across the box.

"Nice picture," said Murdoch, pointing to a page from a popular ladies' magazine that was pinned on the wall. The illustration depicted a golden-haired child leaning against her mother's knee as she listened to a story. The woman's hand rested on the child's curls and her expression was full of tenderness.

"Ettie found it," said Alice with a touch of pride. "She's very artistic." She coughed, glancing about for somewhere to spit.

Ettie perched on the bed. "Are we at a bleeding exhibition or what? Why are you dunning us like this?" she asked. "The girl's shoving off had nothin' to do with us."

119

"We hope not. She didn't die naturally, you see. She'd taken a drug just before she died which caused her to go unconscious. After that she froze to death. We're talking manslaughter at the least."

"What's he mean, a drug?" Alice asked Ettie. She seemed genuinely bewildered.

"Ask His Highness, he'll tell you."

"She'd taken, or been given, opium," said Murdoch.

"Oi, well, she died happy, then, didn't she?"

"Alice!" said her friend. "That's not respectful."

Murdoch spoke to Crabtree. "Let's check the kitchen."

He felt rather than saw the sigh of relief from Bernadette Weston. It was like playing the child's game of seek: "Warm . . . warmer; no, cold . . . very cold." He knew at that moment they wouldn't find anything incriminating in the kitchen. Wherever the plunder was hidden, that place was "cold." He was sure it was these two who'd stripped the dead body, but he thought that was probably the extent of their involvement. Jackey and hot pots was for their sort, not opium.

Ettie said sharply, "Don't forget to put this room back in order."

Crabtree pulled the stained mattress back onto the bedsprings. There was only one greasy blanket and a quilt that was once pretty but was so tattered now the stuffing had almost gone. A tiny feather drifted on the air.

120

Murdoch nodded at the constable. "We'll be getting on, then. Don't forget, we're dealing with a very serious matter here, Alice Black. If there's anything you can help us with, it's your duty to do so."

"Certainly," said Alice. She moved her legs into a provocatively lewd position. Crabtree blushed and bumped into the doorjamb in his hurry to get out of the room. As they walked down the hall they could hear Alice's laughter.

As Murdoch expected, the search of the kitchen yielded nothing. Next, they investigated Samuel Quinn's room, but except for a bag of smelly, rotting meat that was inexplicably tucked in the back of his washstand, they found nothing untoward. Neither Quinn nor the dogs were anywhere to be seen.

The two out-of-work brothers upstairs protested the search with such aggression and anxiety that Murdoch decided to send out a bill on them to Muskoka. Find out if they had guilty consciences. But he found no women's clothes in the untidy, sweat-saturated room the two big men lived in. By two o'clock, he had to declare the search finished. When they came downstairs, both Ettie and Alice were sitting in the kitchen drinking tea, and they followed the officers to the front door. Alice was singing noncha-lantly, a song that turned Crabtree's ears crimson and made even Murdoch uncomfortable. Ettie was quieter, but the wariness never left her eyes. The trail was cold but not totally so.

In the summer, sugar maples lined both sides of St. Luke's and the lush foliage hid the dilapidation of the houses, but the trees were bare now, the branches dark against the dull winter sky. A wagon, drawn by four massive Percherons, lumbered along laden with barrels for the Dominion Brewery, but otherwise the street was deserted.

Murdoch wrapped his muffler tightly to cover his chin, and Constable Crabtree shrugged the collar of his cape higher around his neck.

"That's it, then, sir. I thought for certain we'd find something. Disappointing, isn't it?"

"To be expected, really. Those two women are a shrewd pair. At least that Ettie is. They haven't really had time to get the clothes to the Jews and they're too clever to be using them as yet. Alice slipped up on the boots, which sure as shooting are stolen."

"Could they have an accomplice, sir?"

"Maybe, but it's nobody in the house. We'd better check out the neighbours, but somehow I don't think anybody'd help these doxies. I got the impression when we went around before that Miss Weston and Miss Black aren't too popular."

"Women like that are a disgrace to their sex, if you ask me."

Murdoch didn't comment. He knew many of his

122

fellow officers had similar opinions about prostitutes.

"Shall we start on the next house, then?" asked Crabtree.

Murdoch hesitated. "Let's go back to the laneway for a minute."

They walked down Sumach. The police ropes were still intact, but the curiosity of the locals must have been sated as there was nobody lingering there exchanging misinformation. And it was, after all, a working day.

They ducked under the barricade and walked to the place where the girl had died. Murdoch looked towards the backyard of the lodging house that was directly opposite. A soft glimmer of light shone through a crack in the curtain of the backroom. If he didn't know better, he would have considered it warm and inviting.

"Put yourself in their boots, Crabtree. You're frightened of being seen, you know there will be a search, where would you hide a few clothes?"

Before the constable had a chance to reply, Murdoch exclaimed, "Jesus, Mary and Joseph, I wonder –" He held out his hand to Crabtree. "Lend me your lamp, will you? And I want you to stand guard. Over there where you're out of sight of their room. If anyone leaves the house, detain them."

123

"What are you thinking of, sir?"

"I'm going to the privy."

"I wouldn't recommend it, sir."

Murdoch laughed. "Don't worry. I'm going to give it another look."

"I did check it before, sir."

Crabtree's face was disapproving. They'd done their job. However, he did as he was told and took up a position where he was shielded by the adjoining privy. Murdoch went back through the gate and quickly slipped inside the outhouse. There was only one aperture and the inside was gloomy and so noisome he was afraid to breathe too deeply.

Striking a match, he lit the wick of the lantern and a warm light flared in the cramped space. The rough wooden structure seemed completely bare, just a plank across the rear wall with two holes, one covered by a lid. He bent over the open hole and lowered the lantern into the space. All he could see was human waste not far below. Fortunately most of it was frozen, which cut down on the stench. A fat, black spider scuttled along a thread turned to silver by the light. Its meal waited, neatly wrapped in the centre of the web.

Murdoch straightened, moved the lid over from the second hole. Nothing! Bugger. He had convinced himself he had the right hiding place. He leaned down even deeper into the hole with the lantern.

124 Bull's-eye!

Beneath the neck of the plank he could see the edge of a piece of tartan cloth. He took off his hat, unwrapped his scarf so that it was out of danger and reached in with his gloved hand. The cloth was part of a bundle that had been hooked over a nail. He tugged and, cursing softly, finally managed to pull it back up through the hole. It was a tight fit and picked up some unpleasant smears as he did so but he didn't care.

The bundle proved to be a woollen shawl that was knotted together. He took off his gloves and undid it.

Wrapped inside were clothes: a grey serge skirt, a cotton chemise and petticoat, a black sateen waist. In the centre of the bundle, pathetically squashed, was a black felt hat appliquéd with pink silk flowers.

He replaced everything, tied the ends of the shawl again and went outside, gulping in the fresh air. Constable Crabtree loomed out of the shadows and came towards him.

"I've found them, Crabtree. They're her clothes, all right."

The light behind him suddenly winked as somebody lifted the curtain. The shape was in silhouette but he knew Bernadette Weston was standing there watching him.

Mrs. Letitia Wright and Mrs. Mathilda Kleiser placed their cards on the silver salver in the hall.

"Please give Mrs. Rhodes my condolences. I'm sorry she is indisposed," said Mrs. Wright.

"Likewise," said Mrs. Kleiser.

125

"She wished to express her appreciation to both of you for your kind sympathy," said Foy. "She hopes to be receiving callers next week at the latest."

He had a little trouble getting his tongue around the last few words, and the difficulty was not lost on Mrs. Wright. She knew a tippling servant when she saw one.

"My, that long? Well, Mrs. Kleiser and I will certainly return at a more convenient time. I suppose she has already had a number of callers?"

"Yes, madam. People have been most kind."

Foy opened the door, but the woman hesitated on the threshold.

"Such a tragedy. The entire household must be in a state of shock."

"Yes, we all are, madam."

"Do you know what happened to the poor girl?" asked Mrs. Wright.

"No, I'm afraid not."

Letitia would dearly have liked to winkle more information out of him, but the butler was gazing purposefully somewhere at a point over their heads. Gathering their skirts, clutching their reticules, they allowed him to usher them out. As they walked down the path another carriage was drawing up to the door. The coachman jumped down and helped out a young woman. All three women hovered for a moment, then bowed to each other.

"Good afternoon, Miss Shepcote."

126

"Good afternoon," said Harriet. She proceeded self-consciously to the front door. The older women continued on.

"That poor motherless child is quite the most clumsy girl, although I do regret saying that. And her hat? Wherever have you seen such a fright! A greengrocer could sell it and make a fortune."

Mathilda nodded. "To be utterly frank I cannot imagine what Owen Rhodes sees in her. Donalda has been hinting they are to be engaged in the spring. She would push for it, of course. Harriet is a malleable little thing."

They linked arms, their wide hats almost touching.

"Shall we hire a carriage?" asked Mrs. Wright.

"No, do let's walk a little. It's not as bitter for once."

"That garland on the door was somewhat excessive, wouldn't you say? She was a servant, after all."

"Yes and no."

"What do you mean, Mathilda?"

"I wasn't sure if I should repeat this . . . and you must swear not to tell."

"Naturally. I never do."

"Our nursemaid, Mabel, heard from the Felkins' cook that the dead girl was Cyril Rhodes's love child."

"No!" 127

"That's what I heard. How else can you explain such a fuss?"

"But surely Donalda wouldn't have accepted her?"

"You and I wouldn't have, but she's an odd sort of person, don't you find? Englishwomen often are . . ."

They passed by a tall, dark-haired man who raised his hat politely. He was dressed in a sealskin coat and carrying a brown paper bag under his arm. If they had known it was Acting Detective William Murdoch going to Birchlea to confirm the identification of Therese Laporte's garments, the ladies would no doubt have devised some excuse to return.

Chapter Nine

As Murdoch entered Temperance Hall, the newsboys were in the middle of singing "We Shall Gather at the River," with gusto if not accuracy. Some of them were stamping their hobnailed boots on the wooden floor; others clapped. He squeezed himself onto one of the benches at the back. All around him were boys dressed in the most amazing motley of clothes Murdoch had ever seen in one place: oversized cloth caps with loud checks, felt crushers, fur forage hats and coats and trousers that had all known previous owners. Legally, newsboys were supposed to be at least fourteen to get a licence to sell papers, but many of them were younger. Forced by necessity to hurry through childhood, their faces revealed a premature cynicism that was softened only occasionally with childlike simplicity. The hall was hazy with smoke

129

from their clay pipes and dense with the smell of dirty clothes and bodies.

Murdoch took out his own briar pipe and lit it. Immediately, there was a nudge in his arm.

"Got some clippings to spare, mister?"

The boy next to him on the bench was still so small and young his boots barely touched the floor. His cloth cap was too big, and stringy fair hair almost obscured his eyes. Murdoch handed him a pinch but right away two or three other grimy hands thrust out at him.

"Some for me, mister?" "Hey, what about me?"

He distributed the last of the tobacco from his pouch and was grateful when there was a drum roll from the direction of the stage, indicating the meeting was ready to start. The boys nearby lit their pipes, first borrowing a match from him, and the row was in danger of disappearing into a fug of smoke.

"'Oo are you?" asked his neighbour as he puffed contentedly on a stubby, blackened pipe. Before Murdoch could answer, the master of ceremonies, a rotund man whose bald head shone white in the gas light, trotted onto the stage.

Murdoch had come to the newsboys' meeting in the hope of getting their help. They were denizens of the streets, sharp and ruthless, honed to survive like cubs. If anyone would pay attention to a young girl out on the street on a winter's night, they would. The master of ceremonies had agreed to let him talk from the platform

130

after the guest speaker. No point in stealing his thunder with exciting talk of missing young girls. That suited Murdoch. The speaker was Godfrey Shepcote, and he wanted the chance to study him.

Shepcote was waiting in the wings. The hubbub from the boys excited him, and his round cheeks were even more flushed than usual. His valet, Canning, was beside him and he gave his master a quick brush-down across the shoulders. Shepcote had chosen his wardrobe carefully, a tweed jacket over a fawn waist-coat, beige knickerbockers, brown high boots that his servant had polished to a mirrorlike shine. The impression was of a man of affluence but insouciance. The rewards of the world sat visibly but lightly on his wide shoulders.

In fact, the annual newsboys' meeting at Temperance Hall was one of the bright spots of Shepcote's year. After him on the programme came a fiddler, a juggler and a mind reader, but this was his moment of glory and he knew the boys were waiting eagerly.

The master of ceremonies finally managed to get the audience sufficiently quieted down to make himself heard.

"Thank you, gentlemen, thank you. And a braver bunch of choristers I never did hear . . ."

This elicited cheers and ear-splitting whistles. "All right, then, I know you're all on pins and needles waiting for our next speaker. At least I assume that's why you're fidgeting in your seats like that . . ."

There was great laughter at this remark. Newsboys, plagued by worms and lice, were notoriously itchy.

"Seriously, our man needs no introduction. You heard him last year and loved him; you heard him the year before that and loved him; you begged him to come back this year. So here he is, gentlemen. I give you Mr. Godfrey Shepcote."

The noise was stupendous, the boys only too glad to let off steam, their voices stentorian from long practice.

Shepcote walked out to the lectern, bowed, basked in the din for a moment, then raised his hands for silence. A few whistles more and the throng quieted down, ready to listen. When he was sure he had their complete attention, he began.

"Fellow newsboys – I can say that in all honesty because you and me are fellows . . ." He waited for the cheers to subside. "And even though many years have passed since I stood on those windy corners, I still consider myself a newsboy . . . just a grown-up one." He paused and pointed at somebody in the front row. "I saw doubt on that face . . . and I don't blame him. Who am I to stand up here and say those things?" He patted his paunch. "I don't look like a newsboy. Yes, you may laugh, you may be skeptical, but I tell you, *we are fellows.*" He paused and leaned forward on the lectern. "I know what it's like to be so cold your fingers and toes are dead wood, so cold your ears could snap off like pieces of frozen cabbage. I know because I was there. I know that ever-present companion of newsboys, the dog-fox called Hunger. He that gnaws at your innards 'til you could cry out with it . . . but you don't because you have pride. The pride of those who must fend for themselves and who ask no quarter."

There was now complete silence in the hall.

"I remember the voice of fear. I know that devil who perches on your shoulders and whispers in your ear, 'Where is my next piece of bread coming from?'"

A sigh rippled through the packed ranks like wind through a hay field. Shepcote scanned the rows and it was as if his eyes met those of everyone in front of him. Even the tobacco pipes were laid down. The gathering was under his spell.

Murdoch became aware that a man was standing at his elbow and moved over to give him room. It was Shepcote's manservant, incongruous in this crowd in his sober black suit and grey gloves, dark hair well-oiled and smoothed back from his brow. He nodded in the direction of the stage.

"He's in fine fettle tonight, isn't he?"

Murdoch agreed. "Amazing."

Shepcote took a sip of water, moving slowly and deliberately. He knew how to play an audience the way the fishermen back east had known how to play a big fish, thought Murdoch.

133

Shepcote's voice dropped lower. "I said *my fellows* and I mean *my fellows* because I have not forgotten, nor ever will forget, those many nights when the hard pavement was my bed, the celestial heavens themselves my roof, and my only covers the very newspapers I was selling . . ."

There were some groans of recognition from the boys. Shepcote stepped closer to the edge of the stage, his face glistening with sweat. "Within these walls I have told my story before, but with your permission I would like to tell it again. Because even though it is my story, I know it is not unique to me. It could be the story of you, John Jarvis, you, Tim Black. Among all of you gathered here tonight there are similar journeys yet to be made, lives to be lived that may be even harder than mine was. And if I can be a guide to you, an inspiration, I will fall on my knees and give thanks to Our Father that my pain and my tribulations have not been in vain. So I ask you, brothers, can I tell my tale again?"

He reached out with his arms like a supplicant.

The boy beside Murdoch whistled shrilly, his fingers in his mouth, and others echoed him. Shepcote waved his hands and waited for silence. It came at once.

134

"When I was a boy, so young I was hardly out of skirts, my father died. He was a good, Christian man, hardworking to a fault, but his illness was protracted and when he was finally called to his Maker, my mother was left destitute. I had one sister, a girl so fine of character, so noble of spirit, she had no place on this earth. My mother had barely put off her widow's mourning garb when she was stricken again with grief. My sister went to join the angels, a far more fitting place for her than this vale of sin we mortals call home."

He pulled a white handkerchief out of his breast pocket and wiped at his face. "At the tender age of four, I was left the sole support of a bereaved and poor woman. My mother was so overcome with her sorrows she repined on her bed, unmoving day after day. What could I do? I prayed every night for guidance until my knees ached. It was a bitter cold winter and I made a few pence by sweeping away snow, carrying bags for the wealthy women who shopped on King Street. Some of them were kind, some of them paid me no more attention than if I had been a wheelbarrow . . ."

"Shame," yelled the boys. "Boo! Boo!"

"Come, boys, we must leave their sort to the judgment of the Almighty. Let me continue . . . It was December, one week before Christmas. I had stayed out especially late, hoping against hope to make a little more money so I could buy my mother a gift for Our Lord's nativity. But it was so cold nobody was abroad and I could find no employment at all. I had not eaten. I was exhausted. Finally unable to walk another step, I curled up in a drift of snow against the cathedral. And I tell you, my dear, dear fellows, at that moment I cared

135

not whether I lived or died. Perhaps I fell asleep, I know not, but suddenly I heard a voice, a kind deep voice. I opened my eyes and there was a man standing in front of me. 'Child, you cannot sleep here. It is too cold,' he said. 'You must get home.' Perhaps it was his kindness, the gentle expression on his face, that I was not accustomed to. Whichever it was, it touched my heart and tears sprang to my eyes and sobs tore, red-hot, at my throat. I know what you are thinking: what sort of unmanly behaviour is that? But remember, I was still a mere prattling child and I was close to starving. I will pass on over the words we exchanged, that man and me. All I need to tell you is that he vowed to help me, not through mere charity, although he did that, but by guiding me to where I could earn my own living, to where I could hold my head up with pride. He bade me come early the next morning to a certain corner. I could sell the newspapers I would find there. I determined to do exactly what he ordered and as dawn was breaking I arose and went to that same corner. The stranger was nowhere to be seen, but as he had promised there was a pile of newspapers, neatly bundled up . . ."

There was a hush in the hall. Murdoch could sense the stillness in the man Canning. Shepcote looked up to the ceiling.

136

"Who was he? I don't know. I never saw him again and sometimes I wonder to myself if indeed he was of mortal flesh . . . but no matter. I had my newspapers and I seized my chance to earn my pitiful living. No playmates for me, no hoops and balls to wile away the careless hours. I was still so small the sandwich board was bigger than I was. In fact, on rainy days I would creep inside it for shelter . . ."

This stirred a waft of laughter. Many of those present had done the same.

"But I worked hard. Where other boys walked a mile to sell their papers, I walked two. Where they got up at six to catch the first edition, I got up at five. Where they went home at nine, I stayed until ten. And so we eked out a living. I took home my earnings to my mother, who with that pittance fed us both."

He wagged his hand playfully at his audience. "Unlike many of my friends here, I did not waste one single penny on beer or tobacco."

More laughter and friendly catcalling. Shepcote continued.

"In spite of my best efforts, my mother seemed weaker, more and more frail. Every night when I came home there was a nourishing broth ready, sometimes a hot stew. Oh, not a banquet by rich men's standards, a paltry meal to them, but prepared with such love I felt as if I was eating ambrosia itself, and I left the table sated. Every night I asked her to join me at the meal but she always said she had already eaten. Child that I was, I took her at her word." He pressed the handkerchief to his eyes. "Forgive me, boys, I can never say this part of

137

my story without tears . . . I was fortunate to have such a mother. I know that many of you have never been so blessed . . . that you have never known the joy of a mother's smile or the sweet sorrow as her loving tears fall on your cheeks. My dear mother died. You see, what I did not realize was that with the loving self-sacrifice only mothers can show, she was giving all her food to me and she herself was starving."

He paused, searching the rows in front of him for acknowledgement. He found it on more than one thin face. Some of the boys were crying quietly. One or two put their arms around younger fellows. Murdoch himself felt a lump in his throat. The little boy next to him gave a loud sniff, and he patted his shoulder. The boy smiled up at him gratefully. Canning never moved his gaze from the stage.

"My dear mother passed away. Peacefully and piously, as she had lived. But she left me a gift. After her funeral, overwhelmed by my sorrow, I opened her battered old Bible to pray, and there, tucked inside, was an envelope. Puzzled, I opened it up . . . and took out . . ."

He paused, and one bold youth shouted, "Fifty dollars!"

138   Shepcote smiled good-naturedly. "Exactly. Fifty dollars. She had scrimped and saved and gone without so she could give me this legacy. Not a princely sum by most standards . . . not enough to start a bank . . ."

A lot of laughter now, the boys glad to be taken away from their painful thoughts.

"By the greatest of good fortunes, there was a stall for sale on my street, the owner old and tired. When I went to him with my fifty dollars in hand he laughed in my face. 'Send your father, laddie,' he said, 'then we'll do business.' It took him a long time to believe I was buying the stall myself."

According to Shepcote's narrative, thought Murdoch, he would have been about six years old at this point, but none of the audience was critical and he was never questioned.

"And that's how it began. I worked hard and honourably. No wasting my money on dice . . . yes, you know what I'm talking about. I prospered. I bought another stall, and another, and then I bought the newspaper itself."

He waited while they applauded and whistled.

"Now I have the great honour to represent the good people of our fair city as an alderman. The other day, one of my fellow councillors came to me. I won't name him because it is to his everlasting shame that he said what he did. 'Tell me, Mr. Shepcote,' he said, 'why do you, a busy man, an alderman whom so many people look up to, why do you waste your valuable time going to speak to a group of rowdy good-for-nothings?' It's true, those were the words he used, I regret to say. I looked him in the eye. 'Why? I'll tell you why. Because

139

among these so-called rowdy good-for-nothings might be the future leaders of the city. Wait . . . wait. Among those rowdies are as good men as you will find in your banks and law courts. Among that rough lot are diamonds.'"

The whistles and shouting broke out and he could not continue. Finally he yelled, "All they need is a chance to show what they are made of!"

The boys stamped their feet, awash in the waves of excitement, empty bellies temporarily forgotten. Shepcote knew that the city council was planning to eliminate the grant to the newsboys' lodge this year, but he was not going to tell them that bad news. They would find out soon enough when the lodge door closed to them and indeed the pavement would become their bed.

He waved and bowed as the cheering and whistling continued. Finally the master of ceremonies returned. He shook Shepcote's hand and amidst stomping and clapping the alderman left the stage.

Murdoch turned to Canning. "Excellent speech. Was it true?"

The man's pursed lips relaxed into a small smile. "Some of it."

140   Murdoch would have liked to hear more, but with a nod, Canning stood up.

"I'd better see to him," he said and he left the hall.

Murdoch's pipe had gone out and he stuffed it back

in his pocket, not wanting to arouse the cupidity of his neighbours, who were fast recovering from the mood that Shepcote had engendered. He had to admit to himself that a tear had formed in his own eye at more than one moment. Mr. Shepcote was a persuasive speaker indeed. The master of ceremonies started to call for silence again and Murdoch realized he was up next. He stood up and made his way down the aisle towards the stage. Over on the far side, some boys had started to sing. It could have been "Land of Hope and Glory," but he wasn't sure.

In the wings Shepcote mopped his dripping face and neck and took a quick sip from his whiskey flask. Canning approached him, a towel over his arm.

"Well done, sir. I wish I had a story like that to tell."

Shepcote didn't miss the irony in his servant's tone, and he scowled. "I doubt your life could be told anywhere except in a penal colony."

In fact, a lot of what he had recounted was true. He had been left fatherless at any early age, but the man he generally referred to as his father had been killed in a barroom brawl. His sister had indeed joined the angels at the age of sixteen when she died of venereal disease. It was concerning his mother that there was the most fiction. Destitute, yes, but never for a single moment could she have been termed self-sacrificing. Her last

141

words to him were vile curses because he wouldn't fetch her more gin. It was true that after her funeral he had found money. Hidden under the mattress. Money she had systematically stolen from his trousers, then forgotten about in her sodden mind. With the money, twenty dollars, he had made a down payment on a newspaper stall, cheating a near-blind old man by pretending to give him more than he did. But what was true was that he had worked and clawed his way out of the gutter, driven by a need to be better, to have the kind of comforts he witnessed in the lives of his customers, as distant from that skinny boy as the stars themselves.

And he had done it. He had a fine carriage and horse. A large house. He had married a woman from a better class; his daughter would marry even higher. But in the mixture of lies and half-truths he had handed out this afternoon, there was one total truth. He never forgot he had been a newsboy. Sometimes he awoke at night in a sweat of fear that everything he had built might be taken from him and once again he would be a pauper.

Beatrice Kitchen was darning her stockings, and she held the needle poised in mid-air as she looked at Murdoch.

"Sounds like an improbable story to me. As if angels would soil their hands selling newspapers. It was more likely some Methodist taking advantage of a hungry child."

Her husband chuckled. "Now, Mother, let Will get on with his tale."

It was late by the time Murdoch had got home, but the Kitchens were waiting up for him. Beatrice had made him a salty beef tea and he was sipping it.

"There's not much more to say, really. Mr. Shepcote struggled up the ladder of success by dint of hard work and good morals. I believed him. He made me weep along with all the others."

Arthur started to cough and Murdoch waited until he'd got his breath. Beatrice handed her husband a cloth to wipe his mouth.

"Any luck with the boys?" she asked.

"I think so. Of course there must have been at least three dozen of them ready to swear they'd seen Therese Laporte, in case there's a reward in the offing, but two of them sounded believable. One boy described her exactly. He'd been trying to sell his remaining newspapers at the Somerset Hotel which is at the corner of Church and Carlton. He was turfed out sometime after nine and walked down Church. He says she crossed in front of him at Gerrard Street. She was going east. He said she was, and I quote, 'a tasty bit of crumpet.'"

"Naughty boy!" exclaimed Beatrice. "I hope you gave him a slap to mind his manners."

143

"I did." Murdoch chuckled. "You should have seen him, Mrs. K. His name is Charles Elrod, but he's got a shock of red hair and he's been called Carrots so long he could hardly remember his real name. The other boy's a bit slow-witted and he was vague. However, he was going home and claims he saw the girl at the corner of Berkeley and Queen streets. She was walking towards Sumach, which is about where she was found. His description was close enough. The problem is he can't tell the time and doesn't know when it was he saw her, but he says St. Paul's had just chimed the quarter."

"If it was Therese the redhead saw and if she kept walking, I calculate she'd have been at Berkeley and Queen about a quarter to ten, so that fits," said Kitchen.

Murdoch grinned at Arthur. "We should have you on the force. Yes, that's what I figured."

"She could have hired a carriage," said Beatrice.

"That's true too. We're examining the dockets of cabbies who work in the area."

"Where was the poor child going?" asked Beatrice. "She's nowhere near the train station on Queen and Berkeley."

"I wish I knew. However, I'm going to check at the French-Canadian church on King Street."

"The old Methodist church?"

144   "That's it. There's quite a colony of tanners come down from Quebec and they go to that church."

"Funny how we all gravitate to our own," said Beatrice.

"I'm gambling she was heading there. I'll call on the priest tomorrow. Mr. Shepcote says we can run a picture in his paper free of charge as long as necessary. Somebody will come forward. And at least now we have an exact description of what she was wearing."

Beatrice broke off the wool thread with her teeth and slipped out the wooden egg that was inside the heel. She picked up another stocking from the pile in the basket and started to examine it.

"I can't get over the gall of those two young women stealing clothes from the dead. Heathens would behave better."

Her husband snorted. "They denied everything, I'll wager. Am I right, Will?"

Murdoch nodded. "Absolutely right. According to them anyone could have put the garments in the outhouse."

"Which is true, got to give them that."

"You should just send them to the Mercer and throw away the key," said Beatrice.

"We can't do anything until we have more evidence. We brought them down to the station and Crabtree and I were at them all afternoon, but they wouldn't budge. Problem is, you see, the privy is used by the other inhabitants of the house and it's quite accessible to anyone in the alley. The bundle was well hidden, but it would have taken only moments to put it there. We had to let them go. For now, anyway."

145

Beatrice had found a hole and was busy darning across it. "Have you recovered all of the clothes?"

"There was no, er, undergarment."

"Drawers or chemise?"

"No drawers."

"Hmm. Those are easy things to hide. You just wear 'em."

Murdoch knew for certain that Alice didn't have them. Perhaps Ettie did.

He sneezed. He'd started to feel under the weather, feverish and runny-nosed. Beatrice regarded him over her glasses like a bird contemplating a tasty morsel.

"My oh my. You look as if you're coming down with a cold."

He sneezed again. "'Fraid so."

She got up. "You just sit right there. We'll have you right as rain."

"Don't bother yourself, Mrs. K. I'm off to bed soon."

"No bother. I've got to tend to Father, anyway."

She left him and Murdoch grimaced. He was already familiar with Mrs. Kitchen's home remedies, and some of them were worse than the illness they were curing.

Arthur noticed the expression on Murdoch's face and started to laugh. Immediately the laughter turned into a violent attack of coughing that left him panting and weak in his chair. He spat bloody froth into the cup. Murdoch thought the smell was worse daily.

146

"Can I get you anything?" he asked.

"New pair of lungs is about the only thing that'd do me any good, and I doubt you've got a set of them in your pocket."

"Wish I had."

Kitchen waved his hand in the general direction of the door. "Forgot to tell you, Mother's trying a new cure on me."

The door opened at that and Mrs. Kitchen returned carrying an enamel bowl of steaming water. Murdoch jumped up to help her.

"Here, let me." He took the bowl out of her hands.

"Put it down there close to the fire. Arthur, we'll have to build up the coals a bit. Mr. Murdoch should be warm."

Murdoch started to protest but she cut him short.

"Take off your slippers and socks. Come on."

She sprinkled some mustard powder into the hot water.

"Now put your feet in. Careful, it's hot." He eased his feet into the bowl, watching the skin immediately turn pink.

"Sit back," she said and pulled the mohair shawl up around his shoulders.

He grinned. "I feel like I'm a boy again."

She patted his shoulder. "Good. You could do with a bit of mothering now and again."

She went back to her own chair, unobtrusively

147

moving the tin cup from her husband's side table and putting a fresh one down.

"Arthur said you're trying a new cure."

She nodded. "I was out at the market this morning and there was a new egg-seller at Mr. Howard's table. Apparently he's getting too old to come down from the farm now, so this woman is selling the eggs and chicken for him. Odd thing she was, brown as a berry. Probably got gypsy blood. Anyway, we got to talking and I told her about Arthur here and his sickness. 'That's easy fixed,' she says. 'Make him take twelve raw eggs a day in some heavy cream. Keep him cold at night and don't let up 'til he's cured.' Well, I thinks to myself, it's all very well for you to say that, seeing as how you're in the business of selling eggs. She must have read my mind. 'Cured my father and my own sister,' she says. 'And tell you what, I'll sell you a dozen for the price of ten. How's that?'"

"Course Mother agreed," interjected Arthur. "Even though we can't afford it."

"We'll manage. I'm going to advertise for another boarder. Should be all right if they keep to themselves, don't you think?"

"Anybody who stays here is lucky," said Murdoch. He stirred his feet in the mustard water, making a tidal wave in the bowl. He grinned at the other two. "I used to do this when I was a boy in Nova Scotia with the pools of seawater left behind at low tide. I'd sit on the

148

rocks, put my feet into the pool and pretend I was God sending a storm."

As he watched the water slap in the enamel bowl he remembered his old game vividly. In the middle of the pool he floated a piece of driftwood to represent the *Bluebell*, which was the unlikely name of the fishing trawler his father sailed on. Gradually he stirred the water higher and higher until the waves overwhelmed the flimsy boat and it capsized with all hands on board. He played this over and over, each time with a mixture of Catholic guilt and a pagan delight that he had destroyed his hated father.

". . . dear child, God rest her soul."

Mrs. K. was saying something. He caught the last bit. Ever since Beatrice had heard that Therese was of the faith, her attitude had changed. The girl had risen from one of doubtful character to a child rapidly approaching sainthood.

"Beg pardon, Mrs. K.?"

"You really were off in a brown study, weren't you. I was just asking if there's anything else missing. If she was running away she'd take all her belongings with her, I'd think."

"You're quite right. The housekeeper is sure she had a canvas valise and some extra clothes. Probably a skirt and a waist at least. Her jacket and gloves are also missing. Apparently she had a rosary and a Bible but I searched her room and they weren't there."

149

Beatrice hastily crossed herself. "What wicked person would steal such holy things?"

"I'm sending Crabtree off to check the pawnshops."

"Will she be getting a Christian burial?" Beatrice asked.

"Eventually, but we haven't been able to contact the family yet. They're all snowed in."

"Pity poor them when they hear, losing a pure child like that."

Murdoch had told the Kitchens about the postmortem evidence, but Beatrice hadn't seemed to quite comprehend the full import. Then she surprised him, as she often did. She stopped her darning for a moment and looked at him.

"There'll be folks who'll say she was a sinner, her in the family way like that, but I don't. It's my view that somebody forced connections on her and made her take that opium. Whoever they are, God will punish them. And if in his wisdom He doesn't see fit to do it in this lifetime, I sincerely hope the law will."

Chapter Ten

He looked up at the whore standing above him. Her bare foot was raised and he could see the dirt beneath the ragged toenails. She had splashed on copious amounts of cologne and as always the combination of stale sweat, rank perfume and self-disgust made him want to retch. He'd fought against his need to visit her but finally had capitulated. The defeat, even though it was of his own making, made him angry.

She tapped his nose lightly with her toe. "You don't have to worry about names here. It don't matter to me what you call yourself. You could be the Prince himself for all I care."

He sat back on his heels and took her foot in both his hands. "I'm glad about that. It could hurt both of us very much if anyone found out. Do you understand?"

Grimacing with pain, she nodded.

WEDNESDAY, FEBRUARY 13

ALL WEDNESDAY, SNOW FLOATED DOWN in fat, slow flakes that children caught on their tongues, pretending it was ice cream. When night came the manure-dotted streets lay beneath a blanket of clean, fresh snow that sparkled in the light of the gas lamps. By eight o'clock most of the city's residents were indoors, and even along Queen Street the smooth surface was unmarred by footprints. Only outside the doors of the John O'Neil was the snow heavily dinted.

Samuel Quinn, with Princess at his heels, pushed open the big door of the taproom, and the din and the smoke rushed out together. At the far end a hunchback was thumping out popular music-hall songs on the battered, out-of-tune piano, and a group of men and women, arms linked, stood around him, bellowing out the words.

"And lo it was her father,
Rum ti-iddle ey oh,
And lo it was her father . . ."

One of the women was Bernadette Weston. She was singing at top voice, head thrust back, mouth wide open. The brim of her hat had tilted under such strenuous efforts and settled at an angle across her right eyebrow, and a scrawny green feather bobbed and danced in time to the music. She noticed Quinn and winked at him but didn't break rhythm for a moment.

He waved, then, tugging at the piece of twine attached to his dog's collar, dived into the crowd, heading for one of the long plank tables by the far wall where he could see Alice was sitting. Princess tried to lap at some sticky mess on the floor but he pulled her away. Cuspidors were provided but few used them, and the freshly strewn sawdust was churned into clumps by the mixture of tobacco juice, melting snow and phlegm.

"Heads up!"

A sweating waiter in shirtsleeves, his leather apron stained and wet from splashes, squeezed by Quinn, his laden tray held high. The beer that was brewed at the John O'Neil tended to be sour and weak but it didn't seem to matter. The customers came for the company, not the brew.

"Comin' through. 'Cuse me." Quinn used his elbows for emphasis and the bodies reluctantly yielded. He was known here, and a couple of the men slapped him on the shoulder. There were only a few women and one of them, jammed in the side bench, smiled and beckoned, but he moved on. His eyes were already smarting from the thick pall of smoke from innumerable pipes and cheap cigars.

Alice hadn't seen him yet; she was intent on her companion, a man Quinn didn't recognize. He was burly, clean-shaven with his hair cropped very short. There was a flattened appearance to his face that made Samuel think of prizefighters.

153

He slid in beside Alice on the bench, wrapped the twine around the leg of the table and pushed Princess underneath. She sniffed with interest at the other man's boots.

"Oi, look what the cat dragged in," said Alice. "Where've you been keepin' yourself?"

"Busy working. Not like some as I know of." He gave her a friendly poke in the ribs and she squealed. Her sense of humour was already enhanced by hot gin.

"You're forgetting your manners, Alice. Aren't you going to introduce me?"

"This here's Jack," she said, indicating the man beside her. "He's just passing through. His name's Jack and he's a Jack Tar."

"How'd you do," said Samuel. He called to the beleaguered waiter. "What'll you have?" he asked the other two. "It's on me."

"Oi, come into money, have you? Lucky for you. How'd that happen?"

"Never mind. Do you want a drink or not?"

"Another hot jackey'd go down nice," she said.

The man nodded. "Same. Thanks." His voice was husky and strained as if he had laryngitis.

Samuel gave the order to the waiter, taking a pint of beer for himself. He took a folded newspaper out of his pocket and put it on the table.

"Look at this, Alice. It's concerning that young girl the police were asking us about yesterday –"

154

"I don't want to hear one more word about that sodding mort. You'd think she was the Queen's daughter, all the fuss that's being made."

"What's the story? I don't know nothing about it," her companion said.

Alice sniffed. "You don't want to. Bloody coppers, they're always on at a girl. Ettie and me wasted all yesterday afternoon at the shicey station just because they thought we'd nimmed the girl's clothes."

She stayed her indignation while the waiter banged down two glasses of gin, a pitcher of hot water and a pint of ale. Then she added a couple of splashes of water to the gin and took a deep gulp. "As if we'd do anything like that. What do they take us for? Couldn't prove nothing, we was asleep –"

"If you'll rein in a minute, Alice, I'll tell you what it says in here," said Quinn. "They're offering a reward for information."

He sipped at his beer, wiped the foam from his moustache and prepared to read. At that moment an arm reached over his shoulder.

"Give us a swallow, will you, Sam. I'm fair parched."

Bernadette didn't wait for his answer but seized the glass and drank some beer.

"He's buying tonight, Ettie," said Alice. "Why don't you order one?"

"Won't say no."

Good-naturedly, Quinn flagged down the waiter again

155

and a foaming mug of beer splashed on the table.

"Ettie, sit down and listen to this," said Alice. "There's somethin' else in the paper about that dead girl."

Bernadette glanced quickly at Alice and pulled out the chair. She removed her hat and fanned at her hot face.

"Hard work, all that singing." Princess popped her head up from under the table and pawed at Bernadette's knee. "Hey, lookit who's here." She rubbed the dog's ears affectionately. Then she reached down and offered her mug of beer. The hound lapped at the drink thirstily. Quinn watched.

"That's enough now. Don't want to get her soused."

"First time I've ever seen a dog drink brew," said Jack.

Bernadette took back the glass and finished off the beer. "Ain't seen much, then, have you?"

"Ettie, don't be cheeky. Jack here is a well-travelled man."

"That so? Like where? Where have you been?"

He smiled, a smile that didn't come close to touching his eyes. "Britain, France, China twice. You name it."

"What are you, a sailor?"

"That's right, a saucer and plate."

"What?"

"First mate."

"He's speaking rhyming slang," said Alice. "The cockneys do it in London."

"Sounds like barmy talk to me."

"Ettie," protested Alice. "Jack's a stranger here. You're not being very neighbourly."

"Do you want to see my how-d'you-do?" the sailor asked.

"No."

"I mean my tattoo."

"Yeah. Come on, Jack, let's see," said Alice.

He pulled off his right glove and pushed up his sleeve.

"Lord love us, look at that," gasped Alice.

A red snake curled around his forearm and wrist. The mouth was open and the fangs, which ran along the edge of his thumb and forefinger, were gripping a woman, stark naked and bleeding. He spread his fingers and the woman's legs opened.

"Cheeky," said Alice.

"What d'you think?" the sailor asked.

Ettie shrugged. "Not much. I've seen better." She turned to Quinn and indicated the little white ribbon that was pinned to her velvet jacket. "How do you like me bow, Sam?"

He grinned. "Don't tell me you've joined the Temperance League?"

"That's it. I'm taking the Pledge next week. They stand you to a swell tea, cakes and sandwiches, all you can eat. I've been practising."

She pouted like a little girl, putting her finger to her

mouth. "I pledge that lips that touch liquor will never touch my . . . lips."

The sailor grinned. "You make me want to be an abstainer this minute."

Quinn rattled the newspaper. "Do you want to hear this news or not?"

Jack smiled again. "Let's get another round of blinks first, on me."

Ettie shook her head. "I'm going back to sing in a minute. Sam, get on with it, for Christ's sake."

Quinn swallowed the rest of his beer so he could take advantage of the stranger's offer. He was glad Ettie was being surly with the man. He was too cool a customer by far. But she was like that. Formed strong likes and dislikes right away. God help the man she took a scunner to. She could freeze hell over with one look when she wanted to.

He picked up the paper and read aloud.

Information sought: The investigation continues into the death of Therese Laporte, the lovely young woman who died so tragically last Saturday night. Anyone who saw this young woman on Saturday night between the hours of five o'clock and midnight is asked to report to Detective Murdoch at number-four station immediately. She was known to be wearing –

"Bloody hell, Sam, don't go on with that. We've heard it already, haven't we, Ettie? Get to the bit about the reward."

In the public interest, the owner of the *Signal* is offering a reward of fifty dollars for any honest information that our officers will deem useful in clearing up the mysteries of this tragic episode.

"Fifty dollars!" exclaimed Alice.

Ettie frowned. "Nothin' for us. We didn't see her. Too bad."

Quinn continued.

We must ensure that our streets remain safe for our loved ones and for those who cannot fend for themselves. If we do not eliminate the riffraff that are pouring into our city on a daily basis, we are condemning the fairer sex to a life of perpetual fear.

"What's it mean?" asked Alice in bewilderment. "Who's the riffraff? Do they mean lumberjacks?"

The sailor shook his head. "Haven't you heard of those immigrants coming in from Moldavia?"

Alice laughed. "Where in God's name is that? Oh, never mind. I doubt if I'll be going there in the near future. My carriage has got a wheel missing." She pursed

159

her lips again. "Read that bit once more, Sam. About the reward. Fifty dollars . . ."

Bernadette caught her friend's sleeve. "Alice! Why don't you come and sing with me."

Alice pulled away. "I don't want to, Ettie. Jack and me was having a good chin. Weren't we, Jack?"

She leaned toward him so that her breast was brushing against his arm.

"Why're you so interested in that money? Do you have some information about the girl?" he asked.

"No, she doesn't," said Ettie. "She's just dreaming, aren't you, Alice?"

"No, I –"

"You heard me."

Alice stared sullenly at her friend. "Yeah. I don't know anything. Never have," she muttered.

Bernadette stood up abruptly. "That's my song he's playing. Sam, thanks for the beer. See you, Captain. 'Bye, lovey."

This was addressed to the bitch under the table. Ettie gave her an affectionate caress and returned to the piano, where the hunchback was beginning a plaintive series of chords. Resignedly, Quinn folded up the paper and sat back in his chair to watch.

160   Alice pressed harder on the stranger's arm. "Don't mind her. She's moody."

The piano player thumped out a chord to get attention. The noise in the bar lessened slightly and Ettie began to sing. Her voice was clear and true as water.

"I stand in a land of roses
But I dream of a land of snow . . ."

The room quieted even more.

"When you and I were happy
In the days of long ago."

Alice Black leaned forward, beckoned to her companion as if to whisper and slyly licked the inside of his ear.

He laughed. "Hey, that tickled."

"I'm good at tickling, I am. Here, I'll show ya."

She did so, more slowly this time. He didn't move away. "Did you like that?" she asked.

"Yep. That was real nice, Elaine."

"Alice. Not Elaine. My name's Alice."

He reached over and touched the bead necklace she had around her neck. "That's pretty. Most unusual. Where'd you get it?"

She caught hold of his bare hand and put one of his fingers in her mouth. "Who cares?"

She thrust her tongue in between his fingers and he grinned again.

161

"Tell you what, Miss Alice, why don't you take me somewhere private. Where you can tickle away to your heart's content."

She grinned. "Two dollars?"

"You're dear."

"I'm worth it, you'll see. Where d'you want to go, upstairs or to our place?"

"I've a better idea. You can come to my dodgy figs. Very private. I've got a couple of good bottles tucked away just dying to be opened. Got them in Turkey."

"You're on. I've never had Turkish brew before."

"You'll love it. Come on, pick up your faggot sacks and let's go."

She gulped back the dregs of the gin and they both stood up. Quinn was watching Bernadette and didn't pay any attention. Alice started to lead the way to the door, shoving at the hot bodies that crowded the floor.

"Coming through. Move your carcass, you lumps."

However, as they approached the piano, Ettie was finishing her song. The piano player tinkled the treble keys. A burst of applause came from those who had free hands. Ettie, flushed and excited, bowed lavishly. The hunchback launched into another song and a burly man whose sooty clothes betrayed his calling started to sing an old ballad.

"Where have you been today, Randall my son?
Where have you been today, my beloved son?"

Ettie was about to join in when she saw Alice. She stepped back.

"Where you going?" she asked, grabbing her hard by the arm.

Alice tried to shrug her off but couldn't. "With him." Alice jerked her head in Jack's direction. He was watching them with his flat cold eyes, but the waiter had stopped to serve one of the tables and he was separated from the two women.

"I don't like him," hissed Ettie.

"Well, it's a good thing you're not the one going with him, then."

"Alice, don't go. I wouldn't trust him as far as I could throw him."

"Ha. Since when are you so choosy? If we only went with cullies we liked the look of, we wouldn't do nothing."

"What will you leave your mother, Randall my son?
What will you leave your mother, my beloved son?"

The chimney sweep was warbling in a lovely counter-tenor. All around the room men were laughing, ignoring him.

Ettie scowled. "He's a liar. He's no sailor, his hands are too soft. I had a sailor once. His hands were all rutted and hard. He said it was from the ropes."

"What is he, then?"

"Probably a nark."

Alice looked over at Jack, still blocked by the waiter,

163

who was having a dispute with one of the patrons about his bill.

"No! He can't be."

"Yes, he could. You've been babbling all over him about that girl. We're going to end up in the Mercer if you don't shut up . . . And I told you not to wear that necklace. Not yet. We've got to be careful."

Jack finally got around the waiter and came up to them. "Shall we do a heel and toe?"

Alice looked at him and Ettie, then put her arm through his.

"I can't wait."

They pushed their way to the door. Ettie watched, then shrugged and turned back to the piano. The chimney sweep reached out his grimy hands to her and theatrically she took hold of them and joined in the ballad.

"What will you leave your sweetheart, Randall my son?
What will you leave your sweetheart, my beloved son?"

The hunchback joined in, his voice rich and deep.

"A rope to hang her, mother,
A rope to hang her, mother.
Oh, make my bed soon for I'm sick to my heart,
and fain would lie down."

164

Outside in the street, Alice shivered in the cold and pulled her shawl tightly around her chest. The sailor took her arm.

"I've a friend I'd like you to meet. We'll go there first."

"I thought it was going to be you and me."

"Later. Him first."

"It's all the same to me," said Alice.

Chapter Eleven

THE CARRIAGE LURCHED and Alice almost fell forward into the lap of the man seated opposite her.

"Oops. What'd we do, run over a dead dog?"

"Just a lump of ice."

He pushed her back into her own seat. The sailor had brought her to this man but she didn't fancy him at all. He was as twitchy as a schoolboy, refused to tell her his name, and had barely said a word the entire ride.

She straightened up and sat back, fanning herself. "It's bloody roasting in here."

She started to unbutton her jacket.

166 "No sense being uncomfortable, is there?" She giggled wildly, then hiccoughed. "What'd you put in that drink? I can't feel my nose."

The man sipped at the silver flask he was holding.

"It's just first-quality scotch. Perhaps you're not used to it."

Even well on her way to total drunkenness as she was, Alice picked up the contempt in his voice. She scowled.

"I've had good grog before. Lots of times. Just as good as your Turkey muck."

She was sweating in earnest now.

"Can we open the bleeding window? I'm going to melt, else."

She went to pull up the blind on the window closest to her but the man caught her arm.

"I'd rather you didn't."

"Why not?"

"I value my privacy."

"Nobody's going to see you out here except the ducks."

She had lifted the blind enough to see that they were close to the lake, trotting slowly along a narrow spit.

The man leaned over and lowered the wick on the porcelain lamp that hung from a bracket above the door. The carriage darkened, the shadows so deep she could hardly see his face.

"That's much cozier, wouldn't you say?"

She shrugged. "I suppose so."

She'd had all sorts; some liked daylight, some didn't. She could tell he was one of the play-acting kind. They always wanted you to make out you was enjoying

167

yourself. Ooh and aah and wriggle. When all you could think about was the chops you'd cook for your tea and how long was he going to take to finish the jig. That kind of cully always left red-faced with a couple of dollars on the pillow. "Buy yourself a little present." Sod the fools. She giggled to herself.

Good thing they weren't mind readers.

"Can you share the joke, Alice?"

She yawned. She suddenly felt so tired she thought she could fall asleep right there.

"Wasn't anything. But I'm bloody whacked. Can we go back now?"

"I thought you were enjoying the ride."

Alice sighed. "'S bloody marvellous."

He leaned forward. He was sweating and there was an unpleasant smell coming from him. Maybe she was his first wagtail. The Johnny Raws were always scared out of their nobby drawers.

"I understand you have information about that girl who froze to death . . ."

"Did Jack tell you that? It was supposed to be a secret."

"He tells me everything. Are you going to go to the police and claim your reward?"

168   "I might, 'cept Ettie's all miffy. She doesn't want me to say anything because she thinks it'll get us into trouble."

"I don't see how giving information to the police

could get you into trouble. You're doing your civic duty."

"Don't I always."

"What was it you saw? Perhaps I can tell you if it is worth bothering the police about."

Alice struggled to make sense of what he was saying. He seemed to be going a long way off.

"Stop mumbling," she said. "Course it is. They'd love to know. She got into a carriage, didn't she?"

"Who did?"

"The mort, the girl, who'd you think?"

"Is that so? Where?"

"Yes, it is so, and I saw her on Queen Street. Just past the hotel."

"When was this?"

"'Bout ten o'clock on Saturday night."

"Are you sure it was the same person? Could have been anybody."

"Of course I'm sure. There aren't two women in the whole town with a hat like that. I saw her get into a carriage right at the corner."

"That is very strange. On the other hand there are so many carriages in Toronto I'm not sure if your information will be that helpful."

"Well, you're wrong, Mr. Know-It-All. This one belonged to a swell. I'd know it anywhere . . ." Groggily she shook her head. "Shouldn't be talking . . . Ettie said not to tell anyone . . ."

"So you told Ettie, did you?"

"Course I did. She's my best mate. I love Ettie."

She was having great difficulty sitting upright.

"You seem so tired, Alice. Why don't you put your feet up? Here, let me help you with your boots . . . My, they're tight, aren't they?"

He tugged and the boots came off with a plop, the rancid odour of Alice's dirty stockings filling the carriage.

"It's sodding hot in here. Look at you, you're sweating like a pig." She giggled again. "Do pigs sweat? Can't say I've noticed . . . Wish you'd speak up. It's too dark. Are we in the Other Place? You're not the Devil, are you?"

"Far from it. I'm your Good Angel. In fact, I'm going to send you to Paradise."

He turned and tugged at a short leather thong attached to the upholstery of the seat behind him. A section came away. Behind it was a built-in cabinet.

Alice lifted her head. "Oi. What you got in there, the family jewels?"

"As good as."

He took out a glass vial and a burgundy leather case. Then he rapped hard on the roof of the carriage. Alice heard the coachman call to the horse and they stopped suddenly, the well-sprung vehicle bouncing gently. She watched as her companion flicked the catch on the leather case and opened it. Nestled in a pink satin

170

lining was what looked like a steel tube. He lifted it out, removed a long needle lying beside it and fastened them together. He placed the instrument on the seat and pulled the cork out of the vial.

"What's that?"

"Let's call it the Milk of Paradise."

He plunged the syringe into the vial and drew up the brownish-coloured liquid. "Roll up your sleeve, Alice, and I will make you happier than you've ever been."

She shook her head. "Sod off. I've heard of that stuff. Sends you batchy."

"No, it doesn't, not if used wisely. It's the nectar of the gods."

"That so? Let me see you do it, then."

"I will. But ladies first. Here, hold out your arm."

He caught her by the wrist with his free hand but she knocked him away. "No. I don't want to."

The syringe fell to the floor. The needle broke in half and the brown fluid spread on the beige matting. The man yelped.

"Damn you! You shouldn't have done that. Heaven is costly."

Alice saw his rage, saw the intent. Fear surged through her body, every nerve sensing the danger.

Before he could stop her, she pushed down the handle and thrust open the door and half fell, half rolled to the ground. Desperately, she scrambled to her feet, oblivious to the sharp ice beneath her unshod feet. They were on a desolate strip of shore. She could see the outline of the distillery to the west but it was too far away. Even if she screamed, she knew nobody would hear her. She began to run, not realizing she was heading out on the frozen lake.

The man leaned out of the carriage. "Stop her!" he shouted to the coachman. The order was unnecessary. Jack understood the situation immediately and leaped down from his seat and plunged after the fleeing woman. Even in his heavy cape, he caught up with her easily.

"Hey, wait. Where're you going?"

She turned, gasping, "He's a sodding lunatic . . ."

"Don't be silly, course he's not. Come on, you'll catch your death."

Alice looked over his shoulder and for the first time she could see the carriage completely. The moon was full and gleaming on the snow. It was easy to make out a burgundy chassis. The grey horse shook his bridle and pawed at the ground.

"My God, it's the same bloody carriage. It was you . . . you're the ones who picked up the girl . . ."

She saw the expression on the man's face but before she could move, he caught her shoulder with one hand, twisted her around and slipped a rope noose around her throat. Alice toppled backwards as he pulled tighter.

172

Chapter Twelve

THURSDAY, FEBRUARY 14

JOE SEATON GOT OUT OF BED IN A HURRY. He'd forgotten to pull down the alarm lever on his clock and had slept an hour longer than he should have. The window was already grey with the coming of dawn. He pulled on his trousers, lit his lantern and, rubbing hard at his head to wake himself up, clambered down the ladder to the stable. The horse whinnied softly in welcome and thrust his head over the gate of the loose box. Joe offered him the dried apple he'd pinched from the kitchen the night before, and Silver took it delicately between his big yellow teeth and ground it to pulp. Joe stroked the soft upper lip with its stiff whiskers and the horse nuzzled into his hand in the hope of finding more apples.

"That's yer lot, greedy guts," Joe said affectionately. "Come on, move over. I'm late. They'll be on at me good if I don't get cracking." He pushed the animal aside and went into the box, where he forked some fresh hay from the bale into the feeding trough. Silver was a young horse but sweet-natured and biddable, and Joe was grateful for that. The big Morgan on the farm where he'd first lived in Canada was ornery and unpredictable. He'd landed such a kick on Joe's thigh once he'd near broken the bone. "'Twas yer own fault," said the farmer and cuffed the boy for good measure.

He shivered even though this part of the stable was warm. There was an oil heater in the corner, kept on a low burn, and the horse's body heat helped. Joe's room was up above in the loft. There was only a single layer of wood between it and the elements, and the cracks were so bad, snow sifted in at the corner.

He left Silver to his hay and climbed back up the ladder. The frost on the window shone like silver filigree as the winter sun grew stronger. He put his candle on the wooden dresser, reached under his narrow bed and hauled out the tin strongbox that had come with him from England three years earlier. That, a set of wool underwear and his navy-blue suit were all that remained of his original endowment from Dr. Barnardo's Home. The suit was small for him now. His wrists protruded from the cuffs of the jacket and he was ashamed to wear it. The sturdy boots had gone too, traded to another boy at the Fegan Boys' Distributing Home for a book now stored safely at the bottom of the box.

He lifted the lid. Inside was his scanty clothing, one-piece flannel underwear, two jerseys, a flannel shirt, all neatly folded as he had been taught. Underneath everything was the precious book, *A Handbook of Physiology and Phrenology*. He took it out and laid it aside carefully on the bed, giving it a little pat as if it were a live creature. Although there were a lot of words he couldn't understand, he'd been well schooled in basic reading in the orphanage, and he studied the thin volume at every opportunity. He'd even shown it to Therese and they'd looked at the illustrations together, giggling as they determined that the high bony forehead of Edith Foy was a sign of excessive pride and John Foy's bibativeness, his fondness for liquids, as the book called it, could be clearly seen above his prominent zygomatic arch.

In the far corner of the box, tucked beneath the jersey, was a twist of newspaper which he unfolded. Inside was his hoard of treasures, a gold cufflink, part of a broken onyx earbob, some coins, including two shilling pieces he'd once found on a London street, and a small wooden crucifix. He removed this reverently.

When he first knew that Therese was a Roman Catholic he was afraid. At the Home the word "Romanist" always sat in the same sentence as "wicked" or, at best, "misguided." Once one of the bigger youths had discovered a new boy clutching a rosary, and a group of residents soon gathered, whispering together, solemn and afraid as if they had found the Devil himself in the cupboard. They informed the warden and the poor newcomer was sent away. "To his own kind," said the supervisor. But the incident had shaken everyone and special prayers were offered for the soul of the depraved departed.

Therese was always unobtrusive in her observance, but he'd seen her touching the glass beads on her rosary, muttering in a strange language. Then she'd kiss the little wooden cross that hung from the necklace. She'd shown it to him, the seminaked body of Jesus Christ, arms outstretched, head drooping. The agony of that tiny figure had fascinated Joe.

He propped the crucifix against the candlestick, then dropped to his knees on the hard floor. He'd seen Therese cross herself and he imitated her as best he could, fluttering his hand across his chest. He bent his head in prayer, saying out loud the only Latin he had gleaned.

"Ar vay Maria, Duminee nose tree."

There was no one to hear and make a mockery of him, and he repeated these words over and over.

It was in early December that he'd first crept into her room. There was a severe frost that night and the cold had bitten through his blanket until he woke shivering, unable to sleep. Normally he would have gone down to the stable and burrowed into the pile of straw beside Silver, but he was afraid to. He'd seen two large brown rats vanishing down the drain in the centre of the stable, and them he truly hated. He knew what they were capable of. This particular evening he and Therese were seated at the kitchen table, snug against the wind soughing at the windows. The Foys were on a rare evening out and Joe had basked in the warmth and peace of their absence, and talking what was, for him, "a blue streak," as Tess put it. She soon pried out of him what sort of conditions he was living in.

"You can come to sleep in my bed, if it pleases you," she whispered. "But we mustn't let anyone know."

She hadn't needed to say that. He was quite aware what would happen if they were discovered. So beginning then, on the coldest nights, he climbed through the back window of the house and tiptoed up the back stairs to her room. Infrequently at first, not trusting, only when the cold was unbearable. But always she welcomed him. Always until a week ago. When he came this night she pushed him away like an unwelcome dog and he fell to the floor. Seeing his face, she jumped down and knelt beside him, kissing his cheeks and hands.

"Forgive me, *mon ami*. I regret."

She got back into bed, lifted the counterpane and let him climb into the warm cocoon.

177

"You can place your head here if you wish," she said and guided him to the soft pillow of her young breasts. The feeling was so sweet it made him dizzy and he swelled into uncomfortable manhood, his groin throb-bing. Memories of the coarse jokes he'd heard at the Home came to his mind but he pushed them away. He could not bear anything to sully the purity of his love.

"You cannot come any more," she whispered, her breath warm on his face. But she would not say why, and when he crept away early that morning before it was light, his body hurt as if he had been beaten.

If he had been the one to find her lying in the snow, he would have lain beside her and brought her back to life with his own heat.

He shifted. His knees were aching and his fingers had gone numb with cold. The little room was silent. No voice of God had spoken. No Devil either, for that matter. He thought the Christ stretched out on the cross looked at him with pity, but there was no miracle forth-coming. Stiffly, he got to his feet. He had no idea how long he had been on his knees, but he knew it must be time to prepare the horse and carriage for Dr. Rhodes.

Next to the trapdoor was a washstand where his pitcher and bowl stood. There was a bar of soap in a dish and a razor. Soon after he had arrived, Foy made a scornful remark about the downy hair on his lip and chin, and Joe had immediately purchased a razor and tried to make sure he would never offend again.

He rolled up the sleeve of his jersey, exposing his forearm. A round white scar by the base of his thumb was testimony to his first placement in Elmvale. He'd tried to defend himself against the farmer's belt and the buckle had ripped out a piece of flesh on his wrist.

He picked up the razor in his right hand and drew it firmly down his arm.

A red mark, thin as a pencil stroke, appeared instantly. He clenched his teeth but tears sprang involuntarily to his eyes. He waited a moment, then cut himself again, deeper this time. Then he dropped the bloody razor into the bowl of water, breaking the skin of ice into delicate shards. The water turned pink.

He pulled down his sleeve. Beads of sweat had broken out on his temples and he felt faint. However, the burning pain in his arm was a relief, as if he had transposed the grief that threatened to drive him mad.

Dark plumes of smoke, slow and lazy in the cold air, hung over the tall stacks at the distillery. The old lunatic who lived at the edge of the lake to the east used the smoke as a barometer to the mood of God. If the clouds were white and scattered it meant God was happy, and out-of-doors would be pleasant. If the smoke was dark and still, as it was this morning against the flesh-coloured dawn, God was angry and His breath would burn on your face. It was a time to be careful not to offend Him.

179

So it was with uneasiness he set out to forage for firewood and debris along the shore.

He saw what looked like a bundle of clothes some yards out on the frozen lake. When he went to investigate, he discovered the body.

He circled her once, twice, then poked her gingerly with his stick. In the night, snow had drifted across her body, and beneath that cold blanket she lay with her arms outstretched, legs bent beneath her. Even the confused mind of the lunatic registered that something was terribly wrong, and with a moan of fear he stumbled back over the frozen, rutted ground to the hut of his nearest neighbour. The widow, Maria Jenkins, was deaf and suspicious and he had difficulty rousing her. When she finally opened her door, he was gesticulating wildly, swaying from one foot to the other like a frightened pigeon. She understood him to say that an angel had fallen from the sky.

Later, when Murdoch saw Alice's face, he found it hard to fathom why the old man would have said such a thing.

Donalda had been awake for almost an hour but she lay in her warm bed, not wanting to get up. She had slept badly again, with a terrifying dream of drowning that woke her over and over as if she were rising and falling to the surface of the sea. Finally she willed herself to stay awake. She heard Cyril's door open and close and she slowly got out of bed. She couldn't bear the thought of having breakfast alone, and even her husband's

180

company was preferable. Owen, she knew, wouldn't be up until nine at least, and she never liked to wake him unnecessarily. She slipped on her satin wrapper and went downstairs.

The breakfast room was filled with sun and she could see that the sky was a brilliant, cloudless blue. In the warm room it was as if this were summer and not another cold February morning.

Cyril was seated in the window nook, reading the newspaper, and as she entered he looked up in surprise.

"Donalda, what gets you up so early?"

"I was awake and decided that I was getting tired of seeing only the four walls of my bedroom. It is much more pleasant down here."

"There is no reason you shouldn't take your breakfast here all the time."

"You're quite right. After all, I could eat alone in either place, couldn't I?"

"Please, l-let's not start a quarrel. You're quite aware of my habits. You have chosen not to accommodate yourself to them."

She moved restlessly over to the sideboard. She didn't want to argue with him this morning. She tugged at the bellpull. She could sense Cyril observing her warily and tried to be more pleasant.

"Has anyone come forward with information about Theresa?"

"There is no more m-mention. Shepcote is offering a reward, so that might d-do it."

"Cyril, I –"

There was a tap at the door and John Foy came in.

"I'd like my breakfast served here this morning, Foy."

"Yes, madam. Mrs. Foy was just preparing it. It won't be a moment."

Donalda thought the butler looked as grey as old dishwater and wondered if he was sick.

"May I pour your tea, madam?"

She nodded. Foy went to the sideboard, removed the cozy from the teapot and poured the strong amber tea into a fresh cup. As he handed it to her, she could see his unsteadiness.

"Are you ill, Foy?"

"Thank you, no, madam. Just a touch of my stomach again."

His eyes met hers and for a moment there was no gulf between mistress and servant. She saw the fear reflected in his liverish eyes but, a second before that, utter dislike. Then he blinked and the expression disappeared as if the aperture of a camera had closed. Her butler stood before her, steady and impassive.

182 "I'll bring some more hot water and some toast, madam," he said and left, carrying the jug.

Donalda took her teacup to the table. She wondered if she should mention Foy to Cyril, but she was overwhelmed with inertia. She felt almost as if she were still in her dream, trying to move underwater. She sipped at the hot, sweet tea and regarded her husband. The bright light was not kind. It accentuated the greyness of his beard and the thinning hair at his temples. He looked drawn and tired. She realized he wasn't reading but had gone into a reverie.

"A penny for your thoughts, Cyril."

"What?"

"You were lost in thought. I offered you a penny."

For once, he didn't respond with irritation. He smiled slightly. "I'm afraid even a farthing would be overvalue."

"Do you realize we have hardly set eyes on each other since Monday evening?"

"That so? Hmm, I s-suppose you're right. I have been devilishly busy." He started to fold the newspaper. "And I still am. I must be off."

If he had shown the slightest inclination to stay and talk to her, to share in any way what he was so busy with, Donalda, in her loneliness, would have remained softened towards him. However, his haste to leave stung her and determined her resolve.

"Cyril, I intend to return to England."

He stared at her. "For a holiday?"

"No, I want to go back permanently."

"This seems a sudden decision, Donalda."

"Not really. I've been contemplating it for a long time but I haven't had the courage to follow through."

"I see."

He regarded her bleakly, not making any attempt to dissuade her or question her decision. She continued, trying to hold her bitterness in check.

"Theresa's death decided me. She was such a young girl to lose all promise of a life. She would have liked children and a family, I know that. Since it happened I have been scrutinising myself, and I don't particularly like what I see."

"How so, D-Donalda?"

"There is something wrong when a woman of my age takes most of her comfort from a servant."

"You're talking like this because you are still upset. What h-happened was dreadfully shocking to all of us –"

"Was it? Well, regardless, that event has forced my hand."

"What about Owen?"

"I will suggest that he transfer to Guy's Hospital. It is far superior, anyway. I am confident he and Harriet will make a match, and we could leave after the wedding. Don't worry, we will devise some story to put abroad."

"I am not con-con – er, concerned about that."

184 "Aren't you? You must have changed, then, in the last week. Public opinion has always seemed to matter a great deal to you." She met his eyes. "I have kept your secret, Cyril, and because of Owen I remained, living

this pretext. I can do so no longer. Oh, don't look so alarmed, I'm not going to put a notice in the newspaper. I simply would like to return to my homeland. After a while perhaps we could divorce. I would like the opportunity to live the rest of my life with some honesty." She paused and her voice was low. "I am not that old, after all. It is not inconceivable that I could find love again."

To her surprise, Cyril put his head in his hands, his voice muffled so that she almost didn't catch what he said.

"I am so sorry, Donalda."

When Foy returned to the kitchen, his wife was busy chopping vegetables for the midday meal. Beef stew was on for today.

"She wants her toast."

"It's ready, just needs buttering."

"Shall I do it?"

"I haven't got four pair of hands, have I?"

He took the toast off the fork and slathered butter on one side.

"That's too much," Edith snapped. "You know she likes it spread thin."

His head was throbbing and he was tempted to snarl back at her, but he knew that would precipitate a full-scale war and he wasn't up to it. He scraped off some of the butter, licking at the knife. Edith was slicing at some carrots with an unpleasant vigour.

"She's in a blue mood this morning," he said.

"Has a right to be, if you ask me. Mind you, if I were in her shoes, I wouldn't be blue, I'd be bloody red."

"How'd you mean?"

"Him. Coming in at all hours of the night."

"Dr. Rhodes?"

"That's what I said."

"Was he in late last night?"

Edith demolished a parsnip and dropped the slices into the pot of water on the stove. "Late! You might just as well say it was early. Two o'clock in the morning. I heard him knocking up Joe to put the carriage away."

"I didn't hear a thing."

"No, you wouldn't have, would you?"

Foy winced but didn't pursue the matter. "I suppose he was with one of his patients, then?"

"Ha! Funny how he always has extra work to do Saturdays and Wednesdays. Very convenient."

Her husband was befuddled but had the feeling that it was better to remain quiet. Edith put a hunk of raw meat on the cutting board and began slicing it into chunks.

"Look at the fat on this. And I asked for prime. That man is a cheat if ever I saw one."

186 "The butcher?"

She gave him a withering look. "Men!"

Foy arranged the toast in the silver rack the way Donalda liked it.

Edith continued. "Good thing for Master Owen his father didn't throw the bolt or we'd have had another incident like Saturday in reverse."

"Was he out too?"

"Yes. Came crawling back just after the doctor."

Foy had no real affection for Owen but he felt compelled to counter Edith. "He's a young fellow. Probably out sowing a few wild oats while he can."

Edith hacked the piece of meat in two.

"Men!"

Owen Rhodes knew that he should be getting dressed if he was going to be at his lecture on time, but every movement seemed an effort. He stared into his wardrobe, unable to decide what suit to wear. Courtney had shown up yesterday in a navy mariner's sweater. He said it was practical, considering what they had to do all day. The demonstrator had been furious and would have dismissed him if it had been anyone else. However, Courtney's father and grandfather were both directors of the college, so he got away with it. Owen didn't own a mariner's sweater, but he could wear his brown bicycle jersey. Yesterday he'd got blood on his cuffs when he was doing the dissection and, sickened, threw the shirt away.

187

A female cadaver the colour of lard was ready for them on the table. An old woman, by the look of the wasted limbs and the grey hair, but the information card said she was forty-five, only two years older than his own mother. Illness and poverty had aged her like all the others. Dr. Cavin, the demonstrator, was excited. For the first time the class had the opportunity to see an example of galloping consumption first-hand. Its "ravages," was the word he used. Owen had tried to hover behind his friend McDonough so that his view of the cutting was restricted, but Cavin made him step forward. He pretended to do it in a teasing fashion but Owen could feel the malice. The demonstrator didn't like him and seized every opportunity to goad him.

Cavin pushed aside the flaccid breast, the skin stretched and marked from the suckling of many children, then sliced through the sternum and moved aside the flesh to reveal the ribs, reddened with blood. "Take those pliers and open the ribs for me, Rhodes."

Owen clenched his teeth, determined not to retch or, worse, faint like a green girl. The woman was dead. He didn't know her name or her circumstances. He didn't know who grieved for her, if any did. He pried apart the bones of the rib cage, and Cavin reached in with his snips and severed the arteries and venous system of the right lung. He tugged and the organ came out with a sucking sound as if it were in mud. The blood ran over Owen's fingers and he bit down hard so as not to gag. He was dimly aware that Hugh had stepped to the rear of the group. All the students were quiet.

188

"See the holes that the bacillus had made? She must have gone fast," said Cavin. He held the soggy mass aloft, admiring it. The woman's chest gaped open, empty. "We'll see if there are traces in the intestines, and the bones. Gentlemen, work in pairs. Each take a limb. You have one hour."

There were no traces of disease in the humerus that lay white in its bed of red muscle, but Owen and his partner found that the thoracic vertebrae were riddled with it, the bone crumpling to the touch. Feverell termed the cadaver "TB Tilly," and all the students laughed. They never knew what her name was because it wasn't on the card.

Owen decided on his navy merino suit and pulled off his nightshirt. The wardrobe mirror reflected back his pale, naked body. For a moment he stared at his own image, assessing the slim shoulders and hips. He often wished he was taller and heavier, not so much like his father. Tentatively, he touched his finger to his lips. He could still feel the kiss, the soft tongue inserting itself between his lips. He took the sleeve of his nightshirt, spat on it to moisten it and rubbed hard across his mouth until his mouth burned.

Chapter Thirteen

THE WIDOW JENKINS HAD ROUSED a neighbour to go for help. The man, Jimmy Gallagher, who was not young, ran as fast as he could up the laneway to Mill Street. Excitement gave him strength as he slipped and staggered through the deep snow, but by the time he reached Parliament his chest was close to bursting and he had to stop for breath. A man in a bread wagon was plodding by and, realizing he knew him, Gallagher ran out in front of the horse and stopped him. Through gasps he related what had happened, but Taylor wasn't too willing to give him a ride to the police station.

190

"Rosie isn't so spry any more and I'm not a-going to kill my horse for no strange Jezebel."

"You don't know the poor dead woman was one such thing," said Gallagher.

"Sure she was. Why'd she get herself killed down by the lake, else? Besides, I have my deliveries to make."

"Jesus, Mary and Joseph, they'll wait an hour, surely?"

"Ha! And who'll thank me if I lose my job?"

However, he finally conceded. Gallagher climbed up beside him, and Rosie was persuaded to canter up Parliament to the station. Crabtree had just arrived for his shift and Murdoch was in the orderly room brewing himself a breakfast tea. As soon as the Irishman spit out his story, Murdoch commandeered the police ambulance from the adjoining stables and they galloped off to the lake, Gallagher hanging on to his hat inside the wagon. He hadn't seen so much excitement in many a long day.

Crabtree pulled up the panting horses at the end of the laneway within sight of the ice-pitted shore. The area was deserted. Either from fear or indifference, nobody else had emerged from the ramshackle huts. Only Mrs. Jenkins and the lunatic were there waiting. She was seated on a rock by the marge and had wrapped herself in a voluminous grey shawl. The lunatic was standing beside her, swaying back and forth, muttering to himself. Murdoch walked over to the old woman.

191

"Mrs. Jenkins? I'm Detective Murdoch."

She nodded. "We've been sitting here in the perishing cold. Thought it best to keep guard."

"Thank you. That was very sensible. Is this the man who found the body?"

She cupped her hand to her ear. "Eh? What you say?"

He repeated the question.

"Yep, that's him."

"What's his name?"

"Calls himself Zephaniah. S'not his real name but he's probably forgot that by now. He don't understand much."

The old man's white, matted hair hung down his back, and the grizzled beard reached to his waist. His head was wrapped around in a woollen turban and his stained and torn coat had once been a soldier's greatcoat. At Murdoch's approach, he whimpered and shrank back. He had been jailed barely a month earlier for vagrancy and responded to the police like a beaten dog responds to the sight of the stick.

"She's out there," said Mrs. Jenkins, pointing out to the frozen lake.

The lunatic suddenly shrieked. "I will punish the princes, saith the Lord. All the merchant people are cut down –"

"Mr. Zephaniah . . ."

192

"A cry from the fish gate . . . a great crashing from the hills . . . thick darkness . . ." His eyes were rolling back in his head, spittle coming from his mouth. "Their blood shall be poured out as dust and their flesh as dung . . ."

"Perhaps you could take him back to your cottage," said Murdoch. "I'll come and talk to you shortly."

"Eh?"

He yelled in her ear. Stiffly, she got to her feet and took the old man by the elbow.

"She obeyed not the voice . . ."

They both shuffled off, Zephaniah still shouting.

Gallagher was hovering behind Crabtree. "D'you want me to help with the stretcher, Officer?"

"Probably, but we'll have to wait until the coroner arrives. You can tend to his carriage when he comes. Wait here for now and don't let anybody come near the area."

The old man gave him a soldierly salute and Murdoch and Crabtree set out to the body.

The sky was a brilliant blue and the lumps of ice glittered like glass in the bright sun. Here and there black branches, from bushes that had drowned in the lake before the ice came, reached upwards with desperate fingers. A trail of footprints was clearly visible in the fresh-fallen snow. Murdoch bent down. One pair of prints was wide and flat and would belong to the lunatic, who was wearing clogs; the other, smaller pair that overlapped were no doubt those of the widow Jenkins. He looked closer. Underneath those marks, the snow had earlier been brushed into wide swaths.

"Let's keep to the side," he said to his constable. A gust of wind whipped across their faces, stinging, lifting

193

the snow into a puff of mist that shone in the air like diamond shavings. Murdoch pulled his muffler up around his nose, which was pinching against the cold.

They were about ten feet away when Murdoch realized it was Alice Black who was lying there. There was no mistaking that garish red and black striped jacket and the foolishly overdecorated hat. He felt a pang of pity as they stopped and gazed down on her.

There had been no dignity in her dying. Her brown straw hat had fallen off to the side and one of the dingy yellow feathers, broken in two, lay across her livid cheek. Her swollen tongue protruded from her mouth and the capillaries in her eyes had burst so that the sockets seemed to be swimming in blood. Murdoch knelt down and Crabtree shifted his feet nervously beside him. He wasn't used to this sort of death.

"Nasty, sir," he said.

"It is that. The rope has almost broken through the flesh, it was pulled so hard."

Murdoch found it distressing himself, but he had seen his share of bodies washed ashore. Once, a Norwegian trawler had been shipwrecked off the coast and a young blond sailor had been found jammed in the rocks. A piece of sail rope was wrapped tight about his neck, and he had looked the way Alice did.

"At least we know for sure this one didn't die from natural causes," said the constable.

194

Murdoch nodded. "Too true. Go back to the beach and mark any wheel tracks or prints that you find."

"What do you think she was doing out here, sir?"

"What she was doing is probably not so much the question. How'd she get here is what bothers me. Look!"

Alice was in her stocking feet and the black wool was torn at the soles. He could see lesions on the skin underneath where the ice had scraped her.

"I doubt she walked all the way from home without her boots."

He glanced over at the shore where the half-dozen huts were scattered. To the west was the Gooderham Distillery, the smoke stacks etched against the blue sky.

"I suppose she could have been gaying it in one of these cottages," said the constable.

"It's possible, but she's a long way from her own territory. I'm more inclined to think she came in a carriage. Maybe somebody wanted a winter poke. Anyway, let's search first, then we'll start asking."

"Yes, sir." Crabtree looked down at Alice's body. "She wasn't heading anywhere that could help her."

He indicated the white expanse of lake stretching to the horizon. A flock of gulls were gathered nearby, their underbellies white as the snow, their hooked beaks yellow and cruel.

Suddenly Zephaniah shouted wildly. Gallagher saw them look over in his direction and he saluted again.

"Could it have been the madman as did her in?" asked Crabtree.

"He seems too frail to me, but I suppose we can't rule him out. What I'm wondering is whether or not this has anything to do with Therese Laporte."

"Alice was silenced, you mean, sir?"

"Possibly. On the other hand, with women like this, who knows? She just may have angered one of her customers."

Crabtree nodded and for a minute they both stared down at the dead woman, each with different thoughts. Then the constable saluted and trudged off to begin his search of the shore. Murdoch began a careful examination of the body.

Except for the lack of boots, Alice was fully dressed, drawers intact, no unexpected tears in her clothing that he could see. She was wearing brown leather gloves, old and well mended. Her jacket was undone but none of the buttons were missing or the holes ripped. Her taffeta waist was rose coloured, but he could see dark brownish spots on the bib. She had bitten deep into her lower lip and there was dried blood on her chin. The colour of her face was such that he couldn't make out any sign of bruising, and he'd have to wait for the post-mortem examination to see if she had been marked anywhere else on her body.

Something gleamed in the sun, and Murdoch moved aside the jacket lapels and tugged clear a necklace of

196

green beads. No, not that, not a necklace. The crucifix was missing but it was easily identifiable. Gingerly, he pulled it over the rigid head and stowed it in his inside pocket.

"Mr. Murdoch! I found something, sir. Marks of a carriage. And horse dropping. Fresh."

Murdoch shouted back, "Put in a marker. Watch you don't spoil anything." He waited while the constable edged away cautiously and went to a bush to break off a wand.

Murdoch too stepped away from the corpse. There didn't seem to be much more to be gained here. Whoever had killed Alice had taken care to obliterate their footprints, and all around the body the snow had been brushed smooth.

He made the sign of the cross above Alice's head.

"May God have mercy on your soul, Alice Black," he said.

"So you didn't believe this man was a sailor?" Murdoch asked Bernadette. Her face was taut and pale but she'd shed no tears. Murdoch was sitting with her in the kitchen of the lodging house.

"I knew he wasn't. His hands was as soft as a baby's backside. I didn't like the look of him." She stopped and stared into space for a moment. "I told her not to go with him but she wouldn't listen. When she didn't come home, I knew something bad had happened. I dreamt

197

of spiders, see. They were running up the walls. It's a sure sign that you're going to hear of a death." She stood up and went over to the stove. "Would you like a cuppa?" She spooned tea leaves into a cracked pot, added a ladle or two of boiling water and left it to steep.

Murdoch took out his notebook. "I'll go to the O'Neil, of course, and see if anybody knew this fellow, but I'd better get the names of all the men who've had anything to do with Alice in the last while. Did she ever go down to Mill Street that you know of?"

Ettie shook her head. "Never. She didn't need to. The men she knew were all regulars."

"Did she meet them here?"

"Usually at their lodgings or in the upstairs rooms of the hotel."

She had completely dropped the fiction that Alice made her living mending gloves. "You're not going to give Jimmy a hard time about that, are you?"

Legally, the hotel keeper should have been charged with keeping a house of ill repute.

"Not at the moment."

He could see her shoulders lower in relief. When he did confront the hotel keeper, it might mean the end of Ettie's welcome there.

198

The teapot was still sitting on the stove untended, but she began to stir an enamel pot that was on one of the burners.

"I bought a leg of mutton yesterday. I was cooking

it up for our tea. She liked mutton stew, she did."

A sort of hiccough sob came out of her throat. Murdoch expected her to break into tears. However, she simply stirred the pot more vigorously and the cries never came. He waited a moment, then reached into his pocket and took out the broken rosary.

"Alice had this around her neck. Do you know where she got it?"

Ettie turned around, and when she saw what he was holding she flinched. Her body tensed and her eyes regarded him warily.

"She found it on the street."

"When?"

"I dunno. A few days ago."

"Where exactly?"

"I dunno. Near the O'Neil, I think she said."

Murdoch stared at her but she glanced away and concentrated on the pot again. "Did you know it's a rosary?"

"What's that?"

"People who are Roman Catholics use them to say prayers. Each bead marks a prayer. It probably belonged to Therese Laporte."

"God, you're not going to start up again, are you?"

"How did Alice come to have it?"

"Bleeding hell, you've got a short memory. I just told you. She found it. I suppose that girl must have dropped it."

199

Murdoch got up, went over to her and grasped her by the shoulder, forcing her to face him. He could feel the bone beneath the thin cloth of her wrapper.

"Ettie, listen to me. Alice has been murdered. Brutally. Therese Laporte died in a strange, unnatural way. It is possible the two deaths are connected."

She moved away from his touch as if his hand was hot. "How could they be?"

"You tell me. A strange man shows up at the hotel. He takes off with Alice and next thing, she's dead. Maybe the man knew Therese. She was expecting, after all. Maybe it was him as got her that way and he didn't want anyone to know. Maybe Alice saw something when she was coming home on Saturday night."

She winced again, almost imperceptibly. "Of course she didn't."

"Maybe she found something incriminating on the body when she stripped it –"

"Oh God, stuff it, will ya."

"Come on, Ettie, this rosary belonged to Therese Laporte and it ended up around Alice Black's neck. Just like those clothes ended up in your outhouse. Tell me the truth, for God's sake."

He was shouting at her in his frustration, but she became stubborn and sullen.

"How many times have I got to sodding well say it? Are you deaf or just plain stupid? Alice found the bloody necklace."

He took a deep breath, trying to calm down. Yelling at her wasn't helping. "There is a crucifix that hangs from a rosary. Do you know what that is?"

"No."

"It's a cross with the figure of Jesus Christ on it. This one might have been done in silver or brass. Did you see it?"

She shook her head emphatically. "No."

"You're sure?"

"I'm telling you, the necklace was just like it is now. No Jesus."

"Could Alice have removed the crucifix and put it somewhere else?"

"No."

"How can you be so certain? Could be that she just didn't tell you. She might have thought you would want to take it."

"Sod off. We were like sisters. I wouldn't take anything of hers. Nor her either. I tell you there weren't no bloody cross on that thing."

He tried an abrupt shift. "Did Alice mention to you that she had seen Therese before she died?"

There was a quick flicker of doubt across her face. "What are you getting at?"

"The girl died so close to here. Alice said she was coming home about ten o'clock Saturday night. Perhaps she saw her? Maybe even talked to her? Did she?"

Ettie shook her head.

201

"Look, Ettie, I am giving you fair warning. If I'm thinking that you and Alice were thick as thieves, the murderer is probably doing the same. You could be in danger."

"Go on," she scoffed. "I can look after myself."

"That's what you said about Alice, and –"

At that moment the curtain to the kitchen was pulled back and Samuel Quinn came in, all bundled up in greatcoat and cloth cap, a long muffler wrapped around his neck. Princess was close at his heels, and on a thick leather leash was another dog. It was a big heavy creature, white with brown patches. The skull was wide, set off with long floppy ears, and the eyes were doleful. Princess launched into a few yelps of pleasure at the sight of Ettie, while the other dog gave one deep-throated bark and sat down, drooling copiously. Quinn saw Murdoch and stopped abruptly in the doorway.

"Er, sorry. Didn't know you . . . er . . ."

Ettie bent down, allowing the bitch to cover her face with enthusiastic licks. "Good girl. Did you miss me?"

Murdoch raised his voice. "Can you stay a minute, Mr. Quinn?"

Quinn looked uneasy. "I'm just off to work, Sergeant, er . . . ?"

Ettie silenced Princess by putting down some crusts of bread and patted the second dog on its wide forehead.

"Big old bastard, aren't you? Where'd you come from?"

"My pal's," said Quinn to Murdoch. "Taking care of him for a couple of days."

"Another friend on his honeymoon?"

"What?"

"You said the last dog you were taking care of, the man was on his wedding trip."

"Oh, right. Just forgot for a minute."

Quinn began to twist both ends of his full moustache.

"What's this one's name?" asked Murdoch.

"Titch. His name's Titch."

The enormous dog licked its lips, scattering saliva on the floor.

"What's up?" Quinn asked.

Still stroking the dog, Ettie said, "Alice has been murdered, Sam."

"What!"

"That's why he's here."

"When? Murdered . . . ?"

"Her body was found this morning," Murdoch said. "Over by the Gooderham Distillery."

"What was she doing down there?"

"We don't know as yet. Any ideas?"

"What? No, er, no. Tarnation, I'm sorry, Ettie. The Lord love me, I don't know what to say."

"Were you at the John O'Neil last evening?" Murdoch asked him.

"I was that."

203

"Did you know the man who Alice left with? The sailor? He was calling himself Jack."

"Not me. Never seen him before. Why d'you ask? Was he the one did her in?"

"Let's say he must have been one of the last people to see her alive. Ettie says she didn't like the look of him. Was that your opinion?"

"Can't say as I had an opinion to speak of. He seemed a quiet sort of bloke, really. He was only at the table for a short bit, then they left."

"Can you give me a description of the man?"

"Sure. He was fairish, short hair, a beat-up sort of face like you'd expect for an outdoor fellow."

"He was ugly as the Devil's arse, if you ask me," interrupted Ettie. "Eyes like dead fish."

"One thing I can tell you, Mr. Murdoch," added Quinn, "he had some nobby togs. Best worsted, I'd say, wouldn't you, Ettie?"

She nodded. "Another reason to believe he weren't no Tar. Where'd he get the darby to buy clothes like that?"

Murdoch turned to Quinn. "Where were you last night? After you left the O'Neil?"

"Me? The usual." His fingers kept going at the moustache. "I was working all last night. I went in at eleven. Just got off this morning. You can ask them."

"Sod it, the tea will be like mud," said Ettie. She brought the teapot to the table and plonked down three chipped mugs. Unasked, she poured the strong black brew for Quinn as well. She sat down and he came over and placed his hand on her arm.

"I'm terrible sorry, Ettie," he said again. "Is there anything I can do for you?"

She shrugged. "Nothing to be done, is there? She's gone." Suddenly she slammed down her mug, splashing hot tea on her hand. She put her scalded fingers to her mouth. "Sod it, sod it," she said. With her unburnt fist she started to pound on the table. "Sod it, sod it," she kept repeating.

Mrs. Kitchen added a spoonful of sugar to the tea and handed Murdoch the cup and saucer. He took a cautious sip. "Wonderful, Mrs. K. As usual." She beamed. Making his tea exactly how he liked it was a source of delight for her.

"Ready for your tonic, Arthur?" she asked her husband.

"Now?"

"You've only had seven. We should try to get in at least two more tonight."

There was a jug on the sideboard and beside it a bowl of eggs. She poured thick cream from the jug into a glass, cracked one of the eggs into it and gave them a thorough stir. She brought the yellowish mixture to her husband, who downed it in a couple of gulps and wiped his lips with gusto on the back of his sleeve.

205

"Arthur," she protested, "use your handkerchief. Where were you brought up?"

Murdoch grinned. "I'm tempted to make up a few of those myself."

"You should. Good for you. I tell you I can feel the difference. In two days."

The cheery tone sounded false, not quite masking the underlying desperation. Arthur Kitchen had lived for a long time now with ever increasing debility and the certainty of a painful death. Murdoch fervently hoped this new treatment would work.

As usual they were sitting underneath their quilts and he was relating the events of the day. Beatrice had lit the fire for his benefit but he'd insisted on leaving the window open as Arthur's fever was high tonight.

Beatrice sat down again. She had begun to decorate another box and the smell of glue and lacquer was thick and sweet in the air.

"What's that you're doing, Mrs. K.?"

She daubed some black lacquer onto one of her shells and surveyed it critically. "Mrs. Lewis said there was a call for mourning boxes, so I'm doing a black one for her. I'll see if this works. The lacquer doesn't stick too well . . . Go on, Mr. Murdoch."

206   "Not much more to say, really. Nobody seems to have known the man Alice left the hotel with." He pulled up the sleeve of his cardigan to demonstrate. "He has a tattoo around his wrist and forearm. A snake. Not

hard to recognize, but every last man of them says they never saw him before."

"They that put their hands in evil will perish by evil." Beatrice's metaphor was a little confused, but her expression wasn't. Murdoch drank some more tea. He knew how kindhearted a woman Mrs. K. actually was, but when it came to certain kinds of immorality she knew no compromise. She hadn't evinced any pity for Alice Black.

"We also questioned everybody within a mile radius of the beach, but same story. Nobody saw anything."

"Are they to be believed?" asked Arthur.

Murdoch nodded. "I'd say yes. Her friend, Ettie, swears Alice didn't know anybody in that neighbour-hood and had never been there. It's more likely she was taken to the beach in a carriage. Her jacket was partially unbuttoned and Ettie says she was wearing a shawl, but that's nowhere to be found and neither are her boots."

Murdoch stared into the fire. The dancing flames were making no headway against the cold coming in from the window, but they were soothing to watch. Tomorrow he was going to go to the Rhodeses' house and show them the rosary. There'd been too much to do today.

"How was himself?" asked Arthur.

"A real Cossack. He kept going on about shirking. I wanted to tell him to feel my frozen feet."

Arthur laughed. "In a tender spot, I hope?"

207

"Arthur!" exclaimed his wife, but she smiled too.

"Exactly. He's pushing me to arrest the lunatic but we've got nothing whatever to go on except the fact that the old man found the body. Unfortunately he doesn't help matters by not answering questions. He just keeps yelling Scripture."

Beatrice paused for a moment in her arranging of the shells. "My mother's cousin's son used to do that. Not Scripture but nursery rhymes. Poor fellow got knocked down by a runaway horse when he was a boy, and it damaged his mind. He was never the same after that. No matter what you said to him, he'd rattle off a nursery rhyme. Nobody could make it out at first, but his mother was good with him and she finally figured he was speaking in riddles. The dear child didn't live long. God in His mercy saw fit to take him to Heaven when he was only twelve."

"What do you mean he was speaking in riddles?"

"Well, for instance, if she said, 'Henry, what do you want for your tea?' he'd answer, 'Georgie porgie.' What he meant was that he'd like some pudding. Or if he'd say, 'Mittens,' it meant bread and jam."

Arthur snorted. "Good thing his mother understood him. If it were up to me the fellow would've starved to death."

"If the old man is speaking in code, I don't have the foggiest notion what it is," said Murdoch. "He's telling me we're all damned and will get our punishment, and

208

that seems pretty straightforward to me." He yawned. "Well, it's up the wooden hill for me. I have an early start again."

Arthur said, "I almost forgot, Will. Do you remember you was asking about a little dog, a Pekingese –"

"Or a King Charles," interrupted Beatrice.

"It was a Peke, Mother. Something rang a bell so I looked at some of the back issues of the *News*. Listen to this. It was in Saturday's paper." He opened one of the newspapers that was beside him and read.

LOST DOG. My dog vanished on Friday, while on his regular walk in the vicinity of Church and Queen. He is a purebred Pekingese. Light beige, large eyes. Answers to Bartholomew. Generous reward for information to his return. Contact Mrs. Shaw of Melita Ave.

"I'll make a note of that. By the way, what kind of dog is large as a pony, white and brown with long droopy ears and eyes like this?" He pulled down the lower lids of his eyes, exposing the red.

"Oh, that's a Newfoundland, for sure. Lovely dogs they are, but they drool a lot."

"That sounds right. If you come across any other notice in the paper concerning a dog like that, let me know."

Arthur grinned in pleasure. "I certainly will. They're valuable dogs, they are."

209

"I don't understand," said Beatrice.

"I have a suspicion Mr. Quinn is up to no good when it comes to canines," said Murdoch.

"He has a dog of his own, didn't you say?" remarked Arthur.

"That's right, a noisy hound. Makes a heck of a row all the time."

"Must be a female."

"Arthur! What a thing to say."

"No, no, Mother, what I mean is the fellow's probably using the old trick."

"What's that?" asked Beatrice.

"You want to pinch a dog and hold it for the reward, all you have to do is wait until it's let off its leash, then parade your bitch in front of it. At certain times, she's, er, irresistible. Off runs dog with only one thing on his mind, and the owner is left wringing his hands, ready to pay up to the kind rescuer of dear Marmalade or whatever he's called."

Murdoch laughed. "You've got it, Arthur. On the other hand, we police can suspect our own mothers if we're not careful. He just might have friends who trust him with their expensive dogs."

"Still, I'll keep my eyes open for other notices."

210 Murdoch pushed off his quilt and stood up. "I'm off. Good night to both."

He shook hands and went up to his room. He considered having a pipe but he was too tired, so he undressed quickly and got into bed, shivering as his body touched the cold sheets. Blast, he had forgotten to practise his dance steps, and he'd missed his lesson this week. He'd better do an hour tomorrow or else he'd be a disgrace to the professor at the salon.

The thought of holding a young woman in his arms made him restless again and he thumped his feather pillow into a hollow. Unbidden to his mind came the memory of a thin shoulder beneath his hand, shockingly warm to the touch. He turned over and gave his pillow another punch. Thoughts like that would get him exactly nowhere.

Chapter Fourteen

INSPECTOR BRACKENREID PUSHED ASIDE the reed strips and stepped into the detective's cubicle. Murdoch was at his desk and got to his feet.

"What can I do for you, sir?"

"Bring me up to date on this bloody maid affair. The chief constable himself has sent a telegram wanting to know what is happening."

Murdoch pulled at his moustache. If Colonel Grasett was wondering and if Brackenreid was venturing out of his own office, somebody was turning up the wicks. Probably the alderman, Godfrey Shepcote. He struck Murdoch as the kind of man who liked to find a good cause to make a noise about.

"I don't have much new to report, sir. We're still following up responses to the newspaper article, but so far nothing has opened up."

"And now we've got this other tart to worry about."

"Her name was Alice Black, sir."

"Who the sod cares? Did you get anything more out of the madman?"

"No, sir. But I doubt he's the killer. Zephaniah's an old man. I can't imagine him being able to overcome a young woman like Alice."

"Don't be too cocky about that, Murdoch. Lunatics can have the strength of ten when they need to. Anyway, it's the other business I'm more concerned about."

He nodded over at the wall, which the detective was using as a blackboard. "What've you got there?"

"It's a map of the area pertinent to the scene of the crime, sir."

"I hope that chalk will rub off."

"If it doesn't I'll personally whitewash the wall."

Brackenreid went closer. "Explain it to me, Murdoch."

"Here is where Therese's body was discovered in the St. Luke's laneway." He picked up his ruler and tapped the places as he spoke. "Right here is where the newsboy, Carrots, claims to have seen her. He was at the corner of Church and Gerrard and he says she went past him going east along Gerrard."

"Why would she be doing that? I thought she was supposed to be going home. Surely she would have been heading for the train station? That's at the bottom of Yonge Street."

213

"You're quite right about that, Inspector, but I think I can guess what she was doing."

In spite of himself Murdoch felt eager to show him the progress of the investigation. "The dotted line is the route I believe she took when she left Birchlea. When Carrots saw her it must have been about twenty or twenty-five minutes past nine. Jimmy Matlock, another one of the newsboys, says he saw her crossing the road at Queen and Berkeley and he also remembers her walking east. He is vague about the time but says he'd just heard St. Paul's chime the quarter hour. If we allow her twenty minutes or so to get from Carrots to Jimmy it would put the time at about a quarter to ten, give or take. She has walked south and is still going easterly –"

"So? Get on with it, Murdoch."

"Yes, sir."

Murdoch clenched his teeth to hold back his retort. He knew what Brackenreid was like when he was in one of his moods.

"Therese was a young girl in trouble, and she was French-Canadian. In times of need I think we all seek out the familiar. What represents home to us . . ." He indicated a mark on King Street. "Here is the old Methodist church. Currently, it is being used by a small settlement of French-Canadians who live nearby. I'm guessing that's where she was going."

He knew he was opening himself up to trouble by presenting this theory, and he regretted saying it almost as soon as the words were out of his mouth. The inspector hooted.

"Blamed thin, if you ask me, Murdoch. If you were to find me walking up Bay Street, you couldn't assume I was going anywhere in particular. What if I'd gone that way home on a whim, for a change of scenery?"

"Not quite, sir. If I found you walking north on Bay Street, I'd assume you were going to the National Club."

"What? Oh, I suppose so, but regardless, my point stands."

"I'm just trying to work logically from what we know of the girl's character and her circumstances."

"Are they the only two sightings, two guttersnipes?"

"Yes, sir, so far, but I consider them to be reliable witnesses. They both gave a good description of the girl."

"All right. Go on. Tell me about the rest of your artwork."

"Here, with the blue squares, I've traced Owen Rhodes's route. He left Birchlea at approximately nine o'clock to take Miss Shepcote to her home. He said he travelled across Bloor Street to Church, down to Gerrard, along Gerrard, then south on Berkeley to the Shepcote house, which is just below Queen Street. He claims he dallied there with Miss Shepcote until midnight, then went home via the same path. If in fact this was not the truth and he left Miss Shepcote earlier, he could easily have met up with Therese and taken her somewhere."

215

"Doesn't Miss Shepcote verify his alibi?"

"She does, sir, but she seemed very uncomfortable and I wasn't sure she was telling the truth."

"Don't be ridiculous, Murdoch. She is a well-brought-up young woman. She was probably shy about the fact they were unchaperoned at that hour. Besides, why should she lie?"

"To give young Rhodes an alibi."

He waited for Brackenreid to comment, but he merely grunted and pointed to the map.

"The circles are Dr. Rhodes, I presume?"

"Mr. Shepcote and Dr. Rhodes, actually. The two of them left Birchlea shortly after nine and the doctor was dropped off at his consulting chambers at Church and Carlton. He says he was working on a report for some medical journal until one o'clock. He likes the quiet. Then he walked part of the way home until he found a cab. I've put Constable Wicken onto collecting all the cab driver's dockets for the past week, so we should be able to verify that part of the doctor's statement at least. However, we have only Rhodes's word that he stayed late in his office. He could have had a rendezvous with Therese. She was alone when Jimmy saw her, but if the doctor was walking quickly he could have met up with her on Queen Street. Or he could have hired a carriage. He certainly can come by opium in great quantities if he needs it."

216

"For God's sake, Murdoch, you're snatching at straws. According to you nobody is telling the truth about anything."

"Sometimes it feels that way, sir. However, the girl's condition is not a lie. Somebody impregnated her." Murdoch indicated the wall again. "That is the journey that Mr. Shepcote's carriage took when he left Birchlea. After dropping off Rhodes, he proceeded to his club on River Street. The coachman made a point of telling me that he went via Wilton."

"What do you mean 'made a point'?"

"It seemed rather like that. I didn't ask him, he volunteered. However, that puts the alderman in the same vicinity as Therese and at about the same time. If he had actually gone along Queen Street he could have encountered Therese Laporte here, anywhere between Berkeley and River streets."

"Good Lord, Murdoch, you're not suggesting the alderman has anything to do with this affair."

"I'm not suggesting anything at the moment, Inspector. I'm simply trying to get straight the various movements of the parties who were in any way connected with Birchlea and the life of Therese Laporte. The steward has confirmed to one of my men that Shepcote was at the club from about a quarter past ten until midnight." 217

Brackenreid leaned forward, peering at the wall. "What's that?" He pointed at a small pockmark in the lower part of the map.

"That's actually a hole in the wall, but I thought I may as well use it. I've drawn a balloon around it. I meant to represent that from this point on Therese vanished into thin air."

"You're getting too fanciful for me, Murdoch."

Murdoch kept his voice as flat as possible. "Here is where I believe we're onto something, sir. Constable Wicken is a very capable young officer and he questioned every householder along Queen Street. At number four ninety-five a woman named Philips swears she was sitting at her window from nine-thirty that night until at least midnight. Her husband is a teamster and she was expecting him in from a journey at ten. Apparently one of his horses went lame and he didn't get home until late. Mrs. Philips says Therese Laporte did not pass by. She lives here, on the southwest corner, which means she would have seen anybody turning north or south on Sumach, or continuing along Queen Street."

"I don't understand."

Murdoch couldn't help pausing for a moment for effect.

"This is why I congratulate young Wicken. The woman kept going on as how no girl could have walked by that night. Wicken realizes his questions were a bit too directive and he asks her if had she seen a vehicle, then. Why yes, she says, there were two. A farmer's wagon and a carriage. The wagon went by close on midnight going south on Sumach but the carriage was earlier, about ten o'clock, travelling east along Queen Street. Unfortunately Mrs. Philips couldn't really say what sort of carriage it was, but she thought it might be a hired one. The horse was a grey or white."

"It's hard for me to see this as useful, Murdoch. It's like catching spiderwebs."

"Spiders catch a lot of flies on those same slender lines. You see, Mrs. Philips admitted to seeing Alice Black go by. She hadn't mentioned it earlier because she knew who Alice was and that wasn't what we wanted to know. Wicken kept asking about a strange young girl. But she is positive that Alice went by after the carriage."

For the first time, Brackenreid looked interested. He touched the wall.

"The tart must have seen the Laporte girl."

"I don't see how she could have avoided it. She was home by ten and her route from the O'Neil is along Queen Street."

The inspector was silent for a moment, then he sighed. "The two deaths might be connected, then."

"Yes, sir. I've sent Wicken off to the market to see if a farmer was delivering anything late Saturday night, just to verify, but I don't really think it's important to the case. However, I'd say the carriage is."

Brackenreid glanced around the little room as if it could provide him some sustenance.

"Your zeal is commendable, Murdoch, but don't forget character. A good policeman is a good judge of character. You can draw your dots and arrows 'til Kingdom come, but you're not going to find any murderers or abductors there among these people."

"I beg to differ, sir. Palmer, Lamson and Pritchard were all doctors and young Birchall was a vicar's son." He picked up a compass from his desk. "Dr. Moffat says Therese couldn't have walked far with that much opium in her system." He stuck the point at the place where Therese's body had been found. "If she imbibed it half an hour earlier, maximum, she has to have been within this radius." He moved his pencil in a wide arc. Brackenreid snorted at the extent of the area that covered.

"You've got your work cut out for you, Murdoch."

"I know, sir, we have."

There was a discreet cough in front of the curtain. Murdoch could see the large outline of Constable Crabtree.

"Miss Bernadette Weston is here to see you, Mr. Murdoch."

"Who's she again? Name's familiar," asked Brackenreid.

"She was Alice Black's friend, Inspector."

"I'm leaving," said Brackenreid.

At the threshold he paused, holding back one of the clacking strips. "I'd like a complete written report on my desk by five o'clock this afternoon . . . but you needn't bother with all that nonsense about arrows and dots. Go and talk to the Papists. She must have got friendly enough to let somebody in her drawers. I'll bet it was him who slipped her the opium."

"Yes, sir."

Privately, Murdoch couldn't see any good reason why the two things should be inevitably linked, but not knowing who had seduced Therese was an irritant. It was like trying to start a puzzle. If you could get the corner pieces down you were off and running. He grinned at himself. He didn't even know yet what picture he was trying to put together or even if all his pieces belonged in the same puzzle.

Time to give it a rest. Perhaps Ettie could offer some enlightenment. He went to fetch her.

Crabtree, at Murdoch's request, had brought them both mugs of strong, sweet tea, and Ettie sipped at hers appreciatively.

"'S good."

She was dressed in deep mourning, with a long black cheviot coat and a wide veiled hat that a widow would wear. There was a strong smell of mothballs around her, and Murdoch suspected the clothes, which were too large for her, were rented.

She glanced around the tiny cubicle and indicated his map. "What's that?"

221

"I've been noting everybody's whereabouts the night Therese Laporte died."

She was silent for a moment. "You're taking care about it, aren't you?"

He nodded.

"What's the medal for?"

"I won the mile bicycle race last year at the police games."

"Didn't know they had them. I thought coppers was always serious. All work and no play."

He smiled, but she wasn't joking.

"When you came yesterday, I was what you might call bowled over . . ."

"That's only natural."

"You said you knew what it was like to lose somebody you loved."

"Yes, that's right."

She frowned. "Who was it, then? Your wife?"

"My fiancée. She died of the typhoid fever two years ago."

"What was she? A lady, or what?"

"She was a schoolteacher."

"Clever, then?"

"Very."

222

Whatever it was he said satisfied her. She put down her mug of tea.

"I don't want to spend time in the Mercy but if it means you'll get the cove that did in Alice, I'll do it –"

Murdoch stopped her. "Ettie, let's put it this way. I can guess at what happened. Alice got up to use the outhouse, saw the girl's body just opposite in the lane. Without more ado, she went over there and stole the clothes, hiding them in the outhouse. She kept the boots and the drawers and the rosary. You were asleep in your nice warm bed the whole time. Alice acted alone. Am I right?"

Ettie hesitated, staring at him warily. "Yes, I suppose so."

"Just one question. Did she confide in you afterwards? What I mean is, did she say exactly what the girl was wearing when she found her?"

"Just what you saw in the shawl."

"No jacket or gloves?"

"No. We – I mean, Alice – wondered where she'd been. She saw her earlier, you see."

Murdoch almost held his breath, as if he were approaching a deer in the forest. "Where?"

"When she was coming home from the hotel she saw the girl get into a carriage."

"Did Alice say whether she saw the driver or occupant?"

"No, the blinds were down. But she said the carriage was a reddish colour, or dark brown, and the horse was light coloured. The coachman had a black greatcoat and a tall hat on."

Murdoch stared at her, waiting, but she stared back.

223

"Is that all?" he asked.

"That's enough, isn't it? You'll be able to find the sod."

"Ettie, do you realize how many carriages in this city fit that description?"

"No, how many?"

"Could be over a hundred or more."

"Well, that's your job. At least you know now the girl got into a carriage."

"That's true."

Ettie scowled at him. "I didn't have to come here. I thought you'd be pleased."

"I am, Ettie. I really do thank you."

"Alice thought the girl knew the person who was in the carriage."

"What made her think that?"

"Woman's intuition. She guessed the girl was from the country and that was true, wasn't it?"

"Yes. She lived down near Chatham on a farm."

"I warned Al not to get all leaky but as soon as she heard about a reward she got a gold sign in her eyes. Such a greedy gob and look where it got her."

"You think she was killed because of what she'd seen?"

224 "Course she was. Alice knew how to take care of herself. She wouldn't get no cully customer so aggravated he'd up and kill her. Not even that devil of a Tar. If he's the one done Alice, he's also the one who

did for the young girl."

She stood up and pulled the heavy veil back over her face. "I'm off now. I've got the funeral to get ready for. You know where to find me."

She stuck out her hand to shake and he did so. She was wearing gloves and the leather precluded any sensation of warm flesh, and he was glad.

"Ettie, be careful."

"Course. I always am."

With a faint rustle from her stiff skirt and a waft of camphor, she left.

Murdoch watched the reed strips settle down to stillness.

Chapter Fifteen

FRIDAY, FEBRUARY 15

CYRIL RHODES PACED AROUND his narrow consulting
room. He was still deeply distressed by Donalda's
announcement. Everybody would know it was a marital
separation, and that could be quite detrimental to his
practice. Look what happened to Charles Warden
when his wife ran off with young Jarrod. On the surface
there was sympathy for the cuckolded husband, but
Warden's practice gradually dropped off until he was
seriously considering moving out of the city. It was
sheer good fortune that Clara caught *la grippe* so soon
after and he was able to remarry. Even so, patients
were slow to come back.

Disagreeable as the thought was, he had to admit he
had been having a hard time lately making ends meet. It
was expensive maintaining two establishments, and he
was not as busy as he would have liked. There were

stretches of time when he had nothing to do but wait for the next patient. These days, with the country going through poor economic times, fewer people were coming up the narrow stairs to his consulting room. They were no doubt seeking out physicians whose fees were lower.

He paused for a moment in front of the window and gazed down at the street. To the left he could see the slender spire of St. James's Church, sharp-etched against the drear sky. To the right and opposite was the handsome new Somerset Hotel. A ragged boy was vigorously clearing a walkway through the mound of snow at the curb in front. In spite of diligent truant officers, many boys in the city managed to avoid school, they or their parents needing their meagre earnings to survive. This boy made it his job to carry packages, hold the carriage horses if necessary and, summer or winter, make sure that if the guests wanted to cross the road, there was no offending manure for them to step in. It was a good post and Cyril had seen him fight for it on occasion, the way wild animals will fight off other hungry intruders.

Cyril could sympathize. This stretch of Church Street from Gerrard up to Carlton was jokingly referred to by the trades as "widow's walk." There were seven widows living in large houses on the west side and five on the east, all of them well-to-do. He had jumped at the opportunity to rent an office plumb in the midst of these possibly lonely ladies, but it hadn't brought him the

227

custom he'd hoped for. Initially, they had come in droves out of curiosity, manufacturing trivial ailments in order to assess him, but that hadn't lasted. It was his fault, he knew. He wasn't comfortable with a certain class of women, and try as he might to prevent it, his stammer got worse in their presence. To compensate, he became aloof and impersonal. This was not a good style to have with such ladies, who all wanted to be cosseted and flattered and who expected him to spend considerable time listening to them. Over the years they had drifted away, and nowadays the majority of his patients were from the working classes. They expected their doctor to be remote and took his stutter as a sign of his superiority.

Suddenly Cyril leaned forward, adjusting his pince-nez. My God, surely that wasn't Martha? Not here. She wouldn't dare to come here.

A stout woman in a dark fur cape and wide hat was walking up the street opposite, her skirt lifted indecorously high above her boots. Beside her was a young girl in a bright red tam and matching coat. Quickly, he ducked back from the window and pulled down the blind, just lifting it enough to see. He groaned. It was her. The woman and her daughter were proceeding quite slowly past his office towards Carlton Street.

228   He watched, breath held, as they halted at the corner. What was she doing? Surely she didn't intend to go into the hotel? The livened doorman opened the

door in anticipation, but with a haughty toss of her head, the woman turned back to face the road. Cyril shrank back further but she gave no sign she had seen him. She was concentrating on the electric streetcar that was swaying down the tracks towards them. She flagged it to stop. The urchin gave one last ostentatious sweep at the snow but the woman took her daughter's hand and hurried past him without a glance. They clambered aboard the streetcar, the girl looking over her shoulder at the boy. Encouraged, he started to run after them, but the ticket collector leaned out from his platform and waved him away.

Cyril watched until they were out of sight. His heart was racing and he felt quite ill. He'd long ago realized the situation couldn't be maintained indefinitely, but this was horribly close. Things were getting worse and worse, dreadful scene after dreadful scene. When she heard about Donalda's leaving, it would be even more difficult.

He took out his handkerchief and wiped his forehead. He was actually sweating.

Slowly, he went to his desk and sat down. There was a photograph on his desk of himself and Donalda, taken on their wedding day. He was beaming and she looked lovely, aglow with an inner joy.

229

He turned the picture facedown.

A shrill whistle from the speaking tube startled him.

He seized his notebook and opened it although Mrs. Stockdale, his nurse, wouldn't dream of coming into the inner office unannounced.

"Mr. Shepcote is calling, Doctor. Shall I put him through?"

"Yes."

He pulled the telephone towards him and put the hearing piece to his ear.

"Rhodes here."

The voice on the other end was so low and throaty he wouldn't have recognized it as Shepcote's.

"Rhodes, I have to cancel this evening's salon. I'm not up to it . . ."

Cyril's heart sank. He had promised Charlotte she would meet the famous actress Flo Wortley, and he knew how icy an atmosphere would prevail when he told them it was cancelled. Not from the girl – she was never like that – but certainly from Martha.

"Rhodes?"

"Y-yes, sorry. Woolgathering over h-here. Perhaps anoth-ther time . . ."

"Perhaps," whispered Shepcote. Cyril heard the click of the receiver. He had hung up.

What appalling manners, no polish at all. Surely a person deserved an explanation. Was there anything he could do instead? he wondered. He sat toying with his pen, making scribbles on the blotter. He almost laughed when he realized what he was drawing. A line of stick

230

men, all of them hanging from a gallows. Oh God, what had he got into?

The speaking tube whistled again.

"Yes?"

"Mr. Latimer is here with his father, Doctor."

"Give me a few minutes. And, Mrs. Stockdale, is Mrs. Spoffard on the telephone?"

"I believe so, Doctor."

"Call her up and cancel her appointment. See if she can come tomorrow."

"Yes, Doctor. What shall I tell her?"

"What?"

"Can I give her a reason for the cancellation?"

"I don't have to explain my every move to that woman."

"Yes, sir, of course not. It's just that . . ."

Her voice, thin and tinny over the speaking tube, trailed off.

Mrs. Spoffard was a woman with a lot of influence in the city and she was easily displeased, as Rhodes knew.

"Say I had a crisis to deal with." *It's true enough*, thought Cyril.

"Yes, sir. Shall I bring in the file on Mr. Latimer now?"

"Two minutes."

He pulled his notebook towards him and dipped his pen into the inkwell. He was busy writing when the nurse tapped on the door and entered.

231

Mrs. Mary Stockdale was a tall, willowy woman with fair hair tightly pinned beneath her white, starched bobcap. She wore a grey shirtwaist and darker grey woollen skirt. A silver watch was pinned on her bodice and a discreet straight silver brooch with the twined serpent indicated she was a graduate of the Royal School of Nursing. She had worked in the Toronto Hospital until she married, when she had to leave. No married women were allowed. Four years later she found herself with two children and a useless husband and had been forced to return to work. She was efficient, punctual and invisible. Rhodes knew nothing whatever about her personal life and had no curiosity at all.

She gave the doctor a little curtsy, handed him a buff file folder and ushered in the patient. Latimer was a bent old man who was dressed in a long, foul-smelling goatskin coat. Incongruously, an old-fashioned stovepipe hat, once an elegant green velvet, was perched on his head. Hovering behind him was a big-boned man with the weather-beaten face of a farmer.

Rhodes pretended to finish his notes while Mrs. Stockdale stood quietly by the door. Then he looked up over his pince-nez.

"Please have a seat, gentlemen."

The nurse brought forward two chairs and the younger man half pulled, half pushed his father into one of them. He sported a handlebar moustache, drooping and stained yellow at the tips with tobacco juice. He quickly stowed a wad back into his cheek. Mr. Latimer, senior, was short and scrawny with a long white beard and sidewhiskers. His pale blue eyes were swimmy and vacant and he wouldn't look at Rhodes but shrank down into the chair.

"So, h-how are we today, Walter?"

The old man sniffed but said nothing, and his son answered. "We was better for a few days, Doctor, but the trouble has come back again."

"Only to be expected. Has he been taking the medicine?"

"Yes, sir. Just like you said."

The old man growled. "She's still after trying to poison me."

"Da, she's not."

Mr. Latimer grabbed at his own crotch and scratched himself. "You'd say that 'cos she leads you around by your pisser all the time, but she put something in me tea. I saw her do it."

His son's face turned even redder. "My wife is a good woman, Doctor, and she loves me da. But he was taking poorly and she thought it would help if she gave him some tonic. To build him up. Completely harmless. She got it from the catalogue, sir. We all take it and it helps us. But Da is convinced and nothing will sway his mind."

The old man began to pluck at his beard. "She hit me, too."

233

"Did she now? That doesn't sound too g-good. What happened, Latimer?"

The farmer shifted uncomfortably and twisted his crusher in his hand. "She had to, sir . . . well, you see, truth is me da was after pinching her where he shouldn't."

"I see. Walter, you've been misbehaving again . . . No, don't spit there! Blast. Mrs. Stockdale, would you m-mind?"

The old man laughed, showing blackened gums. The nurse went to get a cloth. Rhodes stood up and went over to the chair.

"All right, let's get on with the treatment. Mr. L-Latimer, will you stand behind your father. Don't forget, during the session there must be no interruption."

He pulled the other chair directly in front of the older man and sat down close to him with his knees on either side and his feet between the man's legs.

"Remember what we did before? Animal magnetism? It helped you calm down, didn't it?"

Latimer shrugged but didn't reply.

"Now. Give me your thumbs, like so."

Rhodes demonstrated by making loose fists with his hands, the thumbs upright. The old man did likewise, and Cyril grasped his thumbs with each hand.

"Close your eyes and relax yourself. No harm is going to come to you here."

234

The old man's callused hands were cold, and Rhodes waited until he could feel the temperature equalizing between his palm and the thumb. Then he let go, inverted his hands, raised his arms above the man's head and made a sweeping movement down his arms, close to his body but not touching.

"You are going into a deep sleep, a deep and refreshing sleep. You are feeling very tired. Very tired and very heavy."

His voice was strong and clear. When he was inducing magnetic sleep he never seemed to stutter.

He made the passing motion again. Up to the head and then in a big sweep down the arms again and along the thighs to the calves, back up and down to the flaccid stomach.

"Sleep. Deeply sleep."

He kept repeating these words and making the passes over the old man's body until twenty minutes had elapsed. The son was by now leaning against the wall looking as if he were mesmerized himself. Mrs. Stockdale stood, waiting calmly. Latimer gave a little snore and his head dropped forward onto his chest.

"Walter Latimer, listen to what I say. When you wake up from this sleep, you will find all your worries have disappeared. They have vanished away like dandelion fluff in a breeze. You will feel in wonderful humour, happy and content. You are with a family that loves

235

you and you have nothing to fear. I repeat, when you awaken, your worries will have all evaporated. They will not return . . ."

He repeated this injunction twice more.

"Now I am going to wake you up. At the count of three you will feel a gentle breeze on your face and you will come completely awake."

Rhodes reached his hand to the nurse, and she handed him a long feather.

"One . . . two . . . three." He leaned forward and lightly stroked the old man's forehead with the feather and at the same time blew on him lightly.

Latimer opened his eyes, which already seemed clearer and more focused.

"Where am I?"

"In the office of Dr. Rhodes," answered Mrs. Stockdale in her crisp voice. The man swivelled around to look at her and caught sight of his son.

"Dickie! What are you doing here?"

"I brought you to see the doctor, Da."

"I've been poorly again, have I?"

"You have that."

"I feel right as rain now."

Rhodes stood up, pleased. Mesmerism was the thing he liked best of all. It almost always worked, could relieve pain and anxiety better than any medicine. He spoke to the farmer.

"Make another appointment for your father for next

236

week. Mrs. Stockdale will make up some more medicine."

Dickie reached out and grasped Cyril's hand, shaking it heartily. "I can't thank you enough, Doctor."

Rhodes withdrew his hand hurriedly and backed away. "J-just doing what's needed. Mrs. Stockdale, give him another bottle of laudanum. Two grams of opium, add some cherry water." He nodded at the son. "If your father shows any return of the delusions before next week, simply give him an extra dose with a shot glass of brandy. Do you have some brandy in the house?"

"No, sir, we're temperance."

"Never mind, then. The laudanum will be sufficient."

His father smiled at him sweetly. "Have you got a plug there, Dickie?"

"When we get outside."

Mrs. Stockdale took the old man by the arm. "Come with me, sir."

He shuffled off with her but at the door he paused and glanced over his shoulder at Rhodes.

"Women'll do you in every time if you let them," he said.

"Da!"

He hurried his father out of the office, and Rhodes went back behind his desk.

They certainly will, he thought.

237

Chapter Sixteen

THE CANDLES AND LAMPS IN THE HOUSES along Lowther had been lit early against the dreary afternoon. Only Birchlea seemed dark and unwelcoming. The curtains were drawn and none of the outside lamps were on.

Like the other houses on the street, Birchlea bespoke quiet affluence. Set back from the street behind a wrought-iron fence, the property was edged with evergreens now laden with snow. Two blue spruce stood sentinel on either side of the door, and the deep bay windows gave a pleasing symmetry. The dark green trim of the dormers and windows was virtually the same colour as the needles of the pine trees.

On the porch, Murdoch scraped the snow from his boots as best he could and waited for somebody to answer his knock. When the door finally opened John

238

Foy stood there, and Murdoch registered the quick look of fear in his eyes.

"I'd like to speak to Mrs. Rhodes."

"I'll see if she's at home."

He hesitated, trying to determine whether he should close the door and leave Murdoch on the doorstep, bring him into the vestibule or send him to the back door. Murdoch solved the problem for him by stepping forward.

"I'll wait inside, shall I?"

Foy retreated down the hall, leaving Murdoch to take care of his own hat and coat. As he hung them up on the oaken hall tree, he checked his reflection in the oval mirror. He smoothed back his hair, wishing he'd worn a fresh collar and trimmed his moustache, which was overhanging his lip a bit too much.

The vestibule itself was almost as large as the entire living room in the house he'd grown up in, and there were more oil paintings hung on the burgundy-papered walls than had existed in the entire village. Most of them seemed to be landscapes full of tumbling clouds and low trees that were distinctively English in charac-ter. He paused in front of one small one. A young woman stood on a desolate beach, staring out across a tumultuous sea. She was holding a shawl tight over her head against the fierce wind, and a curly haired child clung to her skirts. In the distance a lifeboat valiantly climbed the back of a huge wave as it made for the spar

239

of a ship barely showing above the water. A brass plate at the bottom of the frame named the picture. *Sorrow.* Murdoch grimaced. He'd witnessed a shipwreck when he was twelve and he remembered keenly the grief of the women. There must have been a dozen of them, all ages, from young brides up to old women whose sons were on the stricken trawler. They had huddled together against the wind and against the fear that was in all their hearts. It was the sea, as well, who had robbed him of his mother. She was a tiny woman, far too thin, not at all like the young woman in the painting. She'd been found drowned in a shallow pool on the rocky beach. His father put out that she'd slipped on a rock when she was gathering mussels, but Murdoch had grown up with bitter suspicions. He had vivid memories of his mother cowering behind the door to avoid the deluge of his father's drunken rages. There were the three children then. Suzanna, as sweet as the child in the painting but nervous and too quiet, and Albert, barely walking yet, but already showing signs of his affliction. They all knew better than to cling to their mother's skirt. She couldn't protect them.

He touched the brass plate with his fingertip. *Sorrow.*

He moved away. A little farther down the hall was a japanned table with a silver tray in the centre for calling cards. He smiled to himself. His sister had loved to play "visiting" when they were children. Leaves acted as pasteboard and the tray was a piece of tin. He sighed.

240

She certainly didn't need a card tray now. When she was barely sixteen she'd run off and joined an order of cloistered nuns from Montreal. He was allowed to visit the convent once a year and then he could only talk to her through a curtained grid. The priest said he should rejoice that she had chosen a life with Christ, but he grieved. He had looked forward to the sharing of their lives, of her children playing with his, and he constantly reproached himself that he had not been able to take her away from their father in time.

"Detective Murdoch . . ." Foy was standing at the door of the drawing room. "Madam would be happy to receive you." He glanced towards the hall tree but made no apology for his lack of attention. "Mrs. Rhodes and Mr. Owen are both taking tea at the moment."

"Good, that'll save me having to repeat myself."

"This way, if you please."

Man moves like he's got a broom up his arse, thought Murdoch as he followed Foy into the drawing room.

Donalda Rhodes and Owen were sitting next to the hearth and Edith was serving them from the tea trolley. The boy, Joe, was building up the fire with coal from the shuttle. He didn't turn around but the other three did, and Murdoch saw worry in each face. However, Donalda immediately assumed an expression of polite welcome.

"Mr. Murdoch, do come in." She indicated the tea trolley. "May I offer you some tea?"

"No, thank you, ma'am."

He didn't fancy trying to cope with a fragile cup and saucer, cake plate and his notebook.

"Will there be anything else, madam?" asked Foy, about to withdraw.

Before Mrs. Rhodes could answer, Murdoch said, "I'd like everybody to stay, if you don't mind."

"The servants as well?"

"If you please. Makes my job a bit easier. Then I don't have to go over everything twice."

It was also a good way to have all the cards out on the table. It was amazing what people could forget. Saying things out in front of company had a way of jogging the memory and the conscience.

"Well, of course, if you say so."

"We are shorthanded, madam," said Edith. "There is some mending to be done."

"I won't take long," said Murdoch.

Edith looked sour as she wheeled the trolley away from the fireside. Foy remained beside the door, and Murdoch intercepted a quick warning glance between him and his wife.

Murdoch took the rosary out of his pocket. "Do any of you recognize this?"

Owen leaned forward. "That's a rum-looking necklace."

"It's a rosary. We believe it belonged to Therese Laporte. The crucifix is missing."

242

The housekeeper came closer and peered at the rosary. "That's hers, all right. I saw her holding it once or twice. Couldn't understand what she was doing. I'm Methodist myself."

Murdoch glanced around at the rest of them. Owen had returned to his chair. He started to play with the silk fringe on the lampshade, flicking it back and forth. The boy had turned around but was motionless, staring down at the carpet. Murdoch went closer to him, the rosary dangling from his fingers. Joe glanced up and reached out his hand to touch the green beads. Murdoch had deliberately placed himself between the boy and the others, and he alone saw the look of naked yearning on Joe's face.

"Where did you find it?" asked Donalda.

Murdoch faced her. "To tell you the truth, ma'am, it was around the neck of a woman who was found dead yesterday morning. Which is the reason I'm here."

They all stared at him incredulously. *That woke them up a bit*, he thought. Owen stopped in midflick.

"What happened to her?" he asked.

"She was murdered. Strangled."

"I say! How dreadful."

"Yes, it was." Murdoch took out his pen and notebook. "I need to ask where each of you was on Wednesday evening."

"What? Surely it doesn't have anything to do with us," said Donalda.

243

"I hope not, Mrs. Rhodes."

She stared at him in disbelief. The others watched, stiff with wariness.

"The deceased was a prostitute. We know now that she was the one who stole Therese Laporte's clothes."

"Is she the one who gave her the drug?" asked Mrs. Rhodes.

"I doubt it."

Another silence. John Foy was surreptitiously leaning against the doorjamb, looking decidedly under the weather. Edith had stationed herself beside the tea trolley like a warden. Her face was grim and tight with disapproval. As for the boy, Joe, Murdoch almost forgot him, he was so still. He was crouched by the fender, half sitting.

"Are the two deaths connected, Mr. Murdoch?" asked Donalda.

"At the moment, ma'am, I can't say definitely, but I strongly suspect they are."

Owen got up abruptly and went to the trolley with his cup and saucer. "Are you sure you won't have some tea, Mr. Murdoch?"

"Positive, thank you."

Murdoch could see the black crepe that festooned the mantel and the black ribbon around the pictures, the trappings of mourning. He felt a flash of anger. Every last one of them was hiding something. He could smell it. He waited.

244

Suddenly, a piece of coal collapsed with a spurt of flame. All eyes turned to watch as if it were a fireworks display. Murdoch gave them a few more moments, then said, "Mr. Foy, let's start with you. Your whereabouts on Wednesday night?"

"Me? Well, yes, in fact I was out all evening. I had a Masonic meeting and Mrs. Rhodes kindly gave me the evening off. I was at the temple on Yonge Street and I can give you fifty names to prove it."

Foy's normally colourless voice had a distinctly belligerent edge to it.

"Five will do. And their place of residence if you know it."

The butler rattled off half a dozen names and addresses, which Murdoch wrote down.

"Mrs. Foy, can you confirm your husband's statement?"

"Naturally. He left after supper was served, about six-thirty."

"When did you return, Mr. Foy?"

Edith answered for him. "Twelve on the dot. The clock was chiming. Woke me up."

Again her lips tightened, and Murdoch could guess at the welcome Foy had received when he'd stumbled into bed full as a lord.

"You were home yourself, Mrs. Foy?"

"Of course!"

Murdoch turned to the boy. "Joe, my lad?"

245

Surprised, he nodded.

"Were the horse and carriage in the stable?"

Joe hesitated, then almost imperceptibly shook his head.

"Who had them?"

"I don't think you'll get much out of him, Officer," said Edith. "He's slow-witted. Or at least pretends to be."

Joe lowered his head again and his expression returned to dullness.

"Joe?"

The boy shrank back as if he would climb into the fire itself.

"Well? Who had taken the carriage? Was it Dr. Rhodes?"

Donalda interrupted. "My husband never uses the carriage at night, Mr. Murdoch. His office hours are too unpredictable. Joe takes him in the morning and he comes back by hired cab when he has finished."

Edith shifted her position. Her voice was polite but Murdoch saw malice cross her face. "I have to say, Sergeant – knowing as how this is a police investigation – I have to say I overheard Mr. Owen leaving in the carriage. 'Bout ten o'clock it was. I was on the point of retiring for the night."

246   Donalda glanced over at her son. "Is that so, Owen?"

"Yes, I was about to fess up when Edith beat me to the punch."

"You were out on Wednesday night, then, sir?"

"I was. I had some tests to catch up on. I went down to the laboratory to burn the midnight oil. My examinations are coming up before too long."

"Was anybody else with you?"

"Yes, a couple of the fellows."

"Who were they, these friends? May I have their names?"

Owen was looking most uncomfortable. "Good Lord, no. I mean, what am I saying? I was by myself. I'm getting mixed up with other evenings. Yes, that's it. Sorry, no friends."

"So there's nobody who can confirm your statement. A night porter, for instance."

"Er, I doubt it. Old Grant is just that, old. He was asleep, as I recall." He gave an embarrassingly false laugh. "Ha, a whole contingent of thieves could have got in and they wouldn't have woken him. Not that there's anything to steal there. Who wants pickled embryos?"

You're one of the worst liars I've come across, thought Murdoch, *but at the moment I haven't the sod of a notion what you're lying about.*

"What time did you get back to Birchlea, sir?"

"Oh, I don't know. One o'clock maybe."

Murdoch looked at Donalda. "You, ma'am, were you at home?"

"Yes."

"And Dr. Rhodes?"

247

"I cannot answer for my husband, Mr. Murdoch. After dinner I spent the evening in my room. I don't know whether he was in or not."

"He was not, madam," said Edith. "The doctor left the house sometime after Master Rhodes. I believe he didn't return until this morning."

"Father likes to spend the odd night at his club," interjected Owen.

"I'm aware of that, Master Rhodes. I am merely trying to give the officer the correct information."

Murdoch abruptly changed tack, see if they ducked the yardarm.

"What colour is your carriage and horse, Mrs. Rhodes?"

"I beg your pardon."

"We have evidence that Therese got into a carriage shortly before she died. It was described as burgundy or dark brown in colour and the horse light."

Donalda met his eyes without flinching. "Our carriage is walnut and the horse is a grey."

He continued. "Have any of you ever seen a man with a snake tattoo on his right hand? Stocky build, fair short hair, rough sort of face? Says he is a sailor."

248   Blank faces stared at him, and he thought the bewilderment was genuine. He closed his notebook.

"Is that everything, Mr. Murdoch?"

"Not exactly, ma'am. There's still the matter of

Therese Laporte's condition. It might further our solving both cases if we had that mystery nailed down."

"I cannot tell you anything more than I've already said. Theresa had no suitors and frankly no time that I can see when she would have been with anyone."

"If that is the case, then her seducer must be closer to home, wouldn't you agree, ma'am?"

Donalda straightened her back even more. "Let me say I can understand your considering it so."

Edith Foy made a peculiar sound that was a cross between a snort and a cough.

"Is there something you wish to say, Edith?"

"There is, madam."

"For goodness' sake, speak out, then," Donalda said with irritation.

Edith's lips drew tighter together. "You don't have to go far to find the culprit. He's right there." She pointed at Joe Seaton, who had been sitting on the edge of the fender while they were all talking. "He's the one got the girl in trouble, mark my words."

Joe shrank away and covered his head with his arms as if to ward off blows.

"These are serious accusations, Mrs. Foy," said Murdoch. "Can you prove them?"

"He's a guttersnipe and they never change no matter what good is shown them. Besides, he's backward. Can't tell the difference between Christian right and wrong any more than a dog can."

249

Murdoch found it hard not to snap back at the woman. His younger brother had been backward, and until the boy died Murdoch had spent a large part of their childhood defending him against similar ignorance. He moved over to Joe and tried to pull down his arm so he could see his face. The boy yelped in pain.

"What is it, Joe? Have you hurt your arm?"

He shook his head violently. As gently as he could, Murdoch pushed back the boy's sleeve. Two angry red lines ran the entire length of the boy's arm.

"Good Lord, what happened?"

Edith moved closer, and when she saw the boy's arm she said, "Somebody scratched him, that's what. Probably fighting for her life. It's proof."

Murdoch ignored her. The cuts were too deliberate to be the result of a struggle.

"How did you get these marks, Joe?"

The boy wouldn't meet his eyes, just tried to shake his head.

Murdoch crouched down so that he was on the same level and all Joe could see was him.

"Tell me the truth now, lad. Is it right what Mrs. Foy says? That you had connections with Therese Laporte?"

Joe stared at him as if he couldn't comprehend. Murdoch's heart sank. He hoped for Joe's sake it wasn't true.

"See, he's practically admitting it." This time it was Foy who spoke. "They were made for each other. Pair of bastards with no compunction about bringing bastards into the world."

Murdoch could see that the lad's mouth and chin were trembling and there were tears in his eyes.

"Joe?"

"You might as well talk to a brick wall," snorted Edith. "The boy's simple."

"If we stop badgering him, we might get somewhere," said Donalda. She spoke to the boy in a gentle voice. "Answer the officer, Joe. If you're innocent you have nothing to fear."

Joe responded to her like a prisoner to the parson who has come to read the Last Rites. He fixed his gaze on her over Murdoch's shoulder and said, "I didn't have nuffin bad to do with Tess."

His voice was low and shaky as if from lack of use and he had a thick cockney accent, but the words were unmistakable. The others were as surprised as if the horse had answered.

"Hmm. Thought the cat'd got your tongue. You sly little beast, pretending you couldn't speak all this time," said Edith.

Murdoch had had enough. "I'll thank you to hold your tongue yourself, Mrs. Foy. This is still a police investigation, I'd like to remind you, and you, madam, are interfering with the due process." He stepped back, touching Joe lightly on the shoulder. "Go on, lad."

Joe didn't budge from his focus on Mrs. Rhodes.

"Tess didn't write no letter, missus."

"What do you mean?"

"You says as how she wrote to 'er sister but she couldn't have. She couldn't write nor read. I know 'cos I was the one a-teachin' 'er and she hadn't got no farther than her letters."

Murdoch turned to Edith. "Mrs. Foy, you found that note in the girl's bedroom, didn't you?"

"Yes, I did. It was clear as a bell. I don't know what he's talking about."

"Do you still have it?"

"I threw it in the fire. It didn't seem important."

Joe's voice dropped to a whisper. "Tess didn't run away 'cos she was homesick."

Donalda nodded encouragingly. "Why did she, then?"

He cast a quick glance at Foy but returned to her at once. "It was 'cos of 'im. He was after Tess. He wanted to do it with her all the time."

"You bloody little liar," Foy yelled. Before Murdoch could prevent him, he had run at Joe and hit him hard across the face. The boy fell backwards, striking his head against the fireguard with a sickening bang. His eyes rolled up in his head and he lay still. Owen yelled and jumped up to help while Murdoch grabbed the butler's arm, yanking him away, hard.

"Stop it. Behave or I'll charge you with obstruction of justice."

252

Foy kept on shouting. "That boy is wicked, Mrs. Rhodes. I knew we should never have got him. His kind never changes."

Edith pulled at her husband. "Stop it, do you hear? Won't do no good."

Murdoch pointed to an empty chair. "Go and sit over there." His voice topped the butler's. "Don't move again unless I tell you to."

He half shoved Foy towards the chair. The butler seemed to have lost all control and he was shaking, his face crimson with rage. Edith gripped him by his shoulders.

"Try not to make more of a bloody fool of yourself than you've done already," she hissed into his face.

Murdoch waited until Foy obeyed, keeping his eye on him.

"Is the boy all right?" he asked Owen, who had run over to help Joe.

"He lost consciousness for a moment but he's not badly off now." He slipped his arm around the boy's shoulders. "Come on, Joe. Let's get you up."

He lifted him into a sitting position against the fender. Donalda, who had remained seated, spoke to Foy, her voice icy. "Is this true what Joe says?"

"No, madam, absolutely not," he replied. But guilt was written all over his angry face.

Donalda addressed Edith. "How could you have found a letter written by a girl who was illiterate?"

253

"The boy probably forged it."

"Joe? Can you speak?"

A red mark had appeared on his cheek and he was the colour of bread dough, but he met her eyes.

"I didn't write no letter. But Missus Foy knew as what was happening. I saw 'er a-watching Tess all the time. She must of made her run off."

"Madam, I hope you are not going to take the word of a boy like him against that of two respectable people like my husband and me?"

"Frankly, Edith, I don't know what to believe. All I can say is that I am extremely upset at Foy's behaviour. I will not tolerate it." She turned to her son. "Owen, what do you say about all this?"

"I wouldn't trust John Foy as far as I could throw him."

Edith answered for her husband. "How easy for the mighty to accuse those of us who are not so fortunate. Far better the world think my husband was wicked, madam, than that your own son be accused." She whirled to face Murdoch. "Why don't you question him?" She pointed at Owen. "I saw him mooning over that girl all the time. That night she died he was probably with her."

"According to Mr. Rhodes he was with Miss Shepcote all evening."

Edith burst out, "That little mouse would make a pact with the Devil if Owen Rhodes asked her to." She was

254

reckless now, ready to burn her bridges. "He fancied the maid, I tell you. And that Saturday night he was out until the early hours too. Same with this Wednesday. He was probably with that doxie you found."

"Edith, don't be preposterous," Donalda cried.

"Maybe he's the one who did her in. It'd keep her quiet, wouldn't it?"

Owen turned white and Donalda became even stiffer.

"Mrs. Foy, I will tolerate no more of this slander. You are discharged. Both of you. You will leave my employ immediately."

"Don't expect me to be silent, then. You can try to hide all you like but the truth is the truth. Your son was having connections with that girl and I will tell whoever asks."

Murdoch stepped in. "Mr. Rhodes, do you deny this?"

"My God, yes. Of course I deny it."

There was no stopping Edith. "He's a young man, isn't he? Anybody can see he fancies himself. He had his way with her, you can wager."

"Mrs. Foy, will you stop. I had nothing whatsoever to do with Therese Laporte."

"Why is it, then, I saw you coming out of her room? About a month ago it was –"

"That is a lie –"

"Edith, stop this." Donalda tried to stop the spewing. "Mrs. Foy is lying to protect her husband," she said to

255

Murdoch. "She has already forged a letter. She has no compunction about where she flings her mud."

"At the moment, ma'am, it is her word against Mr. Owen's, however, and not much proof on either side."

"I assure you he was not with a prostitute the other night, just as I assure you he was not the father of Theresa's child."

Owen stood watching her, his face filled with agony. "Mother, this is not necessary . . ."

"Begging your pardon, ma'am, you are his mother and it is only natural you would defend him, but I'll need proof. Mr. Rhodes, is there anybody at all who could vouch for your whereabouts on Wednesday night?"

"No, there really isn't."

"Owen, are you insane? Tell him."

"Mother, there is nothing to tell. I was not with anybody."

Donalda's expression was bitter. "This is no time to display some schoolboy notion of honour."

"Call it that if you –" said Owen.

At that moment, the door opened and Cyril Rhodes entered.

"What on earth is happening? What is the shouting all about?" He saw Murdoch and halted.

Donalda swung around to face him. "What impeccable timing, Cyril. Joe has accused Foy of fathering a child on Theresa Laporte. Edith is insisting the real culprit is our son. She claims to have seen Owen leaving the girl's room."

"Indeed!"

"Yes, indeed. And Mr. Murdoch is here investigating the murder of another young woman. He wants to know where we all were on Wednesday night. Apparently the dead woman was a prostitute. Perhaps you could help him."

"W-what do you mean? How could I help?"

"Come now, Cyril, I doubt your tastes have changed that much. Perhaps she was someone of your acquaintance."

Chapter Seventeen

FRIDAY, FEBRUARY 15

MURDOCH BREATHED IN THE FRESH AIR of the street with relief. The drawing room had become overheated in more ways than one. He decided to check on Foy's alibi first. He didn't doubt it was a real one, but he wanted to get a better sense of the man, and his chums might reveal something.

The grey afternoon had moved imperceptibly into night and this outer edge of the city had no street lighting. Trudging through the snow, Murdoch was keenly aware that this had been the street Therese had fled along so recently. Many of the big houses glowed with light and where the curtains were open he could see well-furnished drawing rooms, well-dressed people living their lives. Had she felt the loneliness of an outsider? With an illegitimate child on the way, her prospects must have seemed bleak indeed. Who was the father?

He was betting on Foy but he was too wise to let personal dislike influence him, and he knew the culprit was still uncertain.

At Church Street he checked his watch. It had taken him ten minutes to walk this far, going at a moderate pace. At least his timing was holding up. However, he didn't feel like walking the whole way. He'd had enough shank's mare for one day. He saw a streetcar coming up on the tracks and stepped forward to flag it down.

One of the men named by John Foy was a butcher who lived on Parliament Street, close to the medical school. Murdoch decided to see him first. Light snow was starting to fall, tickling his face, and the wind was gusting. He'd got off the streetcar at Gerrard, exchanged a few words with an excited Carrots, who greeted him from his spot on the curb, and began his walk east, again aware that he was following in Therese's footsteps. The residences that lined Gerrard Street were elegant and well kept. Several of them sat in spacious grounds, and brass plates on the iron fences proclaimed these were doctors' houses.

Just past the corner of Sherbourne there was a charitable home for girls under fourteen who had been in need of rescue. The lamps were lit and he could see into the front room. A half-dozen girls all in neat white pinafores over grey dresses were gathered around an organ. Their mouths were opening and closing like

259

fledgling birds, and he gathered they were singing. Hymns, probably, to judge by their serious expressions. A portly matron was conducting them, waving her arms in awkward dignity. Therese Laporte had not been much older than those girls.

Fred Vose's shop was above Gerrard Street on the west side of Parliament, the end building of a row of three, all newish looking in elegant pink brick. The store adjacent to the butcher's was vacant, the windows shuttered, but the remaining one was lit sufficiently for Murdoch to read the plain, dignified sign: J. CARVETH, MEDICAL BOOKSELLERS. Like the sparrows who chase the crows waiting for droppings, Mr. Carveth had situated himself conveniently close to the medical college, and he seemed to have both a sense of humour and a sense of business. In the window was a skeleton pointing a fleshless finger at a stepladder draped with purple velvet. On each step was a fat tome pertinent to the student's education according to Dr. Osler, including, Murdoch was glad to see, a weighty volume of Shakespeare's complete works. He paused for a moment, reading the other titles the eminent doctor considered necessary to a medical student's mental well-being. The Old and New Testament, of course, Plutarch's *Lives* and, rather surprisingly, *Don Quixote*. Murdoch experienced a twinge of envy for the wealthy young men who could afford to spend five years in uninterrupted studies. Given the chance, he would have loved to enter the university, but it was out of the question for somebody with no means except what his own muscles could earn. He moved on.

Mr. Vose's shop window was hung with several carcasses. Unbutchered pigs, the gash in their throats like second mouths, swayed on big hooks, intermixed with the bloodied bodies of hares and rabbits and sides of beef. Beneath them were displayed various trays of grey tripe, dark red liver and kidneys. Two skinned and eyeless calves' heads sat in the centre.

A bell tinkled as he entered the shop. He glanced around. There was only one sconce lit, and the corners of the store were pools of darkness where he could just make out the sacks of sawdust for the floor and a couple of tubs of brine in which were floating several pig's trotters. The bead curtain behind the counter parted and a man appeared from the backroom. He was brawny, with a broad, red face. Muscular arms swelled beneath his blue flannel shirt. His apron was dark with bloodstains. He was smoking a long clay pipe and the pungent tobacco mingled with the smell of blood and raw meat.

"What can I do for you, Captain? The missus craving a nice fresh roast, is she?"

Murdoch spent a moment to shake the snow off his coat and undid his muffler. "Are you Fred Vose?"

"I am unless my mother was deceiving me."

"I'm Detective William Murdoch, and I'd like a few minutes of your time to answer some questions."

"Lordy, hammer away, Captain."

"I understand you're acquainted with John Foy?"

"I am that. What's up? Has John done something he shouldn't?" Vose's eyes gleamed with curiosity.

"He's not been charged, if that's what you mean, but I'm conducting an investigation and I'd like you to verify his statement."

"Does it have to do with that poor maid as froze to death? She was a maid at Birchlea, wasn't she?"

"That's right." Murdoch chose not to mention Alice Black at this moment.

"John was very shaken by that girl's passing. As soon as my wife and I read about it in the newspaper we went straight over to see him."

"What did he have to say?"

"He couldn't understand how she'd come to die like that. To tell you square, Captain, at one point he was weeping like a woman. I've never seen him like that before."

Foy seemed to show a more delicate side of his nature to his brothers than Murdoch had yet witnessed.

"If you ask me," Vose went on, "Johnny was more bothered even than Edith . . . but then she is a bit of a flinty sort, if you know what I mean. It's understandable, though, isn't it? That maid was hardly more than a child. Still, I suppose, given she was a half-breed, we shouldn't be surprised."

"She was French-Canadian, not of mixed heritage that I know of."

"Oh. Well, anyway, she was a Catholic for certain and you never know what funny thing they're going to get up to."

"I don't follow your logic, Mr. Vose."

"Why d'you think she was out getting herself froze to death?" He stared at Murdoch.

"What's your theory, Mr. Vose?"

"I'll wager she was doing what they call penance. Do you know what that is?"

"Yes."

"Pain is what it is. I've heard that they get nuns and priests to lie stretched out for hours on the church floor. Think it's good for their souls." He waved his forefinger at Murdoch. "Some of them even beat themselves."

Murdoch didn't bother to attempt justification of his church's practices.

"You wouldn't get me doing anything like that," said the butcher.

"What I wanted to know is concerning a different matter. Can you verify Foy's statement as to his where-abouts last Wednesday? He claims he spent the evening at a lodge meeting."

263

Vose concentrated on getting his pipe going, sucking vigorously on the long stem. Finally he exhaled with pleasure.

"Wednesday? For sure. I can tell you straight and true, he was squatting beside me the entire time. Tim Winter was on my right, John Foy on my left."

Suddenly he put the pipe on the counter and wiped his right hand hard down the side of his apron. "Sorry there, Captain, I didn't even give you a proper greeting."

He thrust out his broad hand and, rather puzzled, Murdoch shook it. When he let go he caught an expression of disappointment in Vose's eyes and it dawned on him that there must be a secret Masonic handshake the butcher was testing on him. He had no idea what it was.

Vose went back to fiddling with his pipe.

"Did Foy leave the room at any time?" Murdoch asked him.

"Had to, didn't he? Twice. To let go his water."

"Did he go alone?"

"Nope. Him and me both went. But I can vouch he didn't go anywhere beyond the laneway."

"Drinks a lot, does he?"

Vose's eyebrows rose in surprise. "Not more than any other fellow."

"How would you say he holds his liquor? Like a man or a red Indian?"

Vose puffed on his pipe again, letting out a cloud of aromatic smoke that made Murdoch want to take out his own Powhattan.

264

"Most men gets jolly when we've mashed a few," said Vose. "Foy's no different, that I can recall."

"Has he ever had quarrels or rows with the brothers?"

"Nope. If anything he's the peacekeeper. Bobbie Reynolds and Tim Winter have butted heads a couple of times and John just honey-talked them right out of it."

Murdoch switched tack. "Have you ever met a woman named Alice Black?"

"Never."

"Did Foy ever mention the name?"

Again Vose shook his head emphatically. "Nope. Who is she?"

"*Was* is more like it. She was found murdered early this morning."

Vose whistled. "Great Thor, you're not suggesting John is mixed up in that?"

"Let's hope not."

"Sorry I can't help you, Captain. I've never heard tell of her. How'd she die?"

"She was strangled. Her body was found not far from the distillery on the lake."

"Lordy, Lordy. Was she a jade, then?"

"She was."

Vose was silent, concentrating on his pipe. There seemed nothing more forthcoming. Murdoch started to rewrap his muffler.

"Thank you, Mr. Vose. I won't keep you any longer."

265

"No hurry. To speak square, this is the most excitement I've had all week. I haven't always been a butcher, you see. I used to own a smithy up near the old tollgate on Yonge Street, and I tell you, Captain, I miss it something fierce. I got to shoe the travellers' horses and you wouldn't believe what a grand variety of folks came by my door. They told me such stories. You know, where they'd been, different people they'd met. One man had even saw the Queen herself, right up close. He said she was a little bit of a thing. Pretty as a picture then. This was before the tragedy, of course." The bowl shone red as he sucked hard on the stem. "Not only that, I miss the horses. Beautiful animals, horses are. Some folks say as how they're stupid but that ain't the case. They have a different intelligence from us is all. They'd always know who they could trust. And I never came across a skittish horse that I couldn't calm. D'you want to hear how I did it?"

The butcher looked so wistful Murdoch couldn't say no. He nodded.

"I whistle to them soft like this." Vose started a low trill through his teeth. The tone was sweet and birdlike and Murdoch could imagine it calming the savage beast.

"I did a stint at a lumber camp near Huntsville when I was younger," Murdoch said. "There was a fellow there had charge of two Percherons and he treated them like they was his sons. Combing and brushing them with a silk cloth 'til their coats shone like show horses. And those manes! You'd think you was touching a woman's hair."

He didn't add that Farqueson had whipped his horses quick enough when a load had been about to come crashing down on him. But that was only human nature.

Vose beamed. "Yeah. I understands that. I wouldn't've sold up 'cept I ruined my back from too much bending and lifting. I had to stop. Besides which the wife found the forge awful far up. This shop was her idea. Not that the work's so much easier. Those beeves'd challenge Hercules himself." He waved his pipe for emphasis. "Of course, I don't sell no horsemeat even though there's some as do. Would be like having a pal hanging there."

Murdoch started to edge towards the door. "I'd better be off. I've got other places to check out."

"Hold on a minute," said Vose. He put down his pipe and in a flash wrapped up a rasher of bacon in some brown paper.

"Here you go, on the house."

Murdoch thanked him.

"Come back anytime. I'll have some fresh chickens next week. Raise them myself out back." He followed Murdoch to the threshold. "There is one thing might be worth telling you, Captain, though I probably shouldn't."

Murdoch paused.

267

"At one of our lodge meetings Foy lets drop as how he was having some trouble at home. What sort of trouble, I asks. 'The wife's been acting awful jealous these days,' he says. 'Does she have any cause, John?' I asks, and he gives me a wink. 'Maybe,' he says. 'That's not good, John,' I says. 'Come on,' he says, 'who's gonna resist a taste of fresh meat when all he's had for years is salt pork?'"

"What was he meaning by that, d'you think?"

"I have the suspicion he was dipping his wick in some soft tallow where he shouldn't."

"The maid?"

"More than likely."

"Thank you, Mr. Vose. If anything else occurs, come round to the station. Number four on Wilton. You know where it is, don't you?"

"I do. You've got a couple of fine horses over there, but that bay gelding is favouring his rear leg. You should get him looked at."

"I'll pass that along to the livery constable."

The snow was heavier now, sticking to the ground in a fluffy layer. He walked back to Gerrard Street and turned east towards the medical school.

268   He wasn't surprised at what Vose had said but he felt angry again. He doubted Therese had responded willingly to Foy. He'd probably forced himself on her, and even if it was the cold that had directly killed her, Foy

was still accountable. He'd have to have another talk with the unctuous butler. See how conversant he was with opium.

A footman ushered Owen Rhodes downstairs to the billiard room. The smoke from Hugh McDonough's innumerable cigarettes hung like an autumn fog over the smooth green baize and a fresh cheroot was balanced precariously on the leather corner pocket. He was in the midst of lining up his next shot but when Owen came in he straightened and dipped his cue in a mock military salute.

"Roddy, what brings you out in such miserable weather? God, you look half-frozen. Let me get you some cheer."

"No, not right now. I have to talk to you. Is it private here?"

"Absolutely. What's up?"

Owen explained as succinctly as he could what had been happening, the visit from Murdoch earlier that afternoon and the reason for it.

"He wanted to know where I was on Wednesday night."

Hugh stiffened. "And what did you tell him?"

"That I was in the lab 'til all hours."

"Good thinking."

"Even if he checks, old Grant is such a muddlehead, he wouldn't know for sure if Prince Bertie himself came in."

269

"What if he's positive, though, what then? What will you tell the police fellow?"

"I don't know. I haven't considered that far ahead."

Hugh rubbed chalk on his billiard cue with great concentration. "Perhaps you'd better, Roddy." He poked Owen not too gently in the ribs with the end of his cue. "You're not considering a big confession or anything like that, are you, Roddy?"

Owen frowned. "Do you think I'm insane? Of course I'm not."

"That's good." Hugh smiled. "Come on. Cheer up, you look like a scared rabbit."

"To tell you the truth I feel like one. The fox is sniffing at the door."

"Bosh. He won't find out. And even if he did, what's the worst can happen?"

Owen stared at him. "I take it that is not a serious question."

Murdoch was almost past the hospital grounds before he noticed the man huddled just inside the gate. The man was slumped forward with his head on his knees. For a moment he didn't know if he was alive. Then he looked up and Murdoch saw he was young, barely twenty. He stepped closer.

"You can't stay here."

The young man began to struggle to his feet. "Ja, yust resting."

"Where do you live?"

"No place, zur."

"You're German?"

"Ja."

"How long have you been in Toronto?"

"I yust arrive two weeks since."

"Do you have work?"

"Not yet." He managed a pained smile. "There are many other men to choose. Nobody want foreign fellow."

Like so many immigrants he was hopelessly unprepared for the inhospitable climate. He'd found some sacking to wrap around his shoulders but he had no gloves or hat and he was shaking with the cold.

"You'll freeze to death if you stay here," said Murdoch. He reached in his pocket and pulled out his notebook. The snow immediately began to settle on the page as he wrote.

"Take this note to the police station and ask for Sergeant Seymour. You can stay there for the night. Tomorrow we'll see if we can find you some work."

He tore out the leaf and handed it to the youth, then took him by the arm and faced him in the direction of Sackville Street.

"Go down there and when you get to Wilton, turn right. That way." He indicated the direction. "Keep going until you see the police station. There's a green light over the door. Do you understand me?"

271

"Ja. Danke schön, danke schön."

Murdoch watched to make sure he was going in the right direction, until he was obscured by the swirling snow. Ahead of Murdoch a lamplighter was reaching up with his pole to light the gas lamp on the corner. It didn't make much difference to the darkness of the street; along Gerrard the lights were widely spaced. Murdoch wished he'd thought to bring his own lantern. Huddled into his coat, hat jammed down on his forehead, he trudged on.

Seymour would be good to the German lad, he thought. He wasn't a perpetual vagrant, that was obvious, and he'd be viewed more favourably. It was the chronic paupers that the city despised and caused the city council to be emphatic about forbidding begging on the streets. The police had instructions to charge anybody found doing so. Recently members of the Ratepayers Association had suggested sectioning off fifty acres of High Park as a poor farm where the paupers and vagrants could live and work. Murdoch thought the idea was highly impractical. You couldn't just dump everybody into one huge stew. There would have to be separate accommodations for those with children, for instance. To subject children to the influence of the desperate and destitute was to ensure they'd follow in those footsteps. Besides, he personally was not in favour of the out-of-sight, out-of-mind philosophy. He never forgot that there but for the grace of God went he.

272

By the time he reached the medical school, the street had emptied as people hurried home for their tea. Only one sleigh, bells jingling, had gone by, driven by a young man almost buried underneath the fur wraps, going too fast for the conditions. He was probably on his way to a sleigh party. The horse was blowing hard, its neck pulled in too tightly, its feet high-stepping. Murdoch hated to see animals treated like that.

The school was surrounded by a wrought-iron fence and the buildings were well set back, approached by a wide circular driveway that was rapidly filling with snow. Murdoch could make out the silhouette of the central spire. It didn't soar as high to heaven as the one at St. James's Cathedral, the tallest in the Dominion, but it was a reminder that this place of learning was not godless. There was an appropriate turret at each end of the main block for the studious to retire to, and one or two lights winked through the whirling snow.

To the right of the high gate was a brick lodge. Murdoch could see a soft gleam of candlelight coming through the window. The gate was not locked and Murdoch pushed it open, walked over, brushed away the snow and peered through the glass.

The room within was sparsely furnished, an oil stove in the corner, a wooden chair close to it and a table in the centre. On the rear wall was a board festooned with brass bells. A uniformed man was seated at the table, fast asleep and drooping in his chair. Even as Murdoch

273

watched, he swayed to the side but, without waking, righted himself with a little jerk.

Murdoch went in. The porter was a grey-haired man, thin and worn looking. He could have been old or middle-aged, it was hard to tell. His jaw was slack and Murdoch could see he was virtually toothless. His navy jacket was unbuttoned at the neck and stained down the front. A cap was pushed back on his head. There was a tin tankard beside him and the sweet smell of ale hung in the air.

"Mr. Grant?"

He snorted and his eyes opened. "'Oo are you?"

"Detective William Murdoch, Toronto Police Force."

Alarm shot across Grant's face. "Sorry, I . . . I was just catching a catnap. Never happens usually but, well, I've been a long stretch without sleep."

Quickly, he straightened his cap and fumbled with his buttons.

"I'm on a case right now," said Murdoch. "I want to ask you a few questions concerning one of the students at the college."

Grant blew out his breath with a whistle of relief. "Thank goodness. For a minute there I thought I was getting the gate. Silly of me. They'd hardly send the police to do that, would they?"

274

"Not unless you were breaking the law."

"What? No, no. I do me job like a soldier. Just got a bit tired, that's all."

They both knew he could be fired if he was reported for taking a tipple, but Murdoch guessed that Grant was on call twenty-four hours a day with one day off a month if he was lucky. In his opinion, that issue was between the porter and his employer, and if the man could sneak a bit of pleasure for himself, good luck to him.

"You said it was concerning one of the students. What have they been up to now?" Grant asked.

"What d'you think?" asked Murdoch, genuinely curious.

"Pranks, no doubt. Don't tell me they've gone and built another snowman?"

"Is that so bad?"

"The last one was. Just afore Christmas some of them sneaked over to the Baptist Seminary on Jarvis Street there. Built a ten-foot-high snowman that looked just like the minister. I have to say it was right clever. He's got red whiskers and they dyed some sheep's wool, stuck a pair of spectacles on his nose, the whole bit."

"That seems innocent enough."

The porter snickered. "Oh, yes, that was, but then they added a large pink rubber hose. Put it you know where. Shocking it was. I mean young ladies were walking by every day."

Murdoch tut-tutted in sympathy.

"This student you're enquiring about, broke the law, has he?"

275

Murdoch knew how destructive rumour could be, and he wanted to be fair to Owen Rhodes.

"Let's just say I need to verify his whereabouts at a certain time."

Grant looked uneasy, and Murdoch remembered what Owen had said about his being unreliable.

"Are the students allowed to use the laboratories after class hours?" he asked.

"They are, but not a lot avail themselves. Unfortunately, some of the young gentlemen see their education as a lark. Pity their poor patients, I say. But then that's youth for you. No harm, really. High spirits is all."

Murdoch guessed that the young gentlemen in question made Grant's life miserable. There were at least six bells on the wall and he could imagine the man answering summons after trivial summons.

"You know most of them, do you?"

"Oh yes. See them coming in and out all year."

"But they don't have to sign in after hours."

"They're supposed to, but lookit, they're young. Lot on the mind, as it were. If you gave me a nickel for every Tom and Dick that didn't, I'd be a rich man."

"Can I see the register?"

"Certainly."

He pulled a ledger out of the drawer and opened it, turning it towards Murdoch. Grant was right about the diligence of the medical students. There were no more than four entries on Thursday night and only two on Wednesday. Neither name was Owen's.

"Do you know Mr. Owen Rhodes?"

"Ah yes, sir. I do."

"He says he was here in the laboratory all Wednesday night. Is that so?"

"Certainly is. He's a study, that one. He's here now, as a matter of fact. Came this morning. Been here all day."

"I see. What's he look like?"

"Short, stout fellow, black hair and whiskers. Wears spectacles."

"You're sure that's Mr. Rhodes?"

"Positive. Know him like my own son. That's my job, to know them all. What's he done? Seems like a good sort to me. Doesn't tease like some of the young fellows. But then they're young and –"

Murdoch cut him off. "The Owen Rhodes I'm concerned with is of medium height, slim with copper-coloured hair, no sidewhiskers, small moustache. Favours gaudy waistcoats."

"Ha, don't they all. Quite the fashion these days with the young gentlemen. Those that have the balsam, that is. And most of them do, of course, here." He tapped the bridge of his nose. "Doting fathers. Or mothers, more like. But anyway you was saying this fellow is a carrot-top. Maybe you're thinking of Mr. Beresford. He's a redhead. Quite tall, though, and beefy. Likes his grub."

277

"Mr. Grant, tell me the truth. I wager these young colts lead you a merry chase when they're in the mood."

"That they do."

"You see a lot of them going back and forth. Must be hard to tell one from the other at times?"

Grant looked as ambivalent as a mouse contemplating the piece of cheese in the trap.

"Oh, no, sir. I'm supposed to know who they are. Keep track and so on. I might make the occasional mistake but no, sir, I know them all."

"And you're sure that the raven-haired Mr. Rhodes who is in the college now was here all Wednesday night?"

"Absolutely."

"Do you mind if I look around?"

"Not at all, Sergeant. The place is deserted, anyway, except for Mr. Rhodes. They all went home early on account of the weather. Any excuse if you're young and carefree."

"I've heard stories about the escapades these students get up to. Didn't some of them start experimenting with laughing gas not too long ago? One took too much, I heard, ending up in the asylum for a week or two."

Grant smiled with the true malevolence of the victimized. "That's right. Last November it was. They were supposed to be learning the effects of ether. Always try it out on themselves. Good thing too. They'll know what it's like when they're doctors, won't they? Should

278

do a bit of amputation, if you ask me." He chortled at his own joke. "But no harm intended, Sergeant. We've all been young, haven't we?"

"Do any of them use opium that you know of?"

"Wouldn't be surprised. They've got all sorts of drugs lying around. They make a lot of them theirselves."

More probing didn't elicit further information. Grant was an irritating witness, constantly vacillating between fear of jeopardising his job and the malicious desire to create trouble for the students. Finally Murdoch prevailed on him to show the main building. It took almost an hour to complete the tour. The porter was right about the lone student. He was dark-haired and industrious but his name was Llewellyn and he was of Welsh extraction, with a lilt to his voice. Murdoch hoped he would do well at his studies.

When he finally left and set off again into the blustery winds, Murdoch was sure of one thing. If Owen Rhodes had gone to the college on Wednesday night, he could easily have done so without Grant knowing or anyone else seeing him. His alibi was neither proven nor disproven.

Chapter Eighteen

She rarely went into his study, and even if she did, would have seen nothing untoward. He was careful about that. Except this morning he wasn't. He put the photographs back in his desk but not in the secret drawer. He also neglected to close the lid, so that was the first thing she noticed. She went to close it. There on the blotting pad were the pictures. Four of them, two of women on their own, one of a man and a woman and the fourth, three people. At first she didn't realize what they were, had never in her life seen such a thing, but when she identified what it was, her legs wouldn't hold her and she sat down. She felt a rush of bile to her mouth and had to spit out into her hand-kerchief. That was why she didn't hear the door open, didn't know she was not alone until he was beside her. He leaned over and put his finger under her chin, forcing her to look up at him. His shirtsleeves were rolled up to the elbow and she stared at the garish green and red tattoo that curled down his forearm. There was a naked and bleeding girl in the flat-headed snake's mouth. He whispered in her ear. "Curiosity killed the cat, you know."

FRIDAY, FEBRUARY 15

DONALDA PACED RESTLESSLY IN HER BEDROOM, her whole being so charged with Murdoch's visit she couldn't sit still. Over and over in her mind she replayed what had happened. The Foys were packing to leave and she was glad. She was sure John Foy had forced himself on Theresa, and as far as she was concerned he was culpable in the girl's death. She'd run away and perished.

"If only you'd told me," she burst out loud, but she knew that Theresa had been too frightened to do so.

She poked hard at the fire, breaking the lumps of coal into flame. She couldn't imagine Foy administering opium to the girl, however. So who had? That was the most frightening notion of all.

"Damnation!" she said out loud again. She regretted her angry remarks in front of the detective. There was no point in shaming the family. He, of course, had pounced on what she said but for once both she and Cyril were united. She insisted she had spoken carelessly, meant nothing, and Cyril denied any association at all with what he called "women of the night."

281

Was it true? Even thinking that now made her throat burn, remembering the time so many years ago when he had wept in her lap.

"It will never happen again," he'd said, sobbing like a boy. But she was unrelenting. Her love for him had died with the unborn child, the tiny lump of flesh that she had insisted the midwife show her. It was the same midwife who, nervously, had hinted at the real reason for the miscarriage. Dr. Pollard reluctantly confirmed the truth, and after a stormy confrontation Cyril broke down and confessed. Consorting with prostitutes was a habit he'd picked up in medical school, and it had continued throughout their marriage until the second pregnancy. She was four months expecting and full of joy at the thought of another child. But he'd come straight to her bed from a whorehouse and infected her with gonorrhea. The foetus died and she was ill for weeks, rendered infertile.

He begged for forgiveness but she had none, the rift between them was too immense to repair.

Donalda stood up and clasped her hands together tightly in an unconscious gesture of prayer. Last summer Owen had cried too, his face streaked with tears, his nose running with snot as if he were five years old again. He'd used the same words – "It will never happen again" – but she knew it had. She wanted to deny the truth, to pretend that a marriage to Harriet Shepcote would make all the difference, but after today she knew it would not.

Suddenly she felt in need of comfort so intensely it was a pain in her chest. Owen had left the house at the same time as the detective, using Murdoch as a screen against her anger. Cyril had gone somewhere too, walking out into the winter night as if the darkness could bring him solace. The pale face of her stableboy came to her mind, and with a blind instinct to ease her own pain in the worse anguish of another, she decided to go to him.

A shawl clutched tightly around her head against the bitter cold, she hurried across the snow-covered yard. She hadn't been able to set foot in the stable since the summer but as she entered, the smell of horse and straw thrust the memory upwards.

At first she had not been able to see clearly, coming into the stable from the sunlit yard. Then she saw the two of them. They were lying in the fresh hay, their naked bodies glowing white in the gloom. Initially she'd mistaken the sounds for moans of pain. Then Owen became aware of her and looked over his shoulder, horror on his face.

She lifted her lantern high and as the light struck the horse's head, his eyes gleamed golden. He was placidly chewing his hay but he stamped with his rear leg and shifted. She hesitated, then called out.

"Joe? Joe, are you in here? It's Mrs. Rhodes."

283

There was a thump overhead, the sound of footsteps, and Joe's face appeared in the opening at the top of the ladder. He looked so frightened Donalda's heart went out to him, and she spoke kindly.

"Joe, I'd like to talk to you. I've come to see how you are."

He turned in order to come down the ladder but Donalda stopped him.

"Wait. I'll come up."

He shook his head.

"Why not?"

He started to gesture with his hands.

"You can speak, Joe. You have already."

He gulped, then spoke so softly she could hardly hear him.

"'Tisn't tidied up or anything."

"Don't be foolish, I'm not the house matron."

Joe flinched.

"Come and hold the lantern for me," she said more gently.

He clambered down a few rungs and she handed him the light. Then, gathering up her skirt, she climbed awkwardly up to the loft and stood on the upper rung of the ladder, her head thrust through the opening. Joe moved backwards to the wall, the lantern waving in his hand. He had to bend his head to stand upright because it wasn't a room really, just a space under the eaves. There was a narrow bed made up neatly, with a small

284

wooden crate beside it and a wicker chair. It could have been a passageway in somebody's house. Donalda gazed around in dismay. How could she not know he lived like this?

"You keep it very tidy, Joe."

"I do it like we was taught, ma'am."

The lantern was throwing up long shadows against the walls and his face was in darkness, but his fear was rank in the confined area.

"Help me up, Joe."

"Not much room."

"That's all right. I'll sit."

"Better I come down, missus."

He flapped his hand at her the way you do to shoo away chickens.

"What are you hiding?"

"Nothing, missus."

"Come over here." She was perched uncomfortably at the edge of the trapdoor. Slowly he moved towards her, revealing a metal-bound square box behind him. A tiny cross as if on an altar was balanced against the wall.

"What is that?" she pointed.

"Nothing, missus."

"Shine the light there."

285

"It ain't nothing."

"Do as I say, Joe."

Reluctantly he obeyed, lowering the lantern.

"Give it to me."

He did so, his hand shaking.

"Did this belong to Theresa?"

"Yes, missus."

"Where did you get it?"

Wordlessly, he pointed downwards.

"Use words, Joe."

He hung his head and muttered, "Can't say."

"Look at me. Come on, raise your head. That's better. Now listen. I promise you will not be punished. I know you haven't done anything bad."

She spoke confidently but she felt ill. The crucifix lay cool and heavy in her hand. The Christ figure was made of silver, the cross ebony wood. Joe saw her distress and became even more afraid. She tried to smile to reassure him.

"You must tell me, Joe. Where did you find this?"

Again he pointed down below and whispered.

"In the carriage."

"What? I don't understand."

"Things fall out, money and bits, so I always checks out the seats. I'm sorry, missus, I should've –"

"Never mind that now. What carriage? Who does it belong to? Whose is it, Joe?"

286

Chapter Nineteen

Neither of them were aware of her. There was a peep-hole in the door between the butler's pantry and the dining room so the servants could determine the progress of the meal. The door was solid oak covered with baize and intended to block out sound, so she could barely hear what they were saying. What she saw sickened her and filled her with such fear she could not move, held in place like a rabbit facing a ferret.

His shirtsleeve was rolled up and he had twisted a garter tight around his upper arm. The other man had his back to her but she knew who it was. He was holding a syringe aloft, checking the level of the brownish liquid it contained. He bent over and plunged the needle into the bulging vein in the crook of the other's elbow, and grinned as he winced.

When the syringe was empty he withdrew the needle, and the other man loosed the tight armband

and rolled down his sleeve.

"Do you think that doxy told anybody else that she'd seen us pick up the girl?" he asked, flexing his arm to speed the drug's action.

"Course she did. The only thing looser than a whore's cunt is her tongue. If I know gits, she leaked everything to her chum."

"What shall we do, then?"

"I'll take care of it."

The other man was already having trouble concentrating as the opium took effect.

"W-what are you going to do?" he asked again, his tongue thick.

The second one didn't answer but busied himself replacing the syringe in a blue velvet box.

"Enjoy yourself," he said.

"Where are you . . . going?"

"To take care of the tell-me-when."

"No . . . wait . . . you mustn't . . ."

"No? Are my lugs hearing right? Does my squab have a conscience?" He looked down at the man, whose head was now lolling on his chest. "Don't worry, you and her will soon meet in Paradise. Just what you've always wanted."

288

He grinned at his own joke. Even as the drug pulled him into the Shadow, the man understood. He raised his hand feebly but could do nothing. It was too late.

The man turned to leave, faster than she could move, faster than she expected, so that the door actually banged into her as he pushed it open.

He caught her by the arm before she could run.

"Didn't I tell you, curiosity killed the cat," he spat at her, pinching her arm so viciously she cried out.

"Well, my little pullet, you've really gerried yourself this time, haven't you?" he said.

FRIDAY, FEBRUARY 15

THE YEOMAN CLUB WAS NOT OSTENTATIOUS or well situated like some of the clubs and lodges in the city. The Oddfellows owned a huge chateau of a building on Carlton Street, which was a boast to the world about their wealth. The National Club had a good address on Bay Street. The Yeoman had neither of these. It had been founded fifteen years earlier by a rich brewer who acquired a cheap piece of land at the south end of River Street. In spite of the location, he enticed a significant membership by donating his superb wine cellar, sparing no expense in the decor and, above all, affording complete privacy.

The three-storey building itself was plain, with a flat facade of red brick, the only ornamentation some yellow medallions beneath the cornice and two columns of expensive Italian marble that flanked the door.

289

By the time he reached the club, Murdoch was footsore and his face was burning with the cold. The wind was fierce and the snow was building up on the side-walks, making walking difficult. River Street was a working-class area not fully populated, and there were only a few lights dotting the darkness. At the Yeoman Club a low gas lamp shone outside but the windows were curtained and unwelcoming. Only those in the know would seek out the place.

He tugged on the bellpull and the door was opened at once by a liveried footman. He hesitated, trying to assess the detective's status. Not a tradesman, but not a guest nor likely to be. Murdoch was used to this atti-tude but never reconciled. He stared back at the foot-man and coolly presented his card.

"I'd like to have a word with the steward, if you please."

"That'll be Mr. Keene. He's in his office."

"I'll wait inside, then, while you fetch him. It's maundy cold out here."

Reluctantly, the footman stepped aside to let him in. Then, the card held in his fingertips as if it were dipped in shit, he went off.

Murdoch gazed around curiously at the spacious ves-tibule. There was a log fire blazing in the big fireplace, two fine brocade armchairs facing it and at their feet a tiger-skin rug, fierce head intact, the long teeth bared, ready to bite the unwary. The carpet was a thick Persian, the wallpaper red and green flock, and soft light filtered

290

through porcelain sconces. Murdoch walked cautiously around the tiger's head to warm his hands at the fire. Above the mantel were two framed pictures. One was of Her Majesty holding her orb and sceptre, the other a daguerreotype of a stout man with abundant white whiskers and small eyes. The brass plate declared this was Mr. Lothar Reinhardt, the generous founder and benefactor of the Yeoman Club. Beneath his portrait was a printed declaration of the aims and purpose of the club:

. . . to defend and protect our native land against the encroachment of undue influence from our southern neighbours, to wit the United States of America. To sustain and support our undying loyalty to the throne of England, Her Majesty Queen Victoria and her descendants.

He turned his back to the fire, lifting his coat to get some heat to his cold buttocks. In the centre of the vestibule was a white marble sculpture on an ebony pedestal. It depicted Diana, breasts naked, half woman, half deer, fleeing from her own hounds. The terror carved on the goddess's face made him think of Alice fleeing across the frozen lake.

"Mr. Murdoch. What can I do for you?"

The footman had reappeared, and behind him was a tall man, with grizzled hair cut short. He was dressed in cutaway black jacket and grey trousers, and an immaculate white cravat was at his throat. He had the stiff bearing of a soldier, accentuated by the empty left sleeve of his jacket, which was pinned to his broad chest. Murdoch gaped, recognizing him immediately, but the steward spoke first.

"My name is Keene. Perhaps we should talk in my office. Forsyth, see we are not disturbed."

"Yes, sir." The footman's face was as expressionless as a dummy's. Only the bright curiosity in his eyes gave him away. He stepped back into immobility beside the entrance.

"This way," said the steward. Murdoch followed him into a wide passageway with closed, leather-covered doors along either side. All of them sported mahogany plaques which stated, variously, LIBRARY, SMOKING ROOM, BILLIARD ROOM. The man opened the door labelled STEWARD'S OFFICE and ushered Murdoch inside.

It was actually a sitting room, luxuriously appointed, with a Turkish couch in plush velour and two brown leather chairs. The draperies were chenille and the Axminster carpet thick enough to go to bed on. A massive walnut desk against one wall was the only visible concession to business. There was a blazing fire in the hearth here as well.

The steward closed the door and the two men faced each other. Both broke into broad smiles of delight.

"Willie, my boyo, it's so good to see you again."

Murdoch pulled him into a hug, thumping him hard on the back. "It didn't seem like it back there. What's this 'My name is Keene' stuff?"

"I apologize, Will. I for sure didn't mean to slight you. Gave me quite a shock to receive your card, I can tell you." His Irish brogue was thicker with his excitement. "Truth is I changed my name for practical reasons. I wanted this crib and I suspected that a man named John Keene, Methodist, rather than Sean Kelly, hardened Papist, would be more acceptable to the fat culls."

Murdoch grimaced. "From what I've seen so far, you were probably right."

Kelly stepped back and gave Murdoch an affectionate punch in the arm. "You're fit as a fiddle, I see. Here, now. Let me take your coat and hat. Thank you kindly for being so quick on the uptake and not letting on. Forsyth's a toad-eater if ever there was one. He'd have tattled on me for sure."

Murdoch regarded him, smiling. "Now let me have a gander at you."

Kelly's features were broad and flat, and childhood smallpox had made him cribbage-faced. The general effect was rather sinister. But Murdoch knew, in spite of his appearance, he was a decent man of fierce loyalty and honour. They'd known each other at the lumber camp twelve years before, where Kelly was the manager and Murdoch a young chopper.

"You've not changed a speck."

293

The steward chuckled. "If you think that, it's sure your own eyesight in what's changed." He patted his stomach. "Fifteen more pounds. I married a widow lady last year and she's been doing her best to fatten me up like I was a prize steer worth more by the pound. Lots of bread and potatoes in there."

"So somebody finally snared you?"

"True. A man likes some comfort in his old age. She's a lovely little thing, plump and sweet as a nut with a nice nest egg to boot." He pulled up a chair for Murdoch. "I'd heard up at the camp you'd joined the bulls."

"Were you surprised?"

"Not me. Some of the choppers thought you'd turned your coat, but those as knew you, including meself, said it was good a man as straight as you was looking after law and order."

Murdoch was pleased. He'd always valued the older man's good opinion.

"You're looking perishing, Willie. Let me get you a drop to warm you up? I've got nothing but the best."

He went over to a high bookcase that lined one wall, reached up and pulled out a strip of blank books. A small liquor cabinet was behind.

"Am I to assume you've come about the young colleen that died last week? A young lump of a lad was here asking questions before."

Murdoch nodded. "Something else has happened . . . Ever know a woman named Alice Black?"

294

"Never."

Kelly took a bottle of Glenmorangie, tucked it under his arm and pulled out the cork with his teeth. He got out a crystal glass and poured Murdoch a finger of scotch.

"None for you?"

"No. Minnie made me take the Pledge before we married. The drink made me a hothead all my life. I'm better without it."

He sniffed at the scotch like a besotted man smells his absent mistress's gown. "Beautiful! But go on, Will."

"Alice Black was a prostitute. We found her strangled down near Cherry Beach on Thursday morning."

"Did you now? What a terrible thing."

Murdoch raised his glass. "May the road always rise before you and may you ever have the wind at your back." He took a sip, rolling the silky liquor around his tongue before swallowing.

"Alice might have been offed by a Tom in a rage, but I think it's too much of a coincidence. She stole the clothes from Therese's dead body. I'm wagering she knew something she shouldn't have and was conveniently dispatched to the Grand Silence."

"What can I do to help, Will?"

"Two of the men who were connected with the first girl are members of the Yeoman Club."

"Alderman Shepcote is, and your constable already asked me about him. He was here on that Saturday

295

night. I saw him meself. Came about ten, left at twelve. Who's the other buck?"

"Dr. Cyril Rhodes. Do you know him?"

"For sure. A little cull. Forever tripping over his own tongue when he talks."

"That's the one. He claims he was here on Wednesday night."

"Does he now? I didn't see him meself, but we can ask Forsyth. He could have booked one of the private chambers."

"What are they?"

"Four rooms at the back where the members can stay if they're too tired or too full to go home. Or if they want to do some private entertaining."

"Gigglers?"

"On occasion. Not always. Might be some special business."

"Is the doctor the sort of man who'd pay for his pleasures?"

Kelly hesitated. "I've only been here a month, Willie. It's not a thing I would know."

"His wife spat it out like a fishwife, but then they both shut up tighter than a pair of clams. 'Oh, I didn't mean nothing by it,' says she. 'Oh, I'd never do anything so wicked,' says he. Liars both of you, says I. Anyway, he claims he was here on the night of Alice Black's murder and at his consulting rooms when

Therese Laporte died." He put down his empty glass. "How about showing me these nice private rooms?"

Kelly nodded. "We can go the back way."

"Can't have the members running into a police officer, can we? What'd they think?"

The steward grinned, shamefaced. "That's the truth of it, Will. And sooner or later they'd get around to blaming me."

He led the way down the hall and through a heavy door to a narrow, uncarpeted passageway. At the far end was a second door, and this opened into another wider hall with thick carpeting and rich flock wallpaper. There were four doors on one side.

Kelly opened the first one. Rather to Murdoch's surprise, at first appearance this room was quite plain. It was only when you looked a little closer that you could see the excellent quality of the furnishings. Around the marble fireplace were grouped two armchairs and a sofa, all upholstered in brown suede leather. The tables and sideboard were cherrywood, the lamps fine porcelain. Above the fireplace was a large gilt-edged mirror and, to one side, another portrait of Her Majesty Queen Victoria. On each of the side walls were reproductions of celebrated oil paintings, all depicting royal occasions: the young queen in a white gown addressing Parliament, the wedding of the Prince of Wales to Princess Alexandra of Denmark and so on. Opposite was a beige felt curtain, to the right a louvred door and to the left, double doors.

Murdoch pointed. "Where do they lead?"

Kelly went over and pulled open the double doors. Behind them was a put-away bed.

"Do ye want me to take it down?"

"Not at the moment. And there?"

"That's the crapper room. The water closet."

Murdoch went to have a look. In the small alcove behind the louvred door was a washbasin fitted with brass faucets, a deep bathtub and an oaken water closet. Curious, Murdoch pulled on the chain and watched as the water came swooshing down into the porcelain bowl, swirled and disappeared.

"The members certainly have all the modern conveniences, don't they?"

"That's what they pay for."

Murdoch walked over to the felt curtain. "Is this the back door?"

"That's it."

He drew back the curtain, which smelled of cigars. There was a door behind it, an iron key in the lock. As he opened it a rush of cold air hit his face. He was facing directly onto a laneway. It looked just wide enough for a carriage and had been well used, the ground showing many overlays of wheels. When he leaned out, he could see there was a service bay to

298

his left where tradesmen could bring their carts.

He closed the door, let the curtain drop and stepped back into the room, dusting some of the light snow from his shoulders.

"The members could easily come and go without being seen if they used the laneway."

"That's the idea."

"Is there any way to know if Rhodes used this room?"

Kelly thought for a moment, then slapped himself on the forehead. "May I be taken without shrift for my sins if I'm not an idiot . . . We have chits. The members like it better. They simply sign for their drinks and meals as they have them and pay their accounts at the end of the month. Each chit is stamped. It makes settling up with the waiters easier. I'll fetch them."

While he waited, Murdoch examined the room. The books in the walnut glass-fronted case were properly sober and edifying. There was a beautifully illustrated volume of *Master Thoughts in Poem, Prose and Pencil*, which he'd recently seen in McKenney's Bookshop on Yonge and had coveted. He replaced it carefully and opened the doors of the walnut sideboard. It was empty except for two new packs of cards and a blank notepad. For a moment he was disappointed, but he checked himself. What had he expected? A box of French letters? Syringes and hookah pipe?

The lavatory also revealed nothing personal. A razor, a soapdish and brush and thick satin-damask towels were provided. There was no indication whatsoever in this tastefully furnished room of the kind of activity that Kelly had hinted at.

He sat down in one of the armchairs, sinking back into the soft upholstery. He could see himself sitting there, his crystal glass of Glenmorangie beside him, his leather-bound book of *Master Thoughts* at his elbow.

Kelly returned. "Hey, Willie me boyo, you look right at home. Perhaps one day ye'll be a Yeoman yerself."

"Sure. And one day we'll be able to live on the moon. Come on, what've you got?"

The steward was carrying a stack of papers speared on a metal spike. He pulled half of them off and gave them to Murdoch.

"You take those. They're all the chits for the last week. These rooms are referred to as the Cabinet Section. This particular one is called the Gladstone. The others are the Peel, the Wellington and the Disraeli. Sometimes the waiters will note which particular room they're serving and sometimes they don't."

He held the papers down with his thumb and started to leaf through them. Murdoch followed suit. Many of the signatures were of prominent men. The Yeoman Club admitted only the most eminent of Toronto's Christian citizens.

After a few minutes, Kelly said, "Will you stick to the job at hand? You're oohing and aahing like a chamber-maid at a banquet."

"It's interesting to the policeman in me . . . Alderman Blong ordered *four* magnums of Champagne?"

"He was entertaining his fellow councilmen."

"Speaking of which, here's a chit for McDonough. He's our medical officer."

"Good man?"

"Let's say the colonel likes him because he's very efficient." He imitated the doctor putting his ear to a man's chest. "Hmm, Constable, sounds like the Don River in there. But nothing to worry about. I don't want to keep a young swell like you off the beat. Get yourself some goose grease, rub it on your chest and wear a flannel vest. Next!'"

Kelly laughed. "I know the kind. In the camp it was sheer luck who came in the door first, the physician or the undertaker. But that bill belongs to Hugh McDonough, the doctor's sprig. He's a regular here. He and his friends."

There was a curious tone to Kelly's voice.

"Don't you care for him?"

The steward shrugged. "The Good Lord made many species of animal for his ark."

301

"He was in one of the Cabinet rooms on Saturday. He must have had guests, unless he's in training to oust the Fat Man at the Exhibition. Two magnums of hot

Champagne and a quart of fresh oysters. No, two quarts of oysters."

"He always has company. He has a passion for cards and he's here 'til all hours. I don't know when he does his learning. He's supposedly studying medicine himself, God help us."

"So's the Rhodes scion. Is he a member here?"

"No. Just his father."

"Ever see him? Redhead, lathy build, nobby dresser."

"Can't say I have." Suddenly, Kelly jumped up. "Here we go. Dr. Rhodes ordered a glass of Harvey's cream sherry on Wednesday night. Let's see, that was Humphrey's shift too, which means it was early on in the evening. The man went home with a digestive problem, so I know. Me suspicion is he tipples, but I've yet to catch him."

"Who, Rhodes?"

"No, you daft boyo, the waiter Humphrey."

"Rhodes says he came here about seven o'clock. Do the waiters enter the room when they bring the drinks?"

"Not without permission. They are told to knock and place the tray outside the door."

"So we can't know if the doctor was alone or not."

"No, not unless the waiter overheard someone. Ye're thinking of a female person, I presume?"

Murdoch nodded. He finished his pile. "There's nothing else, and he says he was here from early evening until the next morning. What was he eating, snow?"

302

"Regrettably that doesn't prove anything. He could have gone to the dining room and somebody else paid his meal."

"Did you see him?"

"No, but I was in my office a lot of the time."

"Sean, I'm going to have to ask questions."

"They won't like it, Will. Be careful, me friend. These aren't your usual nocky piss-makers. These are the Uprights. You've got to be very sure of yourself or you're the one who'll get it."

"I'm aware of that." Murdoch sighed. "Unfortunately, we're not much further forward. We've confirmed Rhodes was here at the club Wednesday evening but there is no proof that he stayed the night. And even if he did, it's possible to come and go from these rooms without being seen. He could have slipped off, met Alice Black, killed her and been back to enjoy a good night's sleep with nobody the wiser. We've nothing for Shepcote, but he said he was at home, anyway."

Murdoch leaned back in his chair, lacing his fingers behind his head. He was tired and he hadn't had anything to eat all day. Maybe Sean could stand him a dish of oysters or a plate of roast beef. His friend must have read his mind.

"Come on back to my office. This is a quiet time of the evening. I can order us some lamb chops. The cook is excellent, as you can imagine."

"All right. But let me see the other rooms first."

303

"What are you looking for?"

"I don't know. A ghost to talk to me maybe."

Kelly replaced the chits on the spike and led the way to the adjoining room. The plaque on the door said WELLINGTON but this room differed from the Gladstone only in the choice of wall covering, which was brown, and the oil paintings, which were all military: the Zulu attack on the garrison at Roke's Drift, General Gordon making his last stand at Khartoum.

Murdoch walked around but the room was unrevealing.

"Satisfied?" Kelly asked.

He nodded, about to leave, when his eye was caught by the double doors that hid the bed. They were not totally closed. He went over and opened them up. The bed behind wasn't completely flush with the wall.

"How do I get this down?"

Kelly came over and grabbed a lever at the side. With a hard tug, he pulled the bed down.

The cloth valise had been stuffed underneath the mattress. Murdoch snapped open the bag. Women's clothes. A Bible was sitting on top of the grey jacket and he took it out. Inside was an inscription. *À ma soeur, Therese Laporte. Avec amour. Claudette.*

He felt a flood of white-hot anger.

"Sean, I want to know who was in this room on Saturday last. I'm going to question every fat cull, and they can have my arse on a bandbox for all I care."

As Murdoch started to replace the clothes in the valise there was a sharp rap at the door. Kelly answered it. The imperturbable Forsyth stood there. He made a quick attempt to look over the steward's shoulder but Kelly blocked him.

"Sorry to disturb you, sir, but there's a lady to see you. She said it was a matter of great urgency. I took the liberty of placing her in your office, sir. The members, er, won't have to, er, pass her in the hall."

Women were not allowed into the inner sanctum of the club under any circumstances.

"Did she state her business?"

"No, sir."

"Who is she?"

"She says her name is Rhodes, Mrs. Cyril Rhodes."

Chapter Twenty

DONALDA RHODES WAS STANDING in front of the fire warming her hands, but she turned around quickly as the two men entered the room. When she saw Murdoch, she looked frightened. Kelly spoke first.

"Mrs. Rhodes, I'm the steward, John Keene, at your service."

"I wished to see my husband."

Murdoch interrupted. "He isn't here, and frankly I'd like to locate him myself."

"Why is that, Mr. Murdoch? I thought you had all the information you required."

She spoke haughtily and even though he knew it was a facade, he was irritated. Fed up with the lot of them.

"Mrs. Rhodes, we have found Therese's valise. It was hidden in one of the rooms."

"I see."

306

"You can understand the importance of this discovery. Either the girl was brought here or at the very least somebody from this club was with her in the last hours of her life."

For a moment she appeared to be searching for some denial, an explanation that would remove the danger from her own house. Then she sat down on the edge of the chair by the desk, her back ramrod straight as if she needed to hold herself upright.

She took the ebony cross out of her pocketbook and handed it to Murdoch.

"I believe this is from Theresa's rosary."

"Where did you get it, ma'am?"

"Joe found it in a carriage. He is in the way of fishing down the seats for stray coins and he discovered this."

"Whose carriage would that be, then, ma'am?"

Donalda hesitated, glancing over at Kelly, who was hovering awkwardly near the door.

"Would you rather I left?" he asked.

She considered him. "It doesn't really matter. It will all come out soon, anyway."

"Whose carriage, ma'am?" Murdoch prompted.

"Miss Harriet Shepcote's. She came to Birchlea on Tuesday last, and that's when he found it." She met Murdoch's gaze. "He only showed it to me just now . . . I am sure he is telling the truth, Mr. Murdoch."

He tapped the crucififix lightly in his palm. "Why

307

did you come to the club, Mrs. Rhodes, and not directly to the police station?"

"I hoped my husband would be here. Frankly I felt the need to speak to him. Please believe me, I had every intention of informing you, but I'm sure you can understand my concern. Miss Shepcote is quite closely connected with our family . . . We are hoping for an engagement between her and my son."

Murdoch understood perfectly. Donalda wanted to be fully prepared if scandal was going to burst over their heads. "The girl would make a pact with the Devil if Owen asked her to," were the words Edith Foy had used.

Donalda stood up. "May I offer you the use of my carriage, Mr. Murdoch? It is waiting outside. I'm sure there is some urgency to speak to Miss Shepcote."

She was right. "Thank you, ma'am. That will be most helpful."

"I will accompany you. No, please, Mr. Murdoch, my presence could be an asset."

She was right about that too. He didn't want to be in the position of dealing with an unchaperoned young woman, especially if he was going to arrest her.

Behind Donalda, Kelly beckoned. "Can I have a word?"

Murdoch went closer.

"Willie, let me come too. You might need some help."

"Sean, I can't do that. This is police business."

"You don't have time to get more officers and you've no idea what you're likely to encounter. You don't want the culprit to slip through your fingers, do ye now?"

"What about the club?"

"It's practically my teatime. I can leave for a while."

Kelly's scarred face was as eager as a boy's. Murdoch smiled.

"All right. Do you have any objection to Mr. Keene accompanying us, Mrs. Rhodes?"

"Not at all, but please, let's hurry."

The Rhodes carriage was waiting at the entrance to the club, and Joe Seaton was huddled into a rug on the driver's seat. He was already dusted with snow, which increased his look of pale wretchedness. While Donalda got inside with Kelly, Murdoch climbed up next to the boy.

"Do you know where the Shepcote house is?"

He nodded.

"Off as fast as you can, then. Go along Queen Street. It's been cleared."

Joe cracked his whip and the grey horse set off at a smart canter.

They reached Berkeley Street in ten minutes flat. The house was at the end of a row of four, all trimly gabled with deep bay front windows. The other three houses were warm with lamplight, but the Shepcote

309

house was completely dark. Murdoch was about to jump down when Joe caught him by the arm.

"I want to do something for Tess."

"I'm sure you do, lad –"

Joe interrupted him. "I'll fight anybody if I have to."

Murdoch patted his hand. "The best thing you can do at the moment is stay here with the carriage. We're going inside. If you see anybody leave, man or woman, run in and tell me."

"Y-yes, sir."

The other two were already on the sidewalk, and as Murdoch joined them, Donalda pointed. "The door is open."

"Please wait here, ma'am."

She shook her head. Murdoch didn't want to waste time arguing, but Kelly touched her on the arm.

"Stand behind me, then, if you please."

Because of his disability, he wore a long cape, a dramatic affair of black wool, and he had shrugged both edges over his shoulder, freeing his arm. Murdoch saw that he had also unpinned his left sleeve, which hung down at his side. He was ready for action.

At the threshold Murdoch tugged on the bell, and they could hear the clang in the silent house. At the same time he pushed the door open further. It led into a wide hall, which was in darkness. They waited a moment but there was no response in the house.

Murdoch took a box of lucifers from his pocket and lit the candle in the wall sconce. It gave off sufficient light to reveal velvet portieres on the right and a staircase directly in front. A closed door at the far end no doubt led to the kitchen.

"What's wrong?" whispered Donalda at his elbow. "Why is no one here?"

"Please stay here, Mrs. Rhodes. Kelly, come with me."

This time she obeyed. She looked frightened.

There was an oil lamp on one of the hall tables and Murdoch lit that as well, holding it aloft.

At the drawing room, he pulled back the drawn portieres.

The light shone on the prone figure of Harriet Shepcote, who was lying on the sofa, facing the back. Murdoch went over to the girl. To his relief she wasn't dead as it had first appeared, only very still. Her breathing seemed shallow but not laboured, and when he touched her face the skin temperature felt normal. This close the smell of liquor was strong. Gently, he started to shake her by the shoulder.

"Miss Shepcote. Miss Shepcote . . . it's Detective Murdoch."

She didn't move, but he saw her eyes flutter slightly.

"Sean, help me sit her up."

He slipped his arm beneath the girl and at that moment Donalda entered.

311

"I couldn't just . . . What's wrong?"

"I think she's intoxicated. Perhaps you could call to her."

They got her upright, but her head lolled back against the couch. Donalda knelt down beside her.

"Harriet. Harriet, wake up."

The girl moved slightly but didn't open her eyes. Donalda took a quick breath, then with one swift movement slapped her hard across the cheek. Harriet gasped in shock and her eyes opened.

"Harriet, look at me."

The young woman's eyelids fluttered, but her head started to droop again. Another slap.

"Wake up, Harriet. You must wake up!"

This time she took in the three of them, and suddenly her face crumpled and she started to cry, a soft mewling sort of sound like a baby's. She tried to shrink away from the encircling arm of Sean Kelly.

"I'll hold her," said Donalda. She eased herself onto the sofa and put her arms around the girl. Harriet was trembling and moaning and her voice was barely audible.

"Let me go to sleep. I'm tired. Please let me go to sleep."

Murdoch spoke. "Miss Shepcote. Don't be afraid. You're safe now. What has happened? Where is your father?"

312

The question seemed to frighten her even more, and she huddled into the older woman's bosom, burying her face as if she were a babe in arms. Donalda stroked her hair, trying to soothe her. Murdoch was glad she had insisted on coming. Whatever had happened to Harriet Shepcote, he didn't think drunkenness was familiar to her. He indicated to Donalda to ask the question again.

"Harriet, try to tell us what is wrong."

"Don't let him marry me, Mrs. Rhodes. Please, I can't . . ." Her voice started to rise.

Donalda looked afraid but she said kindly, "Of course you don't have to marry anybody if you don't want to, my dear."

Harriet shuddered and gulped back a sob. "He forced me to drink . . . to celebrate our wedding. He told me . . . he told me."

She couldn't continue. Donalda's face was grim.

"Where is Owen now?"

Harriet looked up at her, bewildered. "Owen? I don't know . . . Oh, Mrs. Rhodes, I don't mean Owen."

"Who, then, Harriet? Who are you talking about?"

It was hard to hear what she said, but Murdoch could just make it out.

"Canning . . ."

"Your coachman?" Donalda asked in astonishment.

Harriet could only nod.

Murdoch leaned closer, speaking as gently as he could. "Miss Shepcote, where is your father?"

"In the . . . dining room . . . Oh, Mrs. Rhodes, what am I going to do?" Her voice began to rise again.

313

Donalda held her closer, rocking her. Even through her concern, her relief was palpable. "It's all right, my dear child. He won't have you. We won't let him. Hush now."

Murdoch signalled to Kelly. "We're going to find Mr. Shepcote, Mrs. Rhodes."

There was an archway from the drawing room to the dining room and the chenille curtains were closed. They went through.

The dining room was lit dimly by a single guttering candle on the table, and the embers from a dying fire threw a reddish glow over everything. They saw a man slumped in the armchair close to the hearth. It was Shepcote.

He was breathing noisily and his arms hung limply beside the chair. Closer, in his lamplight, Murdoch could see his colour was bad, a bluish tinge around his lips.

"What is it, Willie? Is he drunk?" asked Kelly.

Murdoch indicated the empty vial on the nearby table and the open syringe box.

"Not drunk."

"He doesn't look so good."

Murdoch held the lamp close to Shepcote's face. He pulled up the lid of the right eye. The pupil was hugely dilated.

314   "Damnation. Sean, get to the kitchen and make up an emetic. Fast as you can."

Murdoch quickly extinguished the candle that was on the table and held the wick close to Shepcote's nostrils. The acrid smell filled the air but the man didn't stir. Murdoch slapped him hard back and forth across his cheeks and shook him. Nothing. A dribble of saliva was running from the corner of his mouth.

Donalda came through the portieres. Her voice was tight with urgency.

"Mr. Murdoch, I managed to get some story out of Harriet. She says she overheard her father and Canning talking together. Canning murdered that woman you found on the lake. Shepcote was a complicitor."

Kelly came back with a glass of mustard water in his hand.

Murdoch pulled back Shepcote's head and opened his mouth so that Kelly could pour some of the emetic down the man's throat. Shepcote gulped involuntarily but most of the liquid ran out the sides of his mouth. Donalda watched, her body tense and angry.

"Canning told Harriet her father was responsible for Theresa's death." She stared at Shepcote. "I want to hurt him. I want him to suffer likewise."

Suddenly she seized his shoulders and shook him hard. His head lolled to one side. Murdoch was about to restrain her, but she stopped herself.

"It won't do any good, though, will it? It won't bring her back."

"The law will deal with him . . . if he survives that long."

315

Suddenly Donalda caught Murdoch by the sleeve. "Harriet said something about Canning going after another woman – a friend of that dead girl's –"

"Ettie!"

"Can you stop him?"

"I'll try. Will you help Mr. Keene? Try to get Shepcote conscious. Do whatever it takes."

She shook her head. "I have to tend to Harriet first."

It was her punishment.

"Go, Will. I'll be all right," said Kelly. He started to administer more mustard water.

Murdoch left them to it and ran outside to the carriage. He jumped up beside Joe.

"Fast as you can, Joe. St. Luke's Street. SCORCH."

The boy cracked his whip over the horse and they plunged into a full gallop. Murdoch held on with one hand and with the other unhooked the side lantern and began to swing it.

"I wish I had a bell, but this'll have to do," he yelled at Joe. He stood up in the swaying driver's seat and, waving his lantern, bellowed at the top of his lungs.

"Out of the way! Police! Out of the way!"

Silver stretched out his neck and galloped like he'd never run before, Murdoch saying a Hail Mary under his breath that the horse wouldn't falter and that they'd get to Ettie in time.

316

Chapter Twenty-One

BERNADETTE WESTON YAWNED AND STRETCHED. Her shoulders were stiff and her eyes were tired. Trying to do fine sewing in candlelight wasn't easy, but she'd begged extra work from Mr. Webster so she could pay for Alice's funeral. Alice would be buried in style. Black horses to pull the hearse, a proper coffin, black crepe for the house, food after for the mourners. Some of the regulars at the O'Neil had passed the hat but they were such a bunch of piss-makers all she'd got out of it was two dollars and ten cents. Perhaps she should move away from here? Start afresh somewhere else? Who knew, maybe she could get out of the game and join a troupe or something. Everybody said she had a great voice.

She sewed the final stitch and broke off the thread with her teeth. She'd managed to repair half a dozen gloves in the last two days. Mr. Webster was a sour old macaroni, but he might advance her another couple of dollars on the next consignment. Bullocks had agreed to let her pay for the funeral in installments. And so they should, considering what they were charging. She and Alice had talked about belonging to the burial club but, more's the pity, they'd never got around to it. There was a pain in Ettie's throat. She missed Alice something sore. Who'd she have to joke with now? To chin over a pot of chatter broth? She clenched her teeth tight against the sob that was threatening to come up. After dropping off the gloves, she'd go over to the O'Neil for a gin and some company, try to forget for a while.

She tugged the glove off the wooden form and dropped it in the bag with the others. Then she stood up, yawning again. She'd better hurry. Mr. Webster said he'd wait until eight o'clock for the gloves and he'd never stay a minute longer. Bugger, it was a quarter to, now. She grabbed her jacket and shawl off the peg, blew out the candle and tucked the bag under her arm.

At Quinn's room she paused for a second, but there was no light under the door and no sound from Princess. They must be out.

Outside, a light, steady snow was falling and the backyard was clean and white. Ettie wrapped her shawl tightly around her head and shoulders as she trudged down the path and into the laneway. Opposite the house, the police rope blew in the wind, still marking off the spot where Therese Laporte had died. That

318

seemed so long ago now. What she and Alice done was wrong, and look where it had got them. They didn't have the clothes and Alice was dead. Perhaps there really was an angry God up there punishing them like the preachers shouted on the street corner.

She was walking as quickly as she could, but the snow was untouched and slowed her down. Sod it! Webster never waited. She turned out onto Sackville Street.

"Ellie, Ellie, hold on a minute."

Wrapped in her shawl and in the darkness of the laneway, she hadn't seen the man following her. He was wearing a long greatcoat and wide hat and it was only when he was close and pulled the muffler from his face that she recognized him.

"You're a bloody racehorse," he said, panting a little. "Where's the fire?"

"You! Get away from me."

She went to run but he grabbed her by the arm. "Hold on. What's up with you?"

"You know sodding well. You done in Alice."

"What you talking about?"

She struggled to get free but he held on.

"Let go of me. I'll start yelling in a minute."

"Come on, woman. I don't know what you're talking about."

"Alice left with you that night and got herself strangled."

319

He gave her a hard shake. "Ellie. Listen to me. I didn't do anything."

"Why should I believe you?"

She couldn't move out of his grip. "Because it's the truth, you dumb git."

"Don't call me that. And me name's Ettie. Bernadette to you."

"Beg pardon!" He set her free but stood close. "Listen, Miss Trim and Topper, your chum did leave with me and we were all set to go off and have a good bit of jig. Then some swell went past in his carriage. He stopped and without so much as a wink or a wave, she jumped in and off they went."

Ettie stared at him, trying to determine if he was lying or not, but his pugilist's face was impossible to read in the shadows.

"What sort of carriage was it?"

"Nobby, reddish colour."

"Was the horse light?"

"I think so, a bay maybe or a grey. Why? D'you know him?"

Ettie bit on her lip. That was the description that Alice had given of the carriage she'd seen on Saturday. It made sense that it was the same one. Sod it. Had Alice been so stupid as to get in? She probably thought she could put the squeeze on the man. Angry tears sprang to her eyes. What a foolish ignorant tart she was.

320

"D'you know the toff?" the sailor repeated.

Ettie shook her head.

"Listen, even the police believed me," he continued. "I got a visit from them yesterday. Every dick at the tavern must have given them a description of me going off with Alice –"

"What did the coppers look like?"

"One was a Goliath, seven feet at least. The detective was tall too, dark moustache. Fancied himself."

"No he don't. He's a good sort for a frog."

"Ha! Perhaps I should have said he fancies you. His eyes lit up like a gas lamp when he mentioned your name."

"Go on, that's horseshit if ever I smelled it."

"It's the truth, Ellie. He's quite cracked about you."

She shrugged, but she was pleased. "My God, what am I doing here dithering with you? I've got to deliver these gloves."

She set off again, heading for Queen Street, and the man kept pace.

"I was real sorry to hear about Alice. Here's something for the funeral." He pushed a folded five-dollar bill into her hand.

Ettie put it into her pocket. "Thanks."

"Can I stand you a pail and bin at the tavern when you've done your errand?"

"What?"

321

"An ale and gin."

"Throwing it around like a lord, aren't we?"

"There's only one better place I know of to put my money."

"And where's that?"

He touched her on the crotch. "Right in your duck hunt."

"Cheeky."

In fact, she didn't fancy him at all, but beggars couldn't be choosers. Maybe she could toss back enough gin to stomach him.

They were hurrying west along Queen Street to the tailor's shop. Like Alice, Ettie was afraid of the churchyard, but she didn't want the man to know that so she pulled her shawl like a blinker in front of her face and walked faster. She stopped in front of the shop, which was in total darkness.

"Sod it, he's gone. You've made me miss him." She banged hard on the door. "Mr. Webster? Mr. Webster? Bugger, now I won't get my money."

"Maybe he's upstairs."

"Not him. That's the workroom. He lives like a swell over on Jarvis Street."

The store adjoining the tailor's was vacant. Next to it was St. Paul's churchyard, where the snow was slowly creeping up the old tombstones.

"Stay there a minute," the man said. With a quick glance at the empty street he took a knife out of his

322

pocket, opened one of the blades and inserted it between the lock and the doorframe. One quick thrust and the door jumped open.

"What're you doing that for?" Ettie asked.

"Let's see if he's left any money. He owes you."

Ettie hung back. "I'll get in trouble. He'll know it's me."

"No he won't. There's nobody to see. Come on, Ellie. I bet you'd like a bit of best satin for the funeral, wouldn't you?"

He half pushed her into the dark front room of the shop, which was where Webster received his customers. There were two or three tailor's dummies standing by the window, shrouded for the night in white sheets.

"Oi, they're like bloody ghosts," she said.

"You don't have to be scared of the dead, Ellie, only the living. Now let's have a look-see. Where's the cloth kept?"

"Upstairs."

"Let's go, then." He placed his finger on her breast. "I want to see you just the way your own mother did."

It was then that Ettie knew he meant to kill her.

Joe pulled up in front of the lodging house and Murdoch jumped down.

"Get to the station fast as you can. Tell them to send an ambulance to Shepcote's house right away, and have the officer get two constables over here on the run. Speak to Sergeant Seymour."

Joe whipped up the panting horse and galloped off.

Inside the dark hall Murdoch paused, listening. He didn't know if Canning was in here and he was afraid to jeopardize Ettie's life by acting too impulsively. The house was silent as the grave. Hoping against hope he wasn't too late, he crept down the hall. At Ettie's room he halted again. Nothing. With his lantern held high, he opened the door, almost afraid of what he might find. The room was empty, the bed tidy. A candle stub was on the shelf and he touched the wax. It was soft. She hadn't left that long ago.

At that moment he heard footsteps, and Quinn with Princess at his heel appeared in the doorway.

"Hey, what's going on here?" The baker looked alarmed. "Oh, Detective, it's you."

"Have you seen Ettie?" Murdoch demanded.

"No, I haven't. I just got back in myself. What's up?"

"I've good reason to think she's in serious danger."

"Lordy! How?"

"The same man who killed Alice wants to shut up Ettie –"

"The sailor?"

"He's not a sailor, he's a coachman by the name of Canning."

"The hell –"

"D'you think she's at the O'Neil?"

Quinn glanced around the room. "The bag's gone. She was sewing gloves for Webster, the tailor. She's probably gone to his shop."

"Where?"

"Queen Street, right beside St. Paul's Church."

"Come with me. We've got to hurry. Back door. She didn't go out the front."

They set off back down the hall, but suddenly Quinn stopped.

"Just a minute. Hold Princess, will you."

He thrust the twine into Murdoch's hand and dived into his own room, emerging immediately with another dog on a thick leather leash.

"Good Lord, what's that?" asked Murdoch.

"He's an English bulldog. I thought he might come in useful. He's a mild-tempered fellow but he doesn't look it."

The dog stared up at Murdoch. There was a long stream of saliva dripping from his mouth, his prominent eyes were red-rimmed and the lower fangs protruded outside slobbery lips. His face looked as if he'd run into a door.

"You're right about that," said Murdoch. "He'd give Cerberus a fright. Belong to a friend, does he?"

"Er . . . yes, as a matter of fact. His name's Tsar."

"Come on, then."

In the snow-filled yard, Ettie's footprints were clearly visible. The two men and the dogs hurried down to the laneway. Here another set of prints appeared, larger and wider. Murdoch retraced them a few paces. Canning had been standing behind the shed waiting.

They went on again. The dogs had picked up the sense of urgency and they trotted alongside obediently. Tsar sounded asthmatic but managed to keep up a brisk pace.

At the entrance to Sackville Street Murdoch stopped again.

"Canning caught up with her here." He pointed to the prints still visible. "They stood and talked. You can see the snow has melted farther down. There wasn't a fight. They set off again together."

"Would she have gone willingly?"

"The footsteps don't seem to waver at all, so I doubt she was being coerced at this point, anyway. We're right at Sackville Street and there's too much chance of him being seen."

They were jog-trotting down the street now and the few passersby regarded them curiously. In a few minutes the trail crossed to the south side of Queen Street.

"I was right. She's heading for Webster's shop," panted Quinn.

As they approached the graveyard, Quinn tapped Murdoch on the arm.

326

"That's the shop. Next one."

Murdoch slowed down to get his breath. The tailor's was the middle one of three, but the nearest was vacant and boarded up and the far one, a fancy goods shop, was in complete darkness.

"I think I saw a wink of light on the second floor," whispered Quinn. Murdoch stared upwards but saw nothing. However, the footprints they had been following led right into the doorway. None came out. Ettie was in there.

Two of his side teeth on the upper gum were heavy with gold fillings and she noticed that from time to time he tapped them with an air of satisfaction at his own prosperity. She wondered how he could afford gold teeth. His clothes were of good cloth too. It was the snake tattoo that spoiled the effect, peeking out from the cuff on his shirt, purple and malevolent.

Ettie wasn't aware of being afraid. Her mind had gone into a kind of detached clarity, working independently as if she were watching herself from afar. There was an inner voice commenting. *If she screams now, he will cut her throat right here . . . Nobody is close enough to hear and it don't matter to him anyways. He'd do it and run off. Better to keep talking, distract him as long as possible. She's done that lots of times when she wanted the jigger to fall asleep before he docked inside her . . . He don't seem in a hurry. He's excited, though, she can smell it . . . but she can fool him. If he thinks she's just another nocky piece of cattle, he might let down his guard.*

327

The second floor of the shop was used for storage, and along the far wall were deep shelves stacked with rolls of fabric. There were two long tables in the centre where the tailors did their cutting and at the end of each table was a large oil lamp. Canning lit one of them.

Somebody will see the light, said Ettie's inner voice. *The copper on his beat will investigate. She'll be safe soon. Sleeping in her own bed before she knows it.*

But Canning immediately pulled down the window blind and fastened it tight.

He walked over to the shelves and was fingering the different bolts of cloth.

"What's your real name?" she asked.

"You don't need to know, Ellie. Jack'll do."

"You're not a sailor, are you?"

He scowled. "Are we playing 'Forfeit' all of a sudden?"

She shrugged. *Careful, don't crack the egg*, her voice warned. "You seem too nobby for a sailor is all."

That seemed to please him. "I was one once. Not now. Now I'm a gentleman . . . or as near as makes no difference."

So far he hadn't removed his coat or hat, which she took comfort from, but now he unwound his muffler. He looked different but she couldn't at first identify why. Then he removed his wide felt hat. Instead of the close-cropped pate she'd seen at the O'Neil, he sported a head of dark, smooth hair.

328

"Sod me, you've got hair."

"Sod me, but I haven't," he mocked. He tugged off the wig and tossed it to the floor, where it lay like a strange species of animal.

"Frigging thing's hot," he said. Next he removed his greatcoat and placed it on the workbench. "Why don't you get more cozy. I've never taken a flyer before and I don't fancy it now."

"I'm cold."

"I'll warm you up . . . I said to take your jacket off."

The tone of his voice made Ettie's knees quiver. She licked her lips; her mouth was as dry as sand. "Don't happen to have a spot of soother with you, I suppose?"

"As a matter of fact I do." He took a silver flask from his pocket and handed it to her. "You *are* cold, Ellie."

"Ettie! I keep telling you my name's Ettie, from Bernadette."

"What's the difference?" he said.

She unscrewed the top from the flask and took a deep gulp of the liquor. It wasn't gin but something that burned her throat.

"Hey, leave some for me. That's expensive scotch you're swallowing like it was water."

The drink was a fire in her stomach, but every other part seemed to grow colder. In the distance she thought she heard a dog bark but in the room the silence grew deeper, as if her ears were stopping up. He stood, legs apart, contemplating the rows of

329

fabrics. Then he suddenly and violently hauled out a big bolt of crimson satin. In the faint light of the lamp, the cloth was as dark as spilled blood.

"This'll do." He turned back to where Ettie was sitting on one of the wooden chairs at the table. "Didn't I say to take off your clothes? I can't stand gits who won't listen."

She flinched and with shaking fingers began to unbutton her jacket. In the meantime he rolled out the satin, making a pool of crimson on the grimy floor. Then without another word he walked over to her, gripped the back of her neck with one hand and with the other pulled at the collar of her blouse. A button tore off.

"Oi, what are you doing? This is my good waist." But her voice lacked conviction. Her beautiful detachment vanished and she was back in the stuffy room, the smell of new fabric intermingling with the stink of their sweat. Her arms ached as if she had been holding a heavy weight, and her legs had lost all strength. His face was very close to hers, his breath was foul, and she could see a small deep scar by his nostril as if a knife point had been driven in. His chin was rough with reddish hairs. His pale blue eyes looked at her but did not see. He grinned again and the gold tooth gleamed.

330

"I've made you a bed fit for a queen. Come on and try it."

She knew she'd lost.

—

Murdoch extinguished his lantern, relying on the jumping light of the nearest gas lamp. He couldn't risk being detected.

"Go around to the back and wait there," he said to Quinn.

"No, let me come. Ettie may need me."

Murdoch shook his head. The man was distraught and in that state might prove to be more hindrance than help.

"I need you to guard that door." He bent down and picked up a half-brick that was lying against the wall. "If he comes out, hit him."

"My pleasure."

Murdoch slipped off his seal coat and hat and placed it in the doorway, hoping they'd still be there afterwards.

"You take Princess and keep her quiet. Give me Tsar."

Quinn did as he was told. With the bulldog's leash in his hand, Murdoch entered the front room. There was a thin rush covering on the floor which effectively deadened the sound of his boots, but he wished he had some weapon. Then he heard a thump from above and the sound of heavy footsteps across the floor. They were up there.

331

He held Tsar's jaws closed so he could hear better. He made out two voices, one male, the other female. Relief swept through him as he realized she was alive.

Quickly, he crossed to the rear door and as lightly and as fast as he could mounted the stairs, the dog beside him.

"You're going to crash me, aren't you?"

The words were out of her mouth before she could stop them. She felt dizzy but it was a relief to tell the truth. It gave her a strange kind of strength. He stared at her, then stepped away as if she'd violated an unspoken taboo.

"What a fly mort you really are, Ellie. I was wondering when that would occur to you."

This time a wave of anger shot through her body, burning hot but as brief and ineffective as the striking of a match.

"You did for Alice too, didn't you?"

"That's right. She was too leaky for her own good. She told you she saw us pick up the girl, didn't she?"

"Yes."

"So there we are, then, Ellie. Too bad for you."

He yawned like a nervous dog and for the first time she realized he was afraid too.

At that moment, she heard a sound from the landing, a creak.

332   He also heard it.

At the top of the stairs, Murdoch hesitated. The voices had ceased and everything was completely quiet. Slowly, he turned the doorknob. The door wasn't locked and yielded easily.

With a fervent prayer he flung it open and jumped into the room, dropping at once into a crouch.

Canning was waiting for him.

His left hand was covering Ettie's mouth and at her throat he was holding a short sailor's knife. He had pricked her skin and a trickle of bright blood was running down her neck. She was not struggling, but her eyes as they saw Murdoch were wide with terror and pleading.

"Let her go."

Canning scowled. "Nothin' doing. She's my ticket of leave. Now get out of the way. I'm coming down those stairs."

Tsar licked his lips and whined softly, sensing the emotion.

"And don't think of letting that brute go 'cause I'll slit its throat right after I slit hers."

"Turn yourself in, man. You can't get away."

"Wrong. I was a sailor, don't forget. I've got escape hatches you'll never know about. Now move away. Over there! Now!"

Ettie flinched at his voice in her ear.

"Please," she whispered.

Slowly Murdoch obeyed, trying to sense the moment of weakness, the moment when Canning would give him an opportunity to act. He regretted bringing the dog, who had suddenly sat down, panting. Mild-mannered fellow indeed. Unobtrusively he dropped the leash.

"Let go of the girl and I'll give you time to get away."

"The fig you would. Come on. Get over to the corner. If you don't hurry up, I'll start on her now."

The blade dug deeper. Ettie gasped.

Suddenly from the stairs came a deep-throated baying. The door banged against the wall and Quinn burst into the room. Princess was at his heel, howling. Canning turned, momentarily distracted. At the same time, Ettie twisted out of his arm and dropped to all fours, scrambling away. Quinn ran over to help her but as he bent down Canning's boot connected with his jaw, felling him instantly. With a howl, Princess went for the offending leg but Canning landed a blow on her side that flung her in the air. Murdoch lunged forward to grab him but he wasn't fast enough. Canning jumped backwards behind a sewing machine, waving his knife in front of him. Ettie was screaming obscenities at the top of her voice as, still on her hands and knees, she crawled to the injured dog.

It was then that Tsar woke up. He growled deep in his throat, then hurled himself past Murdoch and went full-speed at Canning. The sailor tried to kick at him but the blow glanced off the dog's shoulder. Tsar leapt on Canning's right arm, clamping his jaws around the wrist. With a scream of pain, the man tried to punch

334

the dog in the head with his other hand. He might as well have thumped a pillow for all the impact it had, but it gave Murdoch the chance he needed. He caught hold of Canning's left arm and twisted it backwards, at the same time bearing down with all his weight.

They fell to the ground, the two men and the dog tumbling and rolling among the tables of the sewing room. Neither Tsar nor Murdoch would let go. Dimly he was aware of savage bumps as his spine and shins connected with the iron legs of the sewing tables. Canning was not a big man, but he was strong. Murdoch could not hold him down, and Canning managed to butt him so hard under the chin that Murdoch almost lost his grip. The din was horrific – Tsar was snarling ferociously non-stop, Ettie was screaming and Canning was yelling. Then Princess ran back into the fray, but she didn't distinguish between friend or foe and gave Murdoch a nasty bite on the calf. He tried to protect himself at the same time that he attempted to get his arm around Canning's neck. Then, with a Herculean heave, his assailant staggered to his feet. The bulldog hung on, his stubby paws waving in the air. Blood was streaming from Canning's arm.

"Get him off!" he screamed.

He swung around and Murdoch, who was still behind him, was almost crushed against the shelves. It was only the softness of the cloth bolts that saved him. Canning might have escaped, but at that moment the

335

little hound moved in for another attack and got Canning right above his heel, severing the Achilles tendon. He fell to his knees and Murdoch rolled off to the side. The breath had been knocked out of him and he was gasping for air.

Canning was closer to Ettie and, seeing what was happening, she aimed a savage kick at his ribs, the pointed toe of her boot catching him in the solar plexus. He went white and fell flat on his stomach like a marionette whose strings were cut.

She would have gone on kicking but, panting, Murdoch managed to pull her off.

"Ettie, stop. Stop. Leave him to me."

She struggled for a minute but Princess ran to her aid and she was forced to hold the dog off Murdoch. Canning was retching and gasping on the floor. Murdoch left Ettie, dragged out his handcuffs and snapped them around the fallen man's wrists.

The crimson satin cloth had got wrapped around Canning's legs, and his own blood was making ribbons on the floor.

Epilogue

EVEN AFTER A MONTH, the parlour still reeked of kerosene. When Murdoch had finally limped home, a shocked Beatrice Kitchen had soaked pieces of flannel in kerosene oil and applied them to the multitude of bruises on his arms and legs. The dog bite she had bathed in a solution of carbolic acid, and the initial pain was worth it because no infection had developed. Canning had not been so fortunate.

The Kitchens and Murdoch were sitting in the parlour after Sunday Mass. Arthur had accompanied them to St. Paul's for the first time in almost a year. The egg-seller's cure seemed to be working and although he now looked exhausted his strength was generally much improved. Without complaint he downed his twelve eggs and cream a day.

337

Beatrice poured Murdoch some more tea. He could

see she was dying to tell him something but with the instincts of the born storyteller she was saving the news until the right moment.

What's on your mind, Mrs. K.?" he asked her finally. She put down her teacup, her eyes bright with excitement.

"I have been wanting to chat about my little encounter yesterday but there simply has been no opportunity. You were out."

Murdoch had attended his second salon dance the night before with Professor Otranto's students. It had not been at all satisfying. He had practically destroyed the velvet dancing slipper of one of his partners and she had been most displeased.

"Now's your chance, then, Mother," said Arthur.

"I met the Rhodeses' new cook at the market yesterday," Beatrice continued. "Her name is Doris Winn. She's from down east, your country, Mr. Murdoch. We fell to talking, you know how it is. She was surprised I knew about the family's misfortunes. I didn't say much, of course, merely made an enquiry after Mrs. Rhodes's health."

She glanced rather anxiously at Murdoch, but he smiled reassuringly.

338   "I'm sure you were absolutely discreet, Mrs. K."

"For Mary's sake get on with it, Mother," said Arthur.

"Don't rush me . . . Where was I? Oh, yes, Miss Winn. She told me that Mrs. Rhodes is planning to return to

England in the spring and she's not certain if she will ever come back to Canada. Her son and his fiancée are going to follow as soon as Miss Shepcote is out of mourning. And Mrs. Rhodes is taking the stableboy, Joe, with her. She's made quite a pet of him, by all accounts."

"I'm glad about that," said Murdoch.

"Yes, poor mite. But here is the news. The doctor has moved out of the house! Just two weeks ago, a woman came to the door asking for him. Well, Doris had hardly got her feet wet, as it were, and she didn't know as it wasn't one of his patients, so she let her in. And then there was a dreadful scene. The woman wasn't a patient at all but said she had been living with the doctor as man and wife for over two years. Can you imagine that?"

Arthur glanced over at Murdoch. "Did you have any idea about this, Will?"

"Let's just say I'm not at all surprised. I suspected the good doctor was up to something to give him a guilty conscience."

"According to Doris Winn the woman is completely vulgar. She has a daughter but the girl isn't the doctor's. She said it was because she wanted the girl to be adopted and have a respectable home that she came forward." Beatrice sniffed. "It sounds noble enough, but from what Doris said the woman is just out for what she can get."

"Almost makes you sorry for him," said Arthur.

339

"Not too sorry, Father. A man in his position keeping a mistress should be ashamed . . . Anyway, let me go on. Mrs. Rhodes was home at the time and Doris said she was completely ladylike during the whole thing. Can you imagine? I wouldn't be, I can tell you that." She nodded over at her husband. "Fortunately Arthur's never given me cause. Anyways, in the end she asked the woman to leave. The doctor packed up the very next day." She lowered her voice. "Doris thinks they may even divorce. I feel the most sorry for the Shepcote girl myself. She's had enough scandal to deal with."

She paused and it was clear the real dirt was about to be dished. "Doris said she'd run into that wicked Edith Foy last week who's been saying all manner of dreadful things about the family. A case of the pot calling the kettle black, if you ask me, after what her own husband done, but there you go. Fortunately she's got her head on her shoulders, has Doris Winn, and she took it all with a pinch of salt." She stopped to savour the moment. "I'm referring to young Rhodes."

"What do you mean, Mother?"

"Mrs. Foy claims he's not quite, er, natural. There was some scandal to do with a stableboy last summer. It was all hushed up but apparently his mother found them . . . together. There are whispers he associates with known – what is the word, Arthur? Miss What's-it?"

340

"You're thinking of Miss Mollys, I believe, Mother."

"Yes, that's it. However, the young fellow is going to marry Miss Shepcote, who by all accounts adores him. That's sure to set him to rights. After all, boys do odd things sometimes, don't they?"

Murdoch liked young Rhodes for his kindness to Joe Seaton, and he too hoped his marriage would straighten him out.

Arthur changed the subject. "How's Mr. Quinn doing?"

"Almost recovered. I dropped in to see him yesterday, as a matter of fact. He's eating solid foods now."

"No more dognapping, I hope."

"No, he's sworn off it. He knows what would happen if he tried that again. I can't ignore it next time."

"Thank the Lord for those dogs. You might have been killed and we wouldn't have liked that, would we, Mother?"

"Not at all." She made the sign of the cross over her neat bosom. "Every time I think of you and that Antichrist my blood runs cold."

"He'll hang, won't he, Will?"

"If I have anything to do with it."

"At least he's confessed to doing for Shepcote. Miss Harriet won't have to think her father committed a mortal sin," said Beatrice.

Murdoch thought privately that given everything else Shepcote had been guilty of, that might not be high

341

on Harriet's list of problems. According to Canning, it had been Shepcote who forced opium on Therese. She had managed to run off from the Yeoman Club, where they'd taken her, but the drug and the bitter winter night had overwhelmed her.

"Such a tragedy. And what a dreadful hypocrite that man was," said Beatrice.

"Yes, indeed."

Murdoch thought of the sordid pictures he'd found in Shepcote's desk. He hadn't told the Kitchens.

Suddenly Beatrice clapped her hands together like a child.

"Mr. Murdoch, I almost forgot to tell you. We are getting a new boarder. She's a niece of Doris's. A widow with a seven-year-old boy and she desperately needs a nice lodging. I offered our place. Now that Arthur is getting better there will be no danger, I'm sure. She can have the backroom. Her name is Enid – strange name, it's Welsh, I believe. She is still a young woman, a looker, according to her aunt." Beatrice smiled slyly at Murdoch. "She's probably been lonely without a husband. Perhaps you could interest her in dancing lessons."

"Mother," protested Arthur, "you're not trying to do a bit of matchmaking, are you? Will isn't interested in that sort of thing, are you?"

Murdoch chuckled. "I'd be glad to have a partner at my dance class. Let's hope she's got iron toes."

342

What he couldn't say was that he had a sudden hope that a suitable woman would obliterate the memory of a scrawny, not too clean prostitute, whose tears had wet his cheek as he held her close in his arms.

Acknowledgements

First, I wish to thank Eric Wright, who has been with me on this long journey and helped me more than I can ever say. Also, great thanks to Robert Wright of Robert Wright Books, who kept me supplied with countless treasures of authentic material. The archivists at the Ontario Archives, the most fascinating place in the city, were always courteous and helpful, especially Leon, and I thank them. Finally, my eternal gratitude to my agent, Teresa Chris, and to Ruth Cavin, my editor, for believing in me.

UNDER THE DRAGON'S TAIL

Dolly Merishaw is an abortionist in Victorian Toronto, but her contempt for her clients leaves every one of them resentful. So it's no surprise when this malicious woman is murdered. But when a young boy is found dead in Dolly's squalid kitchen a week later, Detective Murdoch doesn't know if he's hunting one murderer – or two.

"Late-19th-century Toronto comes startlingly alive in Jennings's second gripping tale."
– PUBLISHERS WEEKLY

Trade Paperback
978-0-7710-9597-9

POOR TOM IS COLD

In the third Murdoch mystery, the detective is not convinced that Constable Oliver Wicken's death was suicide. When he begins to suspect the involvement of Wicken's neighbours, the Eakin family, Mrs. Eakin is committed to a lunatic asylum. Is she really insane, he wonders, or has she been deliberately driven over the edge?

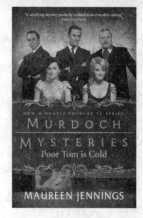

"Jennings has a wonderful feel for the places and tasks that give life and context to a character."
– NEW YORK TIMES BOOK REVIEW

Trade Paperback
978-0-7710-9595-5

LET LOOSE THE DOGS

In *Let Loose the Dogs*, Detective Murdoch's life and work become tragically entwined. His sister, who fled to a convent to escape their abusive father, is now on her deathbed. Meanwhile, the same father calls on Murdoch for help after he is charged with murder. Knowing his father as he does, what is Murdoch to believe?

"Not only the most generously plotted of Murdoch's four cases . . . but the one whose constant reminders of mortality . . . are the most piercing."
– KIRKUS REVIEWS

Trade Paperback
978-0-7710-4676-6

NIGHT'S CHILD

After thirteen-year-old Agnes Fisher faints at school, her teacher is shocked to discover in the girl's desk two stereo-scopic photographs. One is of a dead baby in its cradle and the other is of Agnes in a lewd pose, captioned "What Mr. Newly Wed Really Wants." The photographs are brought to Detective Murdoch, who sets out to find the photographer – and to put him behind bars.

"[Night's Child] *brings to life a violent but vital society of astonishing contradictions.*"
– NEW YORK TIMES

Trade Paperback
978-0-7710-4677-3

VICES OF MY BLOOD

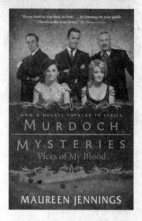

The Reverend Charles Howard sat in judgment on the poor, assessing their applications for the workhouse. But now he is dead, stabbed and brutally beaten in his office. Has some poor beggar he turned down taken his vengeance? Murdoch's investigation takes him into the world of the destitute who had nowhere to turn when they knocked on the Reverend Howard's door.

"Jennings opens a window on the realities of a late-Victorian city. . . . Let Jennings be your guide. There's really none better."
– OTTAWA CITIZEN

Trade Paperback
978-0-7710-4678-0

A JOURNEYMAN TO GRIEF

In 1858, a young woman is abducted and taken across the border from Canada and sold into slavery. Thirty-eight years later, the owner of one of Toronto's livery stables is found dead. Then a second man is murdered, his body strangely tied as if he were a rebellious slave. Detective Murdoch has to find out whether Toronto's small "coloured" community has a vicious killer in its midst – an investigation that puts his own life in danger.

"A Journeyman to Grief is Maureen Jennings's best to date."
– MARGARET CANNON, GLOBE AND MAIL

Trade Paperback
978-0-7710-4679-7

Iden Ford

Born in England, MAUREEN JENNINGS taught English before becoming a psychotherapist. The first Detective Murdoch mystery was published in 1997. Six more followed, all to enthusiastic reviews. In 2003, Shaftesbury Films adapted three of the novels into movies of the week, and four years later Shaftesbury (with CityTV, Rogers, UKTV, and Granada International) created the *Murdoch Mysteries* TV series which now airs on CBC television in Canada and is shown around the world, including in the UK, the United States, and much of Europe. Her new trilogy, set in World War II-era England, got off to a spectacular start with 2011's *Season of Darkness*, followed by *Beware this Boy* in 2012. Maureen lives in Toronto with her husband and their dog and cat. Visit www.maureenjennings.com.